Murder in in Miami

To Jimmy – A man of many talents

Merle Herman PP

MERLE NORMAN

outskirts
press

Outskirts Press, Inc.
http://www.outskirtspress.com

Paperback ISBN: 978-1-9772-5342-2

PRINTED IN THE UNITED STATES OF AMERICA

This book is dedicated to the memory of my mother

Acknowledgements

I wish to acknowledge my sister, Mindy Christiansen, without whose help this book would have never been published.

I also wish to acknowledge my companion, Dee, who has taken care of me throughout this entire endeavor. Without her support and encouragement, I would have given up on this task a long time ago.

Chapter One

It was 8:30 Tuesday morning following a three-day weekend when Carla pulled into her designated parking spot in front of the converted house on the east side of Little Havana, a small suburb of Miami. The two-story house had been converted into law offices 10 years ago which is when Carla began working as the office manager for Mr. Francisco Alfonso de la Carta, a high-powered criminal defense attorney. She was proud to be part of the two-person operation that had rapidly grown into a powerful law firm of 5 full-time Associates and several administrative employees. Carla was always the first one to arrive as it was her job to open the office, turn on all the lights, set the office thermostat to a comfortable working temperature before the rest of the staff arrived at 9:30, check the phone messages, start the coffee brewing, in addition to pulling the daily court cases and placing them on Mr. de la Carta's desk.

After unlocking the front door, Carla stepped

inside, turning to her left to quickly punch in the alarm code and then headed down the hall toward the kitchen. After she started the coffee, Carla continued with her morning routine, noticing that the offices were unusually warm and there seem to be a faint, foul odor throughout the office. Walking down the hall flicking on the lights, Carla passed the beautiful glass-encased conference room, formerly the house's dining area and realized the odor was getting stronger as she approached the stairs leading to the second floor.

It was definitely an odor stronger than someone's leftover lunch thrown away in their wastebasket to rot over the long weekend, especially as Maria, the law firm's cleaning woman of three years, took great pride in her work, never missing a day and would have diligently cleaned all the offices as always.

As Carla climbed the stairs, wondering all the while what was causing the awful odor, the stench became so strong, Carla had to cover her nose and mouth before continuing up to the second floor.

Arriving at Mr. de la Carta's office door, the odor was so putrid that even with her nose and mouth covered, it caused Carla to gag and her eyes to water. Even so, Carla entered the unlocked office, which was odd, since Mr. de la Carta always kept his door locked when out of the office and instantly saw a figure sitting in her boss's chair bent over with their head resting on the desk. At first glance Carla didn't recognize the person at the desk nor did she realize that the slumped body was the source of the now extremely nauseating odor. Wiping her teary eyes, while still keeping her nose and mouth covered, Carla stepped a few feet closer to the desk, suddenly freezing in place. She now saw the body clearly, a bloated, pale, DEAD body!

"Oh, my God!" As Carla became more focused on the corpse in front of her, the realization that it was the dead body of her boss felt like she had just been punched, making her week in the knees and extremely light-headed. Staggering to her office outside of Mr. de la Carta's, Carla picked up the phone to dial 911, however she was trembling so hard, it took several attempts before she was successful in reaching someone.

"911, what is your emergency?" A voice asked, sounding far off in the distance.

"Hello, this is 911. What is your emergency?" The far-off voice repeated.

"Dead." Carla finally responded. "He's dead!"

"Who's dead?" And that was the last thing Carla heard before her body collapsed into a heap at the foot of the desk, with the phone still in her hand.

"Hello? Hello? Can you hear me?" the operator asked, not realizing her voice was falling on deaf ears.

Fortunately, the 911 operator was able to trace the phone call since the line was still open and dispatched two patrol cars to the law firm. Four officers arrived within minutes not knowing what to expect. One officer went to the rear of the building, another waited at the front entrance, while the remaining two entered the building with guns drawn.

The two officers immediately recognized the stench of a decaying human body. They slowly sidled through the bottom floor, clearing each room before heading cautiously up to the second floor not knowing what they would be walking into.

Just past the top of the stairs, they saw the body of a woman lying on the floor. Methodically proceeding, the officers reached Mr. de la Carta's office, where a second body was discovered.

Using his radio, Officer Cruz called in to report what the officers had discovered at the scene and requested a medical examiner be sent to the law firm immediately. Officer Cruz then sent his partner outside to secure the building as a crime scene and await the arrival of the medical examiner. With the smell starting to nauseate him, Officer Cruz decided to greet the soon-to-be arriving homicide detectives outside also. The Medical Examiner arrived first with the crime scene investigating team arriving shortly thereafter.

"What do we have?" Medical Examiner Olsen asked Officer Cruz.

"Two bodies on the second floor. By the smell, I would guess that they have been dead for several days. The building has been secured and no one has touched the bodies."

"Any idea who they are?"

"To be honest Olsen, I didn't check either one of them for identification. One female, one male is all I know."

"Okay, thanks. Be sure to keep everyone out of the building for now." And with those instructions, Medical Examiner Olsen entered the Law Offices of Mr. Francisco Alfonso de la Carta to examine the bodies.

As Officer Cruz strolled toward the now barricaded parking lot, he saw a woman driving one of those small hybrid cars pull to the side of the road, exit the vehicle and walk purposely toward the taped off law firm.

"Excuse me ma'am, you can't go in there."

"Yes, I can! I work here!"

Officer Cruz found it curious that the woman avoided any kind of eye contact and that she didn't even seem curious about what was going on. The parking lot of the law firm was now filled with quite a few squad cars, a medical examiner's van, two CSI units, not to mention yellow police tape around the whole perimeter, yet she doesn't even ask a single question and tries to strut past everyone like she owns the place?

"You say you work here?"

"Yes, I work for Mr. de la Carta."

"What type of work do you do?"

The woman responded unemotionally and without any curiosity, "I am a lawyer."

"What's your name?"

"Abigail Arnold. Why do you ask?"

Chapter Two

A bigail Arnold, or Abbey as she preferred to be called, had sent out hundreds of resumes and went on just as many interviews since graduating from Harvard Law School a year ago. Unfortunately, Abbey suffers from a debilitating shyness causing her to avoid eye contact and speaking in a quiet, almost inaudible voice which keeps her from interviewing well and therefore, despite her stellar resume, not to mention graduating second in her class, the interviews never resulted in a job offer. Despite years of trying to overcome her shyness, Abbey was never able to conquer the issue and as graduation approached, it became quite evident that since she was a straight A student and seemingly first in her class, she may be chosen as the class valedictorian, meaning she would have to give a speech in front of the entire school. The very thought of speaking in public made Abbey physically ill.

During her last semester at Harvard, the school administrator met with both her and Trevor Taylor, another straight A student. And just as Abbey had feared, they were advised that they were both in the running for class valedictorian and should Abbey and Trevor end up with the same grade point average, the Administrative Board would select which of them would be the valedictorian.

Trevor Taylor came from a wealthy, well-respected family, was an excellent student, served as Editor on Harvard Law Review and was clearly the better choice to represent the senior class. However, Abbey had a slight edge over Trevor's exceptional academics and credentials due to her outstanding volunteer work at the Free Law Clinic. Her research, as well as her legal briefs, were legendary at both Harvard and the clinic. Although Abbey never attended a trial or took any credit for her work, the Free Law Clinic prevailed in numerous, seemingly impossible cases to win because of Abbey's in-depth and incredibly detailed research. Abbey reasoned that if she were indeed chosen Class Valedictorian, she would have to find a valid excuse not to attend, allowing Trevor to make the speech. However, Abbey could not do that to her father, a man who spent his entire life working towards the day he would see his only child graduate from law school.

John Arnold worked as a truck driver for an auto parts delivery service weekdays and on the weekends, he worked at a recycling center. And although Abbey was raised in a trailer park located on the outskirts of Memphis, Tennessee, she never felt poor. Her parents raised Abbey to believe that anything is possible and that everyone is equal, no matter their background. When Abbey's mother died of breast cancer during her first year of law school, it was devasting for both Abbey and her father. Abbey wanted to drop out of school immediately to care for her deeply grieving father but he insisted she stay in school and become the great attorney he knew she would be. Since Abbey felt she had no other option but to attend graduation so her father could watch her walk across the stage to receive her degree, she devised a plan that would take her out of the running to be valedictorian. In her last semester at Harvard, Abbey deliberately received a B in a class where she could have easily earned an A, thus giving Trevor a clear path to becoming valedictorian. And even though it meant graduating second in her class, Abbey was deeply relieved that she would not be the one giving the speech.

After graduating from Harvard, Abbey returned home to take care of her still grieving father. Her hopes were that she could join a local law firm as a research attorney which would relegate her to the law library and out of the public eye. Every day she stopped by the local law school, Cecil C. Humphrey, to check the job listings posted outside the administration office.

Finally Abbey's fervent search paid off, finding not one but three positions that looked promising and decided to check them out after dinner.

Abbey always made sure that dinner was ready when her father came home from work. She knew he was saddest at mealtime, so Abbey tried to keep everything the same as it was before she went away to law school. Even though it was never a fancy dinner, it was a hearty meal of meat and potatoes. And just as her mother had always done, Abbey set the table with cloth napkins and a lit candle. They followed the same routine every evening, with Abbey taking her father's hand and saying Grace. While her father wasn't particularly a religious man, what little faith he did have was lost when his wife died. Each night after dinner her father would ask Abbey if she had any luck finding a job and each night when she replied no, the disappointed look on her father's face broke her heart. However, this time, with the hopes of cheering him up, Abbey told him about the three job listings with as much positivity as she could muster.

"Are they local firms?"

"No, however, one is in Miami, Florida which really isn't that far."

Abbey knew how much her father wanted her to stay in Memphis with him and after a yearlong struggle of searching for a position as a lawyer locally, Abbey was at the brink of giving up the idea of being a research attorney or any type of attorney for that matter. Yet, she could not bring herself to walk away from all the sacrifices her father had made to get her through law school. Abbey felt she owed him that, plus so much more and therefore, she simply couldn't quit trying. There must be a firm somewhere in the United States that needs a brilliant legal mind. There just had to be and Abbey was determined to find it.

Abbey cleared the table, did the dishes and began researching the three job listings while her father fell asleep in his recliner watching the nightly news. The following morning after her father left for work, Abbey studied the research she had done on the three law firms that had posted their open positions. The first listing was from a mid-size law firm in North Dakota looking for an attorney willing to re-locate to Fargo. The second listing was from a large insurance law firm in Omaha, Nebraska. Since insurance law doesn't appeal to her nor is she willing to relocate to North Dakota despite her desperate situation, Abbey quickly ruled out the first two listings. However, the third listing from a small law firm in Miami caught her interest. It appeared that the law firm did mostly criminal defense work. While working at the Free Law Clinic, Abbey had developed a strong affinity for constitutional law as it applied to criminal defendants and despite the fact the firm was located in Miami, she impulsively decided to call them regarding the position rather than needlessly sending out another resume.

"Law Offices of Francisco de la Carta. This is Carla. How may I help you?"

"I am calling about the opening for a new associate. Is the position still available?"

"Yes, it is. May I ask how you heard about our firm?"

"I saw a job listing at our local law school here in Memphis."

"Do you currently live in Memphis?"

"Yes, ma'am. If you would like, I could fax my resume to you."

There was something in Abbey's tone that Carla liked. The woman didn't come across as your typical pushy lawyer type, in fact, she sounded almost apologetic, as if she were sorry for interrupting Carla's day.

"What is your name?" Carla asked.

"Abigail Arnold."

Carla found it somewhat amusing that Abigail answered only the questions that were asked of her and offered nothing more. Abigail did not volunteer any information nor was she trying to sell herself, however, for some unexplainable reason, Carla already liked this woman.

"Abigail, while I have you on the phone, may I ask you a few more questions?"

"Certainly."

"Where did you attend law school?"

Suddenly, Abbey's spirits picked up and she became more open in her responses. Abbey told Carla where she went to law school, that she graduated second in her class and even explained how her exceptional legal research at the Free Law Clinic would prove her to be an invaluable asset to the firm.

Carla inquired if Abigail was currently employed at a law firm and was perplexed when Abbey replied that she was not presently employed. Carla could not understand how someone who graduated a year ago from a prestigious Ivy League law school such as Harvard, second in her class no less, was having trouble finding employment.

"Carla, may I ask what exactly the position would entail?"

"Since our firm primarily does criminal defense work, you would be required to prepare cases for trial, research legal points, brief the senior attorneys on any issues and help write motions."

"That sounds perfect!" Abbey replied enthusiastically. "I excel at writing briefs and doing legal research. In fact, I would not mind at all if the firm only needed me to do that type of work."

"Mr. de la Carta will be in the office within the hour, so if you could fax over your resume right now Abigail, I will personally hand it to him to review as well as recommend that he set up a brief phone interview yet this morning. Would you that work for you?"

"Yes, that works perfectly. Thank-you so much Carla. I will fax my resume over to you as soon as we hang-up."

Abbey was always encouraged after speaking to potential employers on the phone but this time felt different somehow. This time Abbey believed she would make it past the complete interview process and be offered the position.

After faxing over her resume, Abbey sat by the phone waiting for the call from Mr. de la Carta. An hour later the phone rang and not to appear too eager, Abbey did not pick up the phone until the third ring.

"Hello, Abigail Arnold speaking."

"Miss Arnold! This is Francisco de la Carta. I am sitting in my office looking over your resume and I must say that it is quite impressive. And even more importantly, my Office Manager Carla speaks highly of you and feels you would be an excellent fit within our firm."

Thank-you was all Abbey could manage to say.

"Please tell me a little about yourself, Miss Arnold."

Panic was Abbey's immediate reaction. Frantic thoughts raced through her head about how to answer. What can I tell him about myself? That I live in a run-down trailer park taking care of my grief-stricken father? That I can't find a job at any law firm despite graduating second in my class from Harvard Law School? That I have no work experience of any kind? That I ....

"Hello? Are you still there?"

"Yes, I'm here. My apologies for not responding right away but I'm not sure what there is to say about myself other than I graduated from law school second in my class and I donated many hours of researching as well as writing legal briefs for the local Free Law Clinic."

Next to graduating from Harvard with honors, Abbey's work for the clinic made her the proudest. Mr. de la Carta could hear the pride in Abbey's voice as she spoke about her work at the clinic. What Abbey did not know was that before Mr. de la Carta phoned her, he had made a call to the Free Law Clinic's director who could not say enough wonderful things about Abigail and even volunteered to send samples of her brief writing.

Like Carla, Mr. de la Carta did not know exactly why but he had a good feeling about Abigail. He liked the tone of her voice, the fact that Carla spoke so highly of her after just a few minutes of conversation, not to mention how impressed he was with the glowing recommendation from the director of the clinic. Mr. de la Carta needed someone who could write brilliant motions. It is hard to find a lawyer who doesn't want to be in the spotlight or isn't constantly asking how soon they would be trying an actual court case and it is even rarer to find one who is not only willing but quite capable of doing the "grunt" work of the firm. It was clear that Miss Arnold was extremely bright without an inflated ego and exactly the type of lawyer he was looking for.

"Miss Arnold, would you have time in your schedule to fly to Miami for an in-person interview early next week?" Before Abbey could utter a word, Mr. de la Carta informed her that he would be sending a round trip ticket. Normally, he wouldn't make such a gesture but he felt being unemployed for the last year probably left Miss Arnold short of funds.

"I would be glad to fly to Miami for the interview."

"Very good. If it is conducive with your schedule, I will send you a ticket for next Tuesday."

"That would work perfectly."

"Is the address on your resume still current?"

"Yes, it is Mr. de la Carta."

"Good. I'll send the ticket to you at that address and expect to see you next Tuesday. Also, Miss Arnold, please call me Frank."

"Thank-you so very much Mr. de la Carta, I mean Frank, for this opportunity."

"Hopefully, this will be a great opportunity for us both. I look forward to seeing you on Tuesday."

While Abbey was excited about the in-person interview, she couldn't help but wonder if it would once again be a waste of everyone's time. Normally, she would have spent the rest of the day searching online for other possibilities, including positions outside of the legal field. Abbey knew that many companies hired management personnel with law degrees yet didn't need them to practice law. However, there was something different about Mr. de la Carta's phone call today that gave her renewed hope. For some reason, Abbey felt that if she continued to look for another job it would jinx the possibility of the Miami position. Therefore, she took the day off from job searching and spent the day thoroughly cleaning the house instead.

Two days later, as Mr. de la Carta had promised, a round-trip First-Class ticket arrived in Abbey's name. Abbey hadn't told her father about the telephone interview as she wanted to wait until she had actually received the ticket. That evening, after sitting down for dinner and saying Grace, Abbey decided it was time to tell her father about her upcoming trip to Miami.

"Dad, I have some good news."

"I could use some good news, Sweetheart."

"I have an interview with a law firm in Miami."

Her father had heard that she had an interview so many times before that he wasn't very hopeful regarding this interview in Miami but decided not to dampen her enthusiasm.

"I spoke to the head of the law firm, Mr. de la Carta, who was impressed enough to fly me to Miami for an in-person interview."

"That really is good news." Her father replied with a genuine interest.

"How soon will you start?"

"Dad! I haven't even had the final interview yet!"

"I can't imagine they would send you a plane ticket if they weren't ready to hire you."

"Actually, it is what most big firms do now when they're recruiting."

"Then this is a big firm?"

"Not really. It appears to be a small-sized firm."

"And yet they spent the money to send you a round-trip ticket?"

"Yes! It sounds encouraging, doesn't it?"

John tried to sound excited for his daughter although the thought of Abbey moving away sadden him deeply. Of course, he could never let her know his true feelings about her leaving, how lonely he would be without her because then she would never leave Memphis and while that may be his destiny, it simply wouldn't be his daughter's!

Abbey could see her father was processing what she had just told him and knew he had to be concerned about her leaving him alone. But what her father didn't know is that Abbey had no intentions of leaving him behind, that once she was hired, they would move to Miami together.

Abbey would never leave her father to live by himself alone, no matter what fate had in store for her!

"When is your interview?" Her father asked breaking the silence.

"Next Tuesday. I leave Memphis at 8:45 am and arrive in Miami at 2:10pm. I have an hour layover in Atlanta."

"Will you be coming back the same day?"

"Yes. The ticket is open-ended which gives me a few options, depending on how long the interview takes. I will try to get home as soon as possible."

"Don't worry about rushing home, Sweetheart. I will pick you up no matter what time you arrive back in Memphis. Please take your time and give a great interview."

"Thank-you Dad."

Abbey got up from the dinner table, threw her arms around her father's neck and gave him a reassuring hug. She knew that even though this was a wonderful opportunity, they were both also a little frightened at the thought of Abbey possibly being offered a job outside of Memphis.

On Tuesday morning, John wished his daughter good luck as he left for work, secretly hoping this interview would end no differently than all the others. Abbey gave her father a kiss goodbye, while struggling to control her emotions. Even though each previous interview had ended in rejection, Abbey was always enthusiastic at the prospect of a new interview. She put on her only dress, a full-length floral print with an empire waist that was a little dated but still looked flattering and headed to the airport.

When Abbey arrived in Miami, she noticed a man holding a sign with her name as Miss Abigail Arnold on it.

"I'm Miss Abigail Arnold."

"Miss Arnold, we have a car waiting for you."

Without further explanation, Abbey followed the chauffer to the waiting limousine, carrying the briefcase given to her as a graduation present from her father. As they drove toward Little Havana and the law offices of Mr. Francisco de la Carta, Abbey began to develop the same nervousness that she had before every interview. This time she told herself, the outcome will be different. When they finally arrived at the law firm, Abbey was surprised to see that the offices were in a converted house in a residential area. She had just assumed the law firm would be in a traditional office building. The casual setting made Abbey feel more at ease as she headed into yet another interview.

"May I help you?"

"My name is Abigail Arnold and I have an interview scheduled with Mr. de la Carta."

"Please have a seat while I let him know you are here."

Within a few minutes Carla came bounding down the stairs from the second floor, extending her hand to Abbey.

"Hello Miss Arnold. We spoke on the phone, I'm Carla. So glad you could make it. Frank is looking forward to meeting you. Please follow me."

Carla led Abbey back up the single flight of stairs, stopping just outside Frank's office. Tapping lightly on the door, Frank motioned for them to enter.

"Frank, this is Miss Abigail Arnold from Memphis."

"Yes, of course. Thank-you Carla. Please be seated, Miss Arnold."

As Abbey walked towards his desk, Frank noticed she looked down at the floor, making no direct eye contact with him. Miss Arnold was average in height, slender and well groomed, even though she was wearing a dress that Frank hadn't seen worn in public since the seventies. He wasn't sure if she was going for a retro look or if it was just an old dress.

"Can I get you something to drink, Miss Arnold."

"No, I'm fine, thank-you."

"Well then, let's get started. I must say, Miss Arnold, I am extremely impressed with your work."

Abbey looked up from the floor in surprise by Frank's statement.

"You know my work?"

"Yes. I took the liberty of contacting the director of the free law clinic where you did volunteer work and he was kind enough to send me a few samples of your writing. And I must say, you are quite thorough in your research findings as well as very detail in your motions and legal briefs."

"Thank-you."

Frank couldn't remember ever meeting anyone as shy and introverted as this young lawyer, nonetheless, he liked her. Of course, Miss Arnold was smart and had tremendous writing skills but it was something more than that.

"Let me give you a little background about the firm, Miss Arnold."

Frank kept expecting her to ask him to call her Abigail but she didn't. He wasn't sure if she hadn't thought to correct him or if she just preferred to be called Miss Arnold.

"As you may have noticed, our law firm is located in the middle of an area known as Little Havana, just outside of Miami. I am of Cuban descent but have lived right here my entire life."

Frank went on explaining his background, telling Abbey how he had started as a sole practitioner and grew his firm to what it is today.

"I have five full-time attorneys and now I am looking for a new associate to primarily do research as well as motions. I have enough lawyers that want to do nothing more than go to court and try cases. No one likes or even wants to do the necessary prep work any more."

"That's what I do best, Mr. de la Carta."

"Again, please call me Frank."

"That's what I do best... Frank."

With a weak whisper and head down, Abbey began trying to sell herself with all the conviction she could muster.

"I truly don't mind spending my entire day in the Law Library helping the other attorneys with any type of needed preparation work. What I don't want to do Frank, is appear in court. I do not do well speaking in front of people but if you have an opening for a lawyer to do nothing but research and write, then I'm your lawyer."

The more Abbey spoke, the more Frank knew she was exactly the lawyer he needed.

"If I decide to hire you Miss Arnold, how soon could you start?"

Abbey sat frozen. No interview had ever gone this far before. She hadn't dared to even think about a start date and actually leaving Memphis. Suddenly, it was becoming all too real.

"Miss Arnold?"

Abbey was startled back to the present by Frank's voice and was astounded to hear her own voice saying that she could start almost immediately.

"Obviously, I would have to find a place to live first as well as make arrangements for my father."

Frank was a little confused by her response.

"I just meant that since I live with my father in order to care for him, I would have to figure out..." Abbey said before pausing mid-sentence.

"Is your father ill?"

"No, my father doesn't have any disabilities or grave illnesses but ever since my mother passed away, he has struggled greatly trying to adjust to living without her. After graduation from law school, I returned home to watch over him."

"I can certainly have one of the associates assist you in finding a place to live and if need be, I could give you an advance on your salary to use as a security deposit once you find a place."

It quickly dawned on Abbey that she had in fact

just been hired. It was clearly no longer a question of "if we should hire you" but rather one of "how soon could you move here?" Thoughts started flooding into her mind. What would she tell her father? Would he be willing to quit both his jobs and move to Miami with her?

After what seemed like an eternity to Abbey, she looked up at Frank and said, "I can start in one week."

"Perfect!"

Frank stood up and reached across the desk to shake her hand.

"Miss Arnold, it has been a true pleasure."

Abbey was surprisingly relaxed after making such a life-altering decision and had no qualms when she replied, "please, call me Abbey."

Frank replied with a slight laugh, "Abbey it is. If you wouldn't mind stepping into Carla's office, she has some paperwork for you to fill out."

As soon as Frank stepped out of his office with Abbey, Carla stood up. And by the smile on both of their faces, she knew Miss Arnold had been hired on the spot.

"Carla, please assist our newest associate in filling out all the necessary paperwork. Miss Arnold will be starting in one week. Thank-you again, Abbey. I look forward to seeing you next week."

Then Frank shook Abbey's hand once more before returning to his office, shutting the door behind him.

Smilingly broadly, Carla turned back to Abbey.

"Welcome to the Law Offices of Francisco de la Carta."

Chapter Three

As the Medical Examiner reached the top of the stairs, he saw the crime scene investigators already photographing the untouched bodies. Dr. Olsen approached the first body, a female lying at the foot of the desk, immediately noticing the healthy color of her skin. Kneeling closer to the body, Dr. Olsen felt for a pulse and discovered the female was actually alive.

"Call for an ambulance!" Dr. Olsen shouted to no one in particular.

He couldn't believe no one had noticed the female wasn't dead. As Dr. Olsen gently rolled the female body over onto her back, he saw no blood or even any signs of trauma. The female body felt warm to his touch and showed no indication of rigor mortis. However, before he could make a more thorough examination of the body, the female opened her eyes and sat up. Her sudden movement startled one of the crime scene investigators so much that he dropped his camera, almost hitting the female on the head.

"Everything is okay. You're safe now." Dr. Olsen

assured her. Then he asked who she was.

"I'm Carla, the Office Manager. Who are you? What's going on?"

But before anyone had a chance to respond, Carla began screaming.

"Oh my God! He's dead, isn't he? Please say it isn't him!"

Carla was becoming hysterical.

"Can you tell us what happened here?"

"Who did this? Why is this happening? Who are you?" Carla just kept screaming the same questions over and over.

As her hysteria mounted, Carla began to wave her arms around as if to defend herself from the people surrounding her.

"Help me! Please, somebody help me!"

"Carla, you're safe. Nobody here is trying to hurt you."

Carla wasn't comprehending what Dr. Olsen was saying and just kept waving her arms in the air while her screaming intensified. Dr. Olsen reached into his medical bag, took out a syringe and injected Carla with a mild sedative. Within seconds, Carla started to calm down. Dr. Olsen instructed one of the crime scene investigators to stay with Carla and to makes sure she did not try to stand up. The Medical Examiner now turned his attention to the body inside of the office slumped over the desk. There was absolutely no doubt that this person was dead. However, after a cursory examination, Dr. Olsen could not determine the cause of death. There was no blood on the body, no signs of physical trauma and definitely no signs of a struggle. It simply could have been a heart attack. The issue with diagnosing a heart attack is that there are no external signs, therefore an autopsy along with a full blood work-up is the best way to determine if it was indeed an acute myocardial infarction.

"Well, what do you think Doc? Natural causes?" One of the crime scene investigators asked.

"I can't really tell without an autopsy. Nonetheless, I think you should continue to treat this office as if it were a crime scene. Take pictures of the entire room, every single detail, including the body from every angle."

"Are you're thinking it could be a homicide?"

"I'm not completely sure but something doesn't feel right. Keep processing the scene while I phone it in."

Homicide Detectives Robert Henderson and Jose Garcia were about to finish their shift when they received the 1045 call.

"Why are we receiving this 1045 call just as we're leaving?" Detective Henderson asked his partner.

"Damned if I know!"

A 1045 call is Miami police code for a person found dead on arrival. If the scene had been declared a homicide case, the call would have been received as a 1031.

"Maybe dispatch got it wrong?" Detective Garcia said questioningly.

"Got what wrong? The code or us?" Detective Henderson replied with a chuckle.

The two detectives arrived at the east end of Little Havana and were surprised to see the address had led them to an office building, rather than a residence. The sign out front indicated they were about to enter the Law Offices of Francisco Alfonso de la Carta. The grounds were meticulously maintained as was the building itself.

"I wonder if it's de la Carta's body that they found."

"Do you know the guy?" Detective Henderson asked Detective Garcia.

"Yeah. A real scum bag defense lawyer. He represents most of the big-time cocaine dealers. Not to mention, raking in a lot of money from the misery of others. I can't stand the guy."

"Sounds like you might have some history with the guy, Garcia."

"A few years ago, I made a clean collar on a major "coke" dealer. The guy was distributing pounds of the stuff throughout the Miami area. We also believed he was sending massive amounts of other illegal drugs up to New York. I worked on the case for almost a year before we were able to make a bust. The dealer hired de la Carta to be his representative and the case finally went to trial. We had an airtight case so there was no way we could lose! However, when I got on the witness stand, de la Carta really tore into me. By the time I stepped down off the witness stand, I wasn't sure whose side I had just testified for. But even worse, "somehow" the lab screwed up on the testing of the drugs. To this day, I still don't know how my airtight case was completely broken wide open! I'm certain there wasn't actual negligence on the lab's part but I was never able to prove it."

"What was the verdict?"

"The cocaine couldn't be submitted as evidence due to the lab's "negligence" and the dealer walked."

"Tough break!"

"You're not kidding!"

"Does this de la Carta ever lose?"

"Depends on how you define lose."

"Like the type of loss that would anger a client enough to want him dead."

"You can't work with the type of clientele that de la Carta did without making a few enemies along the way."

Before entering the building, Detective Henderson

turned his attention to the police officers who were outside interviewing possible witnesses.

"Do we have an identification of the body yet?"

"A woman named Carla Hernandez, Office Manager and personal assistant to Mr. de la Carta has been positively identified."

"Is she the 1045?"

"No. At first sight, the crime scene investigators thought she was a victim but apparently, after finding the dead body, she had simply fainted while attempting to call 9-1-1. When she came to, she instantly became hysterical, so the Medical Examiner sedated her. It hasn't been positively confirmed but we believe the dead body is Mr. de la Carta."

"What do you mean by "believe"? Why aren't you certain?"

"We haven't had anyone who can positively identify him yet. Although there was a wallet in his suit coat pocket."

"Was it his own coat?"

"Well, he was wearing it."

"Are you thinking he was carrying someone else's wallet? What about Miss Hernandez? Why couldn't she identify the body?"

"Apparently, they don't want to upset her again, so the Medical Examiner suggested we find someone else to do the formal identification."

"There certainly seems to be a large group of people out here. Surely, one of them must be an employee that could identify the body."

"We didn't want to let any outsiders enter the building in case this is actually a crime scene."

"So, you're telling me that we don't even know if this is a crime scene yet? Hasn't the Medical Examiner made a determination as to whether or not this person died of natural causes or was murdered?"

"Not yet."

"How about a photo? Couldn't someone have a taken a photo of the guy and brought it out here to see if any of these people recognize him?"

The officer didn't have a response.

"Have you spoken to anyone out here?" Detective Garcia asked as he could see Detective Henderson was getting frustrated by the officer's answers.

"We've interviewed most of the staff that are standing out here as well as the gardener."

"Where's the gardener now?"

"That's him, the man in the hat standing next to the flower bed."

The two detectives headed towards the front door with Detective Henderson giving the officer a directive to not let anyone leave the premises or enter the building.

Walking past the gardener, Detective Henderson asked if he took care of the yard personally.

"Yes, sir." The gardener replied in a heavy Hispanic accent.

"You do one hell of a job!"

"Yes, sir."

"I especially like those blue flowers."

This time the gardener didn't respond. Detective Henderson wasn't sure if it was because the man didn't understand the comment or just didn't like talking to police officers. Once Detective Henderson and Detective Garcia entered the building, a uniformed officer directed them to the body on the second floor.

As they were ascending the stairs, Detective Henderson turned to Detective Garcia.

"No matter how many dead bodies I've seen and investigated, I can never get used to this smell."

"Detective Henderson. Detective Garcia." Dr. Olsen acknowledged the men as they entered the office where the body was located.

"Hey, Doc. What do we have here?" Detective Henderson asked.

I'm not sure yet. It could just be a heart attack."

"Then why are we here? And why is CSI here already?"

"Apparently, the first uniform officers to arrive thought they had found two dead bodies, so when they called it in, it was presumed a homicide. Turns out we only have one body. The Office Manager discovered the body and while attempting to call 9-1-1, she fainted."

"Do we finally have a positive identification on the body?"

"We certainly do. One of the crime scene investigators knew de la Carta from a law case a few months ago."

"How's the office manager holding up?" Detective Garcia asked.

"She's feeling better now that she has been resting."

"Any chance we could interview her?" Detective Henderson asked hopefully.

"Okay but take it easy on her. She's had quite a shock."

"Any signs of foul play?"

"Not exactly."

"What do you mean, not exactly?"

"There's just something about this situation that doesn't seem right."

"Like what Doc?

"Well…for example, even though he is sitting at his desk, he is still wearing his suit coat."

"And that is unusual?"

"Yes, since a person wouldn't normally wear their coat while relaxing at their desk. But it's not just that, if you'll note that on the desk there's a bottle of Tequila and an empty glass. It appears Mr. de la Carta was sitting down to enjoy a drink before leaving the office, so I seriously doubt he would still be wearing his coat. And if he was with someone, there should be a second glass. Sometimes a heart attack victim will grab at their chest and there may be some vomiting. Mr. de la Carta looks too peaceful and the way his body is slumped over the desk just doesn't seem conducive to a heart attack. Of course, I won't know anything for certain until an autopsy is performed."

"That's it? He doesn't look right? Detective Garcia asked.

"I've been the Medical Examiner in this county for nearly twenty years, examining hundreds of bodies, both homicide victims as well as those who died from natural causes and I'm telling you, something about this isn't right!"

"Can you give us the time of death at least?" Detective Henderson asked.

"Sometime between Friday evening when Mr. de la Carta was last seen at the office and this morning when his body was discovered."

"You can't do any better than that?"

"I'm afraid not."

"What about checking his liver temperature? Wouldn't that determine the time of death?"

"It's not that easy. A body drops 1.5 degrees per hour after death until it reaches room temperature. The issue we have here is that someone set the thermostat at 88 degrees, therefore Mr. de la Carta's body reached room temperature in about fifteen hours. However, if I were to venture a guess based on the condition of his body, I would say Mr. de la Carta died sometime Friday evening or early Saturday morning."

Detective Henderson looked around the room, jotting down his observations in his ever-present pocket notepad while directing Detective Garcia to go interview the office manager.

"Miss Hernandez?"

"Si."

"Preferir a Espanol?"

"No, English will be fine."

"I'm Detective Garcia. Do you feel up to answering some questions?"

"Yes."

The sedative had definitely done its job. Carla was much calmer, almost distant.

"I understand you were the one that discovered the body."

"Yes, when I came to work this morning."

"And what time was that?"

"I got here about 8:30, as usual. I unlocked the

front door and immediately noticed how warm the offices were."

"Warmer than normal temperature in the office?"

"Yes, it felt as though someone had turned the heat on."

Detective Garcia couldn't believe someone would intentionally run the heater when it had been so warm and humid the last few days.

"We set the thermostat at 70 degrees and the office is always maintained at that temperature. To keep the office at 70 degrees over a long weekend, we usually leave the air conditioner running. Mr. de la Carta likes it…I mean… Carla's lip began to quiver and tears welled up in her eyes as she quickly corrected herself, …he liked it that way. Sometimes he would come in over the weekend to work and wanted the office cool."

"When was the last time you saw your boss?"

"Friday evening."

"What time was that?"

"Around 7:15."

"Was anyone else in the office when you left?"

"No, being a Friday night, everyone was gone by 6."

"But you stayed until around 7:15? Why so late?"

"Mr. de la Carta asked me if I could stay later since he had an appointment at 6:00."

"Do you know with whom?"

"I have no idea. He'd been out of the office for a few days and had just returned that afternoon."

"Do you know where he had been?"

"No, I don't. I received a brief message when I came into the office last week saying he would be gone for a few days and nothing more."

"Was it unusual for Mr. de la Carta to simply leave, not letting anyone in the office know where he was going?"

"Well, it didn't happen often, but it did happen. Sometimes he would get a call from a client, then fly down to Mexico and wouldn't leave a message as to who he was meeting or exactly where in Mexico he was going."

"Did anything unusual happen on Friday? Did Mr. de la Carta say anything when he returned to the office later that day?"

"Well, there was something a little out of the ordinary. When Mr. de la Carta came in on Friday, he didn't say anything at all. He simply went upstairs and walked directly into his office."

"About what time was that?"

"I don't recall."

"And Mr. de la Carta didn't say anything about where he was?"

"No, he just went into his office, shut the door and sat down. He didn't even say hello."

"How did he seem?"

"Normal, nothing odd. Mr. de la Carta had some files on his desk that he was looking through and it appeared he had something urgent to get out before the end of the day."

"Did he talk to any of the other employees?"

"No one! In fact, everyone else was a little on edge when they saw him."

"What do you mean on edge?"

"It was strange. Everybody just kept their heads down and no one said a word."

"Can you give me a list of the other people who were in the office when Mr. de la Carta returned on Friday?

"Of course."

"And when you left there was no one else here?"

"No one."

"Did you lock the door or set the alarm when you left?"

"No, I didn't because Mr. de la Carta asked me not to."

"Do you know if Mr. de la Carta was expecting anybody?"

"Just the 6:00 o'clock appointment."

"Do all the employees have keys to the office?"

"Not everyone. I do, of course and each of the attorneys also have a key. Maria, the cleaning woman, is the only other person that has a key to the office."

"Was she here when you left?"

"No, she usually doesn't arrive until 8pm."

"Does she come in every night?"

"Just Monday through Friday, never on the weekend."

"Is there any surveillance or security videos?"

"No, Mr. de la Carta insisted we not have any surveillance because of the clientele we represent."

"Do you know if Mr. de la Carta had any health problems?"

"None. He was in perfect health."

"How about a family, was he married?"

"No, divorced."

"Any children?"

"No, that was the reason for the divorce. Mrs. de la Carta wanted children and he didn't."

"Was the divorce amicable?"

"Oh, heavens yes! They stayed on friendly terms, even after Mrs. de la Carta remarried."

"Do you know if Mr. de la Carta was having problems with any of his clients?"

"What do you mean by problems?"

"Such problems as any dissatisfied or threating clients."

"Do you think someone killed Mr. de la Carta?"

Not wanting to upset Carla any more than she already was, Detective Garcia kept his answer intentionally vague.

"It appears as though he may have just had a heart attack. I'm simply asking some routine questions."

"I can't believe Mr. de la Carta had a heart attack. He looked fine when I left Friday night."

Carla began to cry.

Detective Garcia waited a few moments before asking if she felt up to answering a few more questions.

"Detective Garcia, what am I going to do? What am I going to tell everybody? What about our clients? What about all the cases we were working on?"

She put her face into her hands and began to cry harder.

"Actually, I think that's enough questions for now, Miss Hernandez."

Detective Garcia was beginning to feel sorry for her. As he turned around to leave, Detective Henderson was approaching.

"I have a few more questions before we leave ma'am."

Carla slowly lifted her head from her hands and looked up at Detective Henderson.

"When you came into the office, was the alarm set?"

Carla had to think for a minute. Her arrival to the office now seemed like a million years ago, instead of just a few hours. As she thought back to the first moments of her day, Carla remembered unlocking the front door, walking over to the alarm keypad and typing in the code as she did every morning.

"I believe it was set, Detective...?"

"Detective Henderson. What about the lights in Mr. de la Carta's office? Were they on or off?"

"I don't remember if the lights were on or off, but I know for certain that I didn't touch the light switch in his office."

"You mentioned to Detective Garcia that you noticed Mr. de la Carta appeared to be searching through a file when you left his office Friday night. Do you happen to know what he was looking for?"

'No, I don't but it looked like he had been jotting down notes on a yellow legal pad."

Detective Henderson turned around to glance at Mr. de la Carta's desk and saw nothing on it other than an empty glass and a bottle of Tequila.

"Was it Mr. de la Carta's habit to have a drink in his office?"

"Occasionally, he would have a glass of Scotch while working."

"Did he also drink Tequila on occasion?"

"I don't remember him ever drinking Tequila in the office."

"Do you know where the bottle of Tequila might have come from?"

"I can't be sure it is the same bottle, however a

client did bring him a bottle of Tequila a few weeks ago as a thank-you gift for a case he was working on."

"I'll need the name of that client along with any contact information before we leave."

"Certainly."

"And you're sure no one else was in the office when you left?"

"Absolutely sure."

"Thank-you for your time."

Detective Henderson went back into de la Carta's office and took a few more notes. He made sure to also note that the light switch was in the "off" position. Then the detective walked over to the far corner of the office, kneeling to look across the plush brown carpet covering the floor of de la Carta's office.

"Okay if we take the body now?" The Medical Examiner inquired.

The detective got up, walked back over to the desk and looked down at the body of Mr. de la Carta. He had to agree with Dr. Olsen, something just didn't seem right. Detective Henderson had been a homicide detective for over ten years and had earned a reputation for having an uncanny ability in solving the most difficult homicide cases. His instincts were telling him that Mr. de la Carta didn't die of natural causes and that this was most likely a homicide. Detective Henderson also strongly felt that the key to solving the case was within this office.

"Go ahead, Doc. Be sure to let me know the minute you have the lab and autopsy reports."

"I have one case ahead of this one or do you want me to make this a priority?"

"No, I don't think an extra day or two will make a difference. Although, I would like you to run the blood screen right away."

"Will do."

"Thanks."

As Detectives Henderson and Garcia were heading downstairs, they could hear a loud argument coming from outside between a female and one of the uniformed officers.

Hastening their steps, the detectives quickly arrived to help resolve the argument.

"What seems to be the problem, Officer?" Detective Henderson asked.

"This woman is insisting that I let her enter the building and I'm trying to explain why I can't let her, or anyone else for that matter, go in right now."

"He can't keep me out of my office! I have every right to go in there!"

Detective Henderson stepped in and told the irate woman,

"At the moment, you don't have any right to go in there. This is an active crime scene."

"What do you mean it is an active crime scene? What kind of crime? We're all standing out here and no one will tell us anything about what is going on inside."

"What's your name?"

"Rosemarie, Rosemarie Callahan. And you are …?

"I'm Detective Henderson and this is my partner, Detective Garcia."

"Can either of you tell me what kind of crime scene this is at least? What happened? Was there a burglary last night? You can't legally keep me from knowing, so tell me this minute what has happened inside!" Rosemarie demanded loudly as she looked Detective Henderson right in the eye.

"I'm sorry to inform you Miss Callahan…"

Chapter Four

Rosemarie Callahan grew up in the Irish community of Bridgeport, Illinois, located on the south side of Chicago. She was raised in a traditional Irish Catholic family with three older brothers, two of whom became Chicago Police Officers like her father. Rather than follow in the family tradition, Rosemarie's youngest brother joined the Marine Corps. Growing up with three brothers, Rosemarie quickly learned how to be tough and she definitely wasn't intimidated working among strong, powerful men.

Being the only girl, Rosemarie's family was strict with her and overly protective, especially her three brothers. She attended an all-girl catholic school and while she did date a little in high school and college, Rosemarie was still a virgin as a college graduate. Being 5'10', 185 pounds and raised in a mostly male household, she was considered more of a tomboy than a femme fatale, despite having enormous breasts.

After graduating from college, Rosemarie attended

Loyola University, Chicago, School of Law. And even though academics didn't come easily to her, Rosemarie managed to graduate in the upper fourth of her class. However, what did come easily was her aggressive verbal skills which gave her a definite edge in winning the moot court competition. Once she received her law degree, Rosemarie went to work in the City Prosecutor's office but after two years, she felt it was time to move on. When she thought about going into private practice as a criminal defense lawyer, her family did all that they could to discourage her, especially her police officer brothers. They couldn't understand how she could work to set free the criminals that her brothers had worked so hard to put away. Nonetheless, Rosemarie knew she couldn't stay at the prosecutor's office. It was a toxic work environment and in the past two years, Rosemarie had felt compelled to file sexual harassment complaints, even one against her supervisor who continually made comments about her breasts. One of her co-workers had asked her out to dinner several times but Rosemarie always politely, yet firmly, declined. Tired of constantly being rebuked, the co-worker began spreading rumors that she was a lesbian, a prude and a cold-hearted bitch, resulting in Rosemarie feeling ostracized from the rest of the staff, not to mention being passed over twice for a well-deserved promotion. Rosemarie sent her resume to numerous law firms in the surrounding areas yet received no responses, partly in fact that her supervisor refused to give her a favorable recommendation but also because of her mediocre law school grades. In frustration, she decided to look for positions outside of Chicago. After several months of looking for work without a single offer, Rosemarie felt she needed a vacation away from the office and her domineering family to figure out what she was not only going to do about her career as a lawyer but also her life. She certainly couldn't continue putting up with the miserable working conditions at the prosecutor's office. Since Rosemarie had over two months of vacation time accumulated, she decided to take a Caribbean cruise, rationalizing it would be a good way to relax and unwind, clearing her mind to plan the new direction of her life.

When Rosemarie submitted her request for vacation time, her supervisor informed her that he wasn't sure that he could approve it. Obviously, he was just being a jerk since the office was slow and had no immediate trials pending. She told him that either he approves her request or she would quit. Rosemarie knew her supervisor wouldn't call her bluff because even though the office was slow at the moment, they needed her and would be in quite a bind if she left.

"Alright, I'll approve your request on one condition. When you return, you'll show me your tan lines."

Without a moment's hesitation, Rosemarie's hand flew across his face, slapping him with such force, it literally turned his head.

"Forget the vacation! I QUIT!!"

"I was just kidding!"

When Rosemarie saw the red handprint on his face, it felt so satisfying that she wanted to do it again.

"That's exactly why I can no longer work here. I'm tired of your snide comments and offensive "jokes.""

"C'mon, Rosemarie!" Don't you have a sense of humor? Actually, on second thought, I'm glad to see you go, you uptight bitch!"

"Fuck you!"

"You better figure out how to deal with your all your sexual hang-ups and having such huge tits or you'll find yourself in the same situation wherever you go!"

Rosemarie had already slapped him once but was sorely tempted to do it again. Instead, she cleared out her desk and left without saying another word.

Even not knowing what her future held, Rosemarie was certain that whatever it was, it had to be better than her current situation. Upon arriving home, Rosemarie called a local travel agency to book a two-week cruise through the Caribbean. The travel agent let Rosemarie know that if her schedule were flexible enough for her to leave in eight days, the agency could offer her a cruise at half-price. Rosemarie was already aware that cruise lines often gave steep discounts for last minute bookings to fill their ships. Although she was hesitant about waiting eight days to leave, Rosemarie decided she couldn't pass up such a great deal and booked the cruise. Rosemarie asked the travel agent to book her flight to Miami five days ahead of the cruise so she could have a little time to herself before boarding a crowded ship. The travel agent also suggested booking a room at the Fontainebleau Hotel, which sounded perfect to Rosemarie. While arranging her vacation, Rosemarie was beginning to feel more excited than regretful about quitting her job. This was going to be the beginning of a whole new chapter in her life!

Later that day, Rosemarie stopped by her dad's house to tell him she had finally quit. It was the house she grew up in and it still felt like her real home. Walking in without knocking as she always did, Rosemarie was pleased to see her older brother was there also. Now she could tell them both her unexpected news.

"What a pleasant surprise!!" Her dad truly meant it as he loved having her stop by, no matter what the reason.

"What's up, Sis?"

"Nothing too much. I just stopped by to let Dad

know that I was taking some vacation time. I'll be in Miami for a few days and then off for a two-week Caribbean cruise."

Rosemarie surprised herself when she didn't tell them the bigger news of quitting her job.

"Why Miami? Why a cruise? Her dad asked.

"And why now? Is everything okay?" Rosemarie's brother chimed in.

It was the perfect opening for Rosemarie to them both about everything, instead she responded by saying that she just needed a little R & R.

"Are you sure you are all right?" Her brother asked again.

"Of course!"

Rosemarie didn't know why she couldn't bring herself to tell them that she had quit her job since they were going to find out eventually anyway but whatever the reason, she kept the news to herself while she filled them in on the details of her upcoming trip.

"I'll be staying at the Fontainebleau and I'll call you with the room number once I check in."

"When are you leaving?"

Her Dad began to ask more questions but Rosemarie cut him off.

"I have to get going since I have a lot of last-minute details to take care of before I leave."

And before either of them could ask her another question, Rosemarie was out the door.

Two days later, she was in Miami checking into the Fontainebleau Hotel.

Once she was in her room, Rosemarie found herself siting on the edge of the bed contemplating her rash decision to not only quit her job but then travel to Miami and take a two-week cruise. What was she thinking? Yet, even with no job, no prospects for employment in the near future and not enough savings to live on for very long, she was oddly unconcerned.

"I need a drink." And she headed downstairs to the hotel bar.

Even though it was still early in the day, the bar was surprisingly quite crowded. Rosemarie went up to the bar, ordered an Irish Coffee with no whipped cream and scanned the room for a table. Every table was taken, however she happened to notice a party of three stand up and appear to be leaving. Rosemarie quickly headed toward the table, hoping to grab it before someone else did. She had just about reached the table, when one of the members of the party sat back down. As Rosemarie turned to scan the room once more, the man seated at the head of the table spoke up.

"Would you care to join me?"

The man was wearing a nice suit, well-groomed

and very handsome. His voice was welcoming and Rosemarie felt at ease accepting his invitation to join him.

"If you wouldn't mind. There seems to be a shortage of seats."

"Not at all. I certainly don't need an entire table."

"Thank-you, that is so kind of you. I don't normally sit with strangers in a bar or anywhere for that matter but you seem okay." Rosemarie said with a laugh.

"Well, I don't normally invite people to join me but you seem harmless enough." He laughingly replied.

"By the way, I'm Frank." And he extended his hand.

"Pleased to meet you, Frank. I'm Rosemarie." She said as she firmly shook his hand.

"So, what brings you to the Fontainebleau Hotel Rosemarie?"

"I'm down here on vacation." She replied without wanting to offer more, especially to a stranger, even a nice one.

"Down here from where?" Frank asked, determined to know more about Rosemarie.

"Chicago." Again, not elaborating in her reply.

Frank genuinely liked the way she responded to his questions. Very confidently. Without knowing anything about her background but simply by the way she conducted herself, Frank felt Rosemarie would make a great lawyer. There was no doubt that this woman would be able to hold her own with any prosecutor.

"What do you do for a living in Chicago?"

"At the moment, I'm unemployed."

"No better time to take a vacation then when you're unemployed." Frank joked.

"What line of work were in before you became unemployed?"

"I was a prosecutor for the City Attorney's office."

Suddenly Frank's interest piqued.

"And what line of work are you in, Frank?"

"You probably aren't going to believe this but I'm a criminal defense lawyer."

Now it was Rosemarie's interest that was piqued. For the next three hours, she and Frank discussed the law, prosecution, criminal defense and the constitution. Rosemarie was surprised at how much she had in common with someone practicing criminal defense. Meanwhile, Frank was thinking about what a great asset an ex-prosecutor would be to his law firm, especially such a dynamic woman. He had been toying with the idea of hiring another attorney to help with the firm's rapidly growing trial caseload. How fortuitous an attorney just happened to be sitting across the table from him! And not just a capable attorney but one firm in her beliefs with the mind of a good defense lawyer rather than a prosecutor. Frank liked Rosemarie as well as the fact that she had family in law enforcement which was something that might come in handy someday.

Rosemarie was surprised at how much she agreed with the things Frank was saying considering their careers had them representing opposite sides of the courtroom. Being so in sync with Frank's line of thinking only solidified what Rosemarie had long suspected, she was not meant to be a prosecutor.

"Have you ever thought about relocating to Miami?" Frank asked suddenly.

"Not until just now." Rosemarie responded without any hesitation.

After all that she had put up with at the City Attorney's office, Rosemarie appreciated how Frank never hit on her, never made any inappropriate comments and hadn't stared at her breasts even once during their entire conversation. He had been nothing but professional.

"Rosemarie, I would like to offer you a position with my law firm here in Miami."

"Just like that?" Rosemarie questioned somewhat surprised.

Frank had not only surprised Rosemarie by the unexpected offer but himself as well.

"Just like that. That's the one of the advantages of being the head of a law firm, I don't need to get approval from anyone else. In case you're interested, here's my business card." Frank handed Rosemarie the card that he had taken out of his suitcoat pocket after he had made the job offer.

"The office opens tomorrow at 8:30 am but most of the staff arrives between 9:00 and 9:30 am. Please feel free to stop by any time that is convenient for you to meet the rest of the firm. Rosemarie, this is a serious offer. The job is yours if you want it."

Standing up to leave, Frank apologized to Rosemarie for having to leave so abruptly.

"I'm sorry I can't spend more time going over the details of the position right now but I have an appointment that I have to keep. I hope to see you tomorrow and we can seal the deal then."

With that, Frank left the bar, never looking back. A few minutes later, the server brought Rosemarie a drink.

"Thank-you but I didn't order this." Rosemarie said.

"The drink is compliments of Mr. de la Carta."

"Who?"

"Frank de la Carta. You know, the man you were sitting with."

It was the first time EVER that a man in a bar had bought Rosemarie a drink who didn't have expectations of something more.

Chapter Five

Nick overheard what Detective Henderson told Rosemarie and walked over to her.

"I suppose you heard what the detective just told me."

"Hard to believe but not at all surprising."

"Why would you say that?"

"Just think about our clientele. We've had a few losses lately and our clients haven't been too happy about that."

"Are you suggesting one of our clients did it?"

Detective Henderson was watching the dialogue exchange between the two associates and although he couldn't hear the actual conversation, he did notice how unemotional they were while discussing the death of their employer. They seemed so unaffected. It was as if the two lawyers were simply talking about something they had heard on the morning news. And then there was the other associate that avoided any eye contact and was clearly more concerned about getting into her office than hearing about the death of her boss. No one seemed to care about the death of Mr. de la Carta except the office manager. He decided to direct his attention to the outside police officers and strode over to the one in charge of the scene.

"Sergeant, did you find out anything?"

"Nothing much. The entire staff is here, no one is unaccounted for and they all seemed to have liked working for the victim."

"Anyone mention a client that may have had a beef?"

"One of the secretaries mentioned a heated argument de la Carta had with a client a few weeks ago. She said they were shouting at each other in the entryway. Mr. de la Carta tried to move the "conversation" upstairs but the client turned and stormed out."

"Did you get a name?"

"She wouldn't give it up. Declaring "attorney-client" privilege."

"Bullshit! Did she at least tell you what they were arguing about?"

"Apparently, the firm lost a case involving one of the client's associates."

"The client a drug dealer?"

"The secretary refused to say."

"Where is she now?"

The Sergeant pointed her out and Detective

Henderson headed towards the woman but then suddenly stopped, turning back towards the sergeant.

"By the way, did anyone happen to mention if something was going on between the office manager and de la Carta?"

"When I asked that very question, no one knew of anything or if they did, no one was admitting it. Damn lawyers! Do you suspect something was going on between the two?"

"Not necessarily. She just seems to be the only one who cares that he's dead."

As Detective Henderson neared the secretary who had cited "attorney-client" privilege, Nick stopped him.

"Excuse me, Detective…?"

"Henderson. Who are you?"

"Attorney Nicholas Constantine. I work here and I want to know if we can enter the building now."

The detective couldn't help but notice that the young attorney's voice was firm and full of self-inspired confidence.

"No." And with that, Detective Henderson walked away.

"What an asshole!" Nick said as he turned back to Rosemarie.

Working with law enforcement during legal trials left Nick with a great distaste for anyone with a badge as he believed they were all liars and would say or do anything to get a conviction.

"He's just doing his job." Rosemarie calmly replied.

After a brief conversation with the smug secretary, Detective Henderson headed back to the sergeant. As he passed by Rosemarie and Nick, he noticed the two attorneys whispering to each other.

"Hey, Hotshot! I'll need your itinerary from the weekend. Yours too, Miss."

"Be glad to." Nick replied with a touch of sarcasm aimed at the detective.

Nick knew he didn't have to tell or give Detective Henderson anything but he also knew that the detective could take him to police headquarters for intense questioning on a whim.

"Sergeant!" The detective yelled, scanning the crowd.

"Yes, sir?" The Sergeant replied as he quickly appeared by Detective Henderson's side.

"Have someone take pictures of everyone here, get all their id's and then let them leave. No one and I mean NO ONE goes into the building until we know how the guy died. Keep two officers posted around the clock until I tell you differently."

"You got it, Detective. Think it was a homicide?"

"Don't know yet but I'm not taking any chances. Keep your people away from all the files until we know something for sure. I wouldn't want any cases dismissed because we accessed privileged files."

Detectives Henderson and Garcia left the scene and headed towards downtown Miami.

"Where are we going now?" Detective Garcia asked his partner.

"The Criminal Courts building. I want to look at who de la Carta was representing in the last few months. I understand he lost a case recently involving someone close to one of his "big" clients."

Meanwhile back at the crime scene, Abbey approached Nick, looking down at the ground as usual.

"What are we going to do now, Nick?"

"Nothing."

"I mean about our clients, their cases, court appearances…"

Before Abbey could finish her sentence, Nick rudely interrupted.

"I'll have Carla make a list of all the active cases and we'll call those clients in for a meeting. Hopefully, they'll want to stay with the firm."

"Will there still be a firm?" Abbey asked with genuine concern.

"Of course! We will definitely keep it going." Nick replied confidently. "I will contact the Court on all the cases currently set for hearings or trials and apply for continuances. I hardly think anyone would object under the current circumstances."

Abbey admired how Nick could always confidently take charge of any situation. He made her believe everything was going to be all right. As Abbey walked towards her car, Nick turned his attention once again to Rosemarie.

"Would you like to discuss all this over dinner with me tonight?" Nick asked, already certain of Rosemarie's answer.

Rosemarie had dined with Nick several times since joining the firm and genuinely enjoyed his company. He never made a pass at her or acted inappropriately like her co-workers at the City Prosecutor's office.

"I think we should ask Abbey to join us." Rosemarie replied.

"Absolutely!"

Nick saw that Abbey was about to get into her car but before he even had a chance to say anything, Abbey spoke up.

"I can't make it."

"Why not?" Rosemarie pressed, knowing Abbey didn't have any type of life outside of the law firm.

"My dad will be moving here soon and I need to have everything ready."

Both Nick and Rosemarie knew this was just a lame excuse, one Abbey had used so many times before.

Abbey had begged her father to move to Miami ever since she joined the firm but he steadfastly refused.

"Abbey, this is important. It's about our futures, yours included. We will even pick you up. I am not taking no for an answer." Nick said insistently.

"Where are we dining?" Abbey hesitantly asked.

Nick wanted to scream out that it really doesn't matter where they go but instead replied that Abbey could choose the restaurant.

"Would pizza be okay with everyone?" Abbey asked shyly.

Nick was hoping to go to an upscale steakhouse, however, it was Rosemarie who quickly replied as she understood Abbey better than anyone else at the firm and was glad that Abbey had finally agreed to dine out with them.

"Sure! We'll go to Luigi's Ristorante. Their pizza is excellent!"

"Meanwhile, we should all start working on a list of things that we need to do immediately to keep this firm going and we'll compare notes at dinner." Nick said, once again taking charge.

Chapter Six

Nicholas Cornelius Constantine III was born in West Granby, Connecticut, the only child of an extremely wealthy Greek family. Nicholas's, or Nick as he preferred to be called, grandfather immigrated to America with his family after the end of WW1 where they settled on the coast of Connecticut near Long Island Sound. And since fishing was all that Nick's grandfather had ever known, shortly after arriving in Connecticut, he bought a small fishing boat, equipped it with a bit of fishing gear and embarked on a career that became quite profitable and the envy of any immigrant. One small fishing boat soon turned into a fleet of fishing vessels, specializing in anchovies. Nick's grandfather's anchovy business was so successful that he ultimately founded a cannery and became the leading provider of anchovies in the United States.

Nick's father grew up working in the family business even though he loathed the fishing industry but as a dutiful son he felt that there was no other option. As head of the family, Nick's grandfather refused to allow his only son to attend college as he strongly believed you couldn't learn the fishing trade in some fancy school, you needed to learn the business from the ground up. Therefore, Nick's dad started by working on the boats, then running the boats, eventually working his way up the ranks to finally operating the cannery. And even though Nick's dad did everything that was asked of him, Nick's grandfather never believed his son was good enough to take over the business completely. Eventually, Nick's grandfather let Nick's dad do what he liked to do best, spend the family fortune, in which he excelled. Nick's dad and mom, Barbara traveled the world and became fast members of the "Jetsetters" club. However, a year after they were married, Barbara became pregnant which was definitely not in their plans. The young couple discussed having an abortion until Nick's grandfather heard about the pregnancy. He was ecstatic at the thought of having a grandson and hopefully a more willing heir to the family business. That the baby might be a girl never even occurred to him. Nick's grandfather threatened his son that if they ended the pregnancy, he would completely cut them off, monetarily speaking. The threat worked and Nicholas Cornelius Constantine III was brought into the world.

From the day he was born, Nick's grandfather focused all his attention on his new grandson, grooming him from day one to eventually take over the family business. As Nick's parents had no interest in parenthood, they hired a full-time nanny to care for him and Nick was either with her or his grandparents until he was old enough to go to boarding school. The only time he even saw his parents was on holidays, that is if they weren't traveling around the world with their friends, or during summer breaks.

Then one summer everything changed. Nick was 15 and staying with his grandparents for the summer when he got the news that his mother had drowned in a bizarre diving accident in the Caribbean. After hearing about his mother's death, Nick announced to everyone that he was never going back to boarding school, never! His mind was made up, he wanted live at home to attend public school. No one argued with him as they felt he had enough to deal with in losing his mother. Besides, his grandfather was excited to have him home and his father needed him. No one ever asked and Nick never told anyone why he refused to go back to boarding school, but what happened to him there would shape the course of his future. That fall he enrolled in public school for his freshman year. Nick was a big kid for his age, already over 6 feet tall and solidly built. He was recruited for football and as a freshman made the varsity team as a backup quarterback. He became the starting quarterback his junior year and led his team to the state championship.

Nick's father had settled down and was helping Nick's grandfather run the business and to everyone's surprise, he was quite good at it. During the summers between his junior and senior years, Nick worked the boats, just as his dad had. But unlike his dad, Nick enjoyed the experience. By the time he had graduated from high school he had grown to 6'4", 220 pounds, thanks in part to his summers as a fisherman. Despite his low grades, Nick was recruited by numerous colleges and offered athletic scholarships. He chose a PAC 10 school, where they were more interested in your physical abilities than your intellectual prowess and attended all four years on an athletic scholarship. Sadly, during Nick's senior year, his grandfather had a stroke, leaving him unable to work. His grandfather died two months later but by that time Nick's father was in full control of the family business. Upon his grandfather's death, Nick was informed by the company's attorney that he had been set-up with a $25 million trust account which he could access for a maximum of one million dollars a year until he turned 30, at which time he would receive the balance. Nick also inherited one half of the business, but without a voting interest. His father received the other half with complete control of the operation.

During his senior year, Nick decided on law as a career choice. He took the LSAT and surprisingly scored fairly well. He wanted to return to Connecticut for law school and had three to choose from. Yale, which was quickly ruled out due to his low grades and the fact that they weren't interested in him athletically. He applied to the University of Connecticut School of Law, considered one of the leading public law schools in the United States, but wasn't accepted. He settled on Quinnipiac University in Hamden. The good thing about Quinnipiac, it was close enough that he could still live at home, enabling him to be near his aging father. Nick also wanted stay in Connecticut so he could learn other aspects about the family business, although he couldn't see himself ever taking over from his father.

During his senior year in law school, he read about a high-profile criminal case being tried in New Haven. A drug kingpin, as he was described by the media, was accused of killing three members of another drug organization for attempting to hijack a boat load of drugs coming into Connecticut. It wasn't the murders themselves that made headlines, it was how they were carried out. The local news stations were alerted that exactly at midnight, they would witness something spectacular happening at one of the freeway overpasses. With all the media on hand, wondering what they were about to see, no one could have anticipated what happened next. Out of nowhere, three bodies fell over the edge of the overpass, hanging by their necks. And as if that weren't enough, they suddenly burst into flames and hung there like human torches in full view of the entire world through the eyes of the media. Several days later, a Columbian drug smuggler was arrested and cut a deal with the New Haven Prosecutor for leniency in return for giving up those responsible for the "Overpass" murders, as they became known. The defense lawyer was a man from Miami by the name of Frank De la Carta.

Intrigued by the case, Nick traveled to New Haven to watch the trial. When he arrived at the courthouse, Nick was told that there was limited seating for spectators since most of the seats were taken by the media. There was a lengthy line outside the courtroom of spectators hoping to get in to watch the trial. Nick took the bailiff aside, explained that he was there to do a story for the law school Law Review and if he could get Nick a seat in the courtroom, the article would mention him by name and in a very favorable light. Nick also pointed out that the bailiff's name would forever be cemented in the annals of Quinnipiac's Law School. The lie worked and Nick was given a seat in the media section. Watching the trial unfold proved to be another life changing moment for Nick. From the very minute the trial began, Nick finally knew what he wanted to be, a defense lawyer. The trial lasted two weeks and the drug dealer was acquitted.

After the verdict had been read and the courtroom emptied, Nick waited outside until all of the media interviews were over and Mr. de la Carta was about to leave for the airport in his limo before approaching the formidable lawyer.

"Excuse me, Mr. de la Carta, my name is Nick Constantine. I am graduating from law school this semester and I would like to work for you, money is not an issue. If you take a chance on me, I promise you won't be sorry."

Frank liked this kid's confident demeanor and his instincts told him that he definitely wouldn't be sorry.

"Call me when you graduate. I'll let you intern while you wait for the Bar results." Frank said while handing Nick his business card.

As he was getting into the limo, Frank turned to Nick saying,

"And just so you know, money is ALWAYS an issue."

With that being said, the limousine pulled away leaving Nick standing at the curb holding the business card of Mr. Francisco de la Carta.

Chapter Seven

"Thought we were going to the courthouse." Detective Garcia asked his partner.

"Changed my mind. I decided it would be more fruitful to go straight to the U.S. Attorney's office and speak to someone who has handled any of de la Carta's cases."

When they arrived at the U.S. Attorney's office, Detective Henderson asked the receptionist if Paul Flintmore was available.

Taking his partner aside, Detective Garcia asked him,

"How do you know if this Paul knows anything about de la Carta's cases?"

"I don't. However, Flintmore is one of the supervisors so he should be able to lead us to someone who has the information we need."

"Excuse me gentlemen, may I ask who's calling?"

"Detectives Henderson and Garcia."

"Is Mr. Flintmore expecting you?"

"Flint is an old friend of mine and I'm just stopping by to say hello." Detective Henderson replied.

The receptionist picked up the phone and called Mr. Flintmore while indicating to the detectives to take a seat in the reception area.

"What exactly are we looking for in de la Carta's court cases?" Detective Garcia asked his partner.

"I'm not sure. I have a bad feeling about that crime scene. Something is nagging at me about de la Carta just dropping dead from an apparent heart attack. It doesn't seem to add up."

Before Detective Garcia could respond, a middle-aged man wearing a white shirt with the sleeves rolled up and his tie loosened, strode through the doors of the reception area. He was about 5'7" with bright red hair and a lot of freckles.

"Henderson! What brings you in?"

"Can't a guy simply stop by and say hi to an old friend?" Detective Henderson replied.

"Yes, of course he can, yet you never do." Flintmore responded laughingly.

"Flint, this is my partner, Detective Garcia."

"AUSA Paul Flintmore."

The two gentlemen shook hands without saying anything else before Mr. Flintmore turned back to Detective Henderson.

"So, Henderson, do you want to tell me what this is really all about?"

"Is there some place we could talk in private?"

Detective Henderson asked, while furtively looking around.

Mr. Flintmore led the two detectives down the hall to a small conference room.

"What do you know about any recent cases of a Mr. Francisco de la Carta's?" Detective Henderson asked.

"His most recent case involved Manuel Neves. You may have heard about it. Neves is the guy that was convicted of an alien smuggling charge." Mr. Flintmore answered.

"I did hear about that case. The verdict was all over the news. What can you tell me about this Manuel Neves?"

"Well, I can tell you that we prosecuted Neves for transporting undocumented immigrants in an eighteen-wheeler. We caught him carrying 32 aliens in the back of the sealed rig. However, I can't tell you much more than that."

"Are you able to tell us who prosecuted the case?" Detective Henderson inquired of his friend.

"Yes, it was one of our young lawyers, T. J. Ahmed. Would you like me to see if he's here today?"

"If you wouldn't mind Flint. I'd like to ask him a few questions about the case."

"No at all. I'll see if he's in."

A few minutes later, Mr. Flintmore returned with

a young lawyer in a pinstriped suit with a fashionable silk tie with a Windsor knot and Italian leather dress shoes. As the two men walked toward the detectives, their contrasting style of dress definitely stood out.

"T.J., this is an old friend of mine, Detective Henderson and his partner, Detective Garcia. They have a few questions regarding the Neves case. Please feel free to answer any questions that they ask of you."

T.J. simply nodded as he shook hands with each detective.

"Henderson, Garcia, I have a few things on my desk that need my attention so I'll leave you in T.J.'s capable hands to discuss the case."

"Thank-you for your time, Flint."

"Not a problem. Stop by any time."

"So, Detectives, what would you like to know about the Neves case? It was a simple open and shut case. Mr. Neves was pulled over by the Highway Patrol on the Interstate as he was leaving the Miami area driving a rig with Texas license plates."

"Why did the Highway Patrol stop the truck?" Detective Garcia asked.

"Apparently, the brake lights were inoperable on the trailer. Mr. Neves presented a bill of lading showing that the truck was hauling electrical components. While the officers were examining the paperwork presented by

Mr. Neves, they heard what they believed to be people moving around inside the trailer. The trailer was sealed as is the custom when the trailer is "loaded," so one of the officers knocked on the trailer door and heard voices asking for the door to be opened. Mr. Neves was immediately taken into custody. When the trailer door was unsealed, there were 32 undocumented immigrants inside the trailer."

"I take it this Neves person wasn't the head of the operation." Detective Henderson mused.

"We're certain he was not. And despite our attempts to flip Mr. Neves, he wasn't willing to give up any information."

"Do you have any suspicions on who might be behind the transport?"

"Yes, we strongly feel it might be a local drug lord named Javier Cortez."

"What makes you believe it might be him?"

"In this area, everyone knows no one does business without the okay from Cortez. He's been under investigation for years by the US Government, especially the DEA and now the newest branch of government, Immigration and Custom Enforcement, which as you know is mostly referred to as ICE. We have long suspected Cortez of operating a large smuggling ring of drugs and undocumented immigrants. The problem is trying to prove it. Cortez never gets his hands dirty and isolates himself just far enough so that no one can rollover on him."

"One interesting fact, the truck is owned by a corporation that is run by Cortez's people. And even though the corporation owns the vehicles, they are leased by independent haulers. When any trucks are impounded, the corporation sends their attorney to claim the trucks. The position of the corporation is that they merely lease the vehicles and are not responsible if the lessee uses the truck for illegal purposes. The Court agrees and releases the trucks back to the corporation."

"How many of this so-called corporation's trucks have you impounded?" Detective Garcia questioned.

"During the last two years, we have impounded six trucks which were all promptly returned to this so-called corporation."

"How were you able to get a conviction on Mr. Neves?"

"We weren't sure we were going to be able to since Mr. Neves had taken the position that he was nothing more than a driver, hired by the lessee to drive the truck to New York, however we caught a lucky break. Five of the undocumented immigrants testified that the driver was the one who actually loaded them into the trailer. The lawyer overseeing the defense for Mr. Neves argued that the five illegals were only testifying for the government in order to obtain favorable treatment. Fortunately for our side, the jury believed the testimony of the five illegals. Even after his conviction, we tried again to get Mr. Neves to flip on his boss but he wasn't the least bit interested."

"Who was the defense lawyer?"

"A woman I hadn't met before but who is extremely capable in a courtroom, Rosemarie Callahan."

Chapter Eight

Frank had called Nick into his office, asking that the door be shut behind him.

"Nick, a friend of mine has hired our firm for a special endeavor. An exceptionally good friend by the name of Mr. Javier Cortez."

Of course, Nick had heard of Mr. Cortez, he was a legend around the office. Mr. Cortez was one of Frank's first clients and it was strongly rumored that he "owned" Frank. No one was quite sure what exactly Mr. Cortez had on Frank or if it was simply Frank's deep gratefulness for his assistance in getting him started as a young lawyer, but whenever Mr. Cortez called, Frank jumped. It was also a known fact that most of Frank's clients still came from Mr. Cortez. What exactly Mr. Cortez's business was no one knew for certain but everyone presumed it was not legal. The vast majority of clients referred by Mr. Cortez had either been arrested for trafficking in undocumented immigrants or narcotics, sometimes both. Today was the first time Nick had actually seen Mr. Cortez in the office.

And what came next took the young attorney completely by surprise.

"Nick, I am about to discuss a proposition with you that has to stay between us and our investigator, Raul. If, after hearing what I am about to ask, you would prefer not to be involved, I will understand and it will not affect your position within the firm. If you do decline, it will never be mentioned again. I am only asking because I trust you and believe that you would be capable of pulling it off."

Nick did not really want to know what the "endeavor" was, yet he was intrigued by Frank's mysterious tone. He was also flattered Frank had chosen him to perform this task, whatever it was. Still, Nick couldn't help but wonder if Frank had asked other associates first and they had turned it down. Nonetheless, whatever the proposition turned out to be, Nick wanted in, at least he thought so. Nick waited for Frank to continue without responding.

"As you know Nick, Mr. Cortez is an excellent client. With his numerous referrals, he single-handedly keeps our firm in business. And now, Mr. Cortez needs our assistance. As he has no documents, no visa, no passport, is wanted in nearly every country in the world and will never be eligible to obtain any type of legal identification, Mr. Cortez has devised a plan to be smuggled into the United States. Our task would be to implement his plan and once he is safely in the United States, our obligation would end. Other than trusting you completely, the main reason I am offering you this opportunity, and only you, because you are not just extremely smart but you excel at thinking outside of the box. Your part within the plan would be to put all the pieces together to make it work, not carry it out. There are unlimited funds and endless resources at your disposal but make no mistake Nick, the plan MUST work!"

Nick's mind was reeling, surprisingly not from the audacity of Frank's request but rather at the thought of how he could accomplish such a task. Numerous scenarios were rushing through his mind at that very moment. As soon as an idea came to him, he immediately saw a flaw, dismissed the idea and it was just as quickly replaced with another. Frank sat there quietly staring at Nick and instinctively knew he was on board.

"I'm in. How much time do we have?" Nick asked.

"One week." Franked replied.

"I can use our investigator, Raul, correct?"

"Absolutely! You may use any of the staff that you need, however they can't know what is going on. And Nick, everything will be going through me. You'll have no direct contact with Mr. Cortez."

Nick barely heard Frank as his mind was already

straining to find the perfect scenario to carry out Mr. Cortez's outrageous "endeavor."

"I will reassign your caseload so that you can devote all your time and energy to this project."

"I'll need a recent photo of Mr. Cortez."

Nick wasn't sure why he asked for the photo but felt that he might need it for one of the possible scenarios he was considering.

"Okay, I'll see what I can do. Thank-you Nick. I knew you were the perfect person for the job."

Nick took that as his cue the conversation was over. As he left Frank's office, his head was still spinning with possibilities. Nick couldn't believe how excited he was about committing a crime.

By the following morning, Nick had already figured out a foolproof way to implement the plan. First, he needed to enlist Abbey's assistance because he knew that she wouldn't ask any detailed questions. Nick found her in the law library which is where Abbey did most of her work. She had a table with a computer, printer, reams of paper, pens and anything else you might expect to find in an office, set up at the far end of the room. Abbey had an actual office next to Nick's on the first floor but she rarely used it except to store case files.

"Hey Abbey, do you have a minute to talk? I need a favor."

"Sure Nick. What do you need?" Abbey replied without looking up from her work.

"I want you to check the schedules of all cruise ships leaving Miami in the next six days with Port of Calls in the Caribbean. I'll need to know where they dock, the days they port as well as times of arrival and departure."

"Should I do this on my own time?"

Only Abbey would think to ask such a question Nick thought to himself. She would never consider doing a personal favor on company time.

"No, this is a business matter for our firm."

"How soon will you need this information?"

"Sorry for the short notice but I need it by noon today. I wouldn't even ask if it wasn't so urgent."

"No problem. I'll start on it right away and you'll have all the information shortly."

"Thanks Abbey. You're the best!"

It never even occurred to Abbey to ask why Nick wanted the information. If Nick asked for it, then he simply needed it. Abbey liked Nick as he always showed her respect, along with treating her like an equal. Her other colleagues acted like she was a freak and never showed any appreciation for all the work she did for them. However, Nick was different. He always thanked her for her assistance and had even invited her to lunch as a thank-you on several occasions. Although Abbey never accepted, she always appreciated the gesture, especially since no one else ever thought to thank her, not even once.

Nick left the law library but before heading to Frank's office, he stopped off at the men's room. Nick was standing at the urinal when Bruce walked in.

"Hi there, Big Boy." Bruce said in a highly exaggerated feminine voice.

Bruce was gay and knowing Nick was homophobic, he would always go out of his way to be as flamboyant as possible in Nick's presence.

"You need to be in here now Bruce? Can't you see I'm using the restroom?"

"Really Nick? You need the entire restroom?" Bruce replied while twirling around the room.

As Bruce approached the urinal, Nick stopped mid-stream and quickly zipped up his pants.

"Are you sure you are even in the correct restroom Bruce?"

"You know Nick, I wasn't always gay. I only caught my "gayness" about five years ago."

"What the hell are you talking about?"

Nick wanted no part of this conversation and could hardly believe he was actually in the men's room speaking with a queer.

"I mean I was born straight just like you Nick. Then one night around five years ago, I was spending time with a gay friend of mine and I am sure I caught my gayness from him. I don't exactly know how but maybe when we were playing basketball some of his sweat fell on me."

"That's bullshit and you know it, Bruce! You can't catch "gayness," if that is even a word!"

"Well, I did! So, you better be careful Nick or you might catch it too!"

"You're full of shit Bruce!"

As Nick opened the door to leave, Bruce yelled out in a sing-song voice,

"You didn't wash your hands!"

"Fuck you, Bruce!"

"That would be just fine with me!" Bruce loudly replied still using his sing-song voice.

Bruce was sure Nick was on the computer checking to see if you could catch being gay through sweat, laughing to himself at the thought of Nick researching "gayness."

Chapter Nine

You could see the look of anger on Rosemarie's face as she bounded up the stairs to Frank's office.

"Frank, do you have a minute?"

"Sure. What's up?"

"Remember the Carlito Lamas case?"

"Of course. By the way, how is the case coming along?"

"The case goes to trial next week."

"Already? I wouldn't be too concerned since the wife didn't even show up to testify the last two times and both cases were dismissed."

Carlito Lamas had been arrested twice in the last two years for beating his wife. This time his wife was hospitalized with a broken jaw, a broken nose, two front teeth knocked out, her left eye socket broken as well as the complete loss of her right eye.

"She'll be there this time!" Rosemarie told Frank with certainty in her voice.

"I highly doubt it."

"Well, she's currently in protective custody Frank!"

"What??!! Rosemarie, you have to do something! With Mr. Lamas' record, he'll get over ten years if his wife shows up to testify."

"If he's lucky! Unfortunately, the prosecutor won't deal the case, saying that Mr. Lamas will eventually end up killing his wife and he doesn't want that on his head. On the other hand, the prosecutor feels if a jury sets Mr. Lamas free, then it will be on them."

"Rosemarie, you know how important winning this case is to our firm, right?"

"Of course, I do! Mr. Lamas is one of Mr. Cortez's men."

"Then you also know that Mr. Cortez refers more clients to us than all our other clients put together."

Although it was a slight exaggeration, Rosemarie understood the point Frank was trying to make. Mr. Cortez was an extremely important client with a steady stream of referrals, so losing this case was not an option.

"Who is the prosecutor?" Frank asked, clearly concerned.

"Donald Davidson."

"Donnie?! That little weasel!! You'll eat him alive!"

"Frank, you should see the photos of Mr. Lamas' wife. They're horrific! The jury will convict him the minute those pictures are shown."

"What does Mr. Lamas say?"

"Naturally, he maintains that he didn't do it, stating

that he came home from work and found out his wife had been taken to the hospital by paramedics."

"Who called the paramedics?"

"It was an anonymous call."

"Who has the 911 tape?"

"The police. From the tape, it appears, a woman made the call. When the police questioned Mr. Lamas upon arrival to the house, they noticed his hands were bruised along with having several cuts, so they arrested him on the spot."

"What does Mr. Lamas say about his hands?"

"He claims he had been in a fight with someone who owed him money. Apparently, the guy went to the hospital all beaten up but wouldn't press charges or even speak to the police about what happened. However, he's willing to testify that it was Mr. Lamas who worked him over."

"If Mrs. Lamas doesn't testify, that defense might just work."

"The prosecutor told Mrs. Lamas that if she doesn't testify this time or claims her husband didn't beat her, he would prosecute her for perjury, obstruction of justice, contempt of court and any other charges he could think of." Rosemarie explained.

"The prosecution would never prosecute a victim of spousal abuse."

"I think Davidson would Frank. This is the worst beating of a defenseless woman I have ever seen. And I prosecuted plenty when I was with the District Attorney's office."

"Davidson has to make an offer. He wouldn't want to chance an acquittal, especially if there is a strong alibi. There's always the consideration that the jury might just buy Mr. Lamas' story."

"That's what I actually came in to talk to you about Frank. Davidson does want to make an offer."

"I knew it! What's the offer?"

"Davidson wants to tell me over dinner."

"What are you talking about Rosemarie?" Frank asked confusedly.

"He wants to meet me at Chez for dinner."

"The little Italian restaurant located in that boutique hotel downtown?"

"That's the one."

"Well, what did you tell him?"

"I told him he could kiss my ass!!"

"I bet he loved that! Frank couldn't keep from chuckling. "He probably responded with some snarky answer like, maybe after dinner."

"You men are all the same! You're all PIGS!"

"Hey, don't put me in that category! I'm not the one trying to get you into bed!"

"Okay, maybe not *all* men. However, do you know this guy's reputation regarding women?"

"I have heard that he considers himself quite the ladies' man, using his position to get whatever he wants. I also heard it usually works."

"Not this time it won't! Not with me!!"

"Rosemarie, it wouldn't hurt to just have dinner with the ass and hear the offer."

Rosemarie couldn't believe what she was hearing.

"Frank, you're joking, right?! You're not really asking me to fuck this jerk to help get a wife-beater acquitted?" Rosemarie's anger was obvious, especially so as she emphatically emphasized the words fuck and wife-beater.

"I'm not asking you to fuck anybody. I'm simply telling you to have dinner with Davidson, get the offer and then make an excuse to leave. Just don't shoot him down *before* you get the offer."

"You want me to intentionally lead him on?" Rosemarie asked incredulously.

"Well…."

"Fuck him and Fuck YOU!! I'm not doing it!! Rosemarie yelled before stomping out of Frank's office.

Rosemarie was sitting in her office fuming and the more she thought about it, the angrier she became. How many other lawyers did Frank force into sexual encounters for the sake of saving a client? Then suddenly a calm came over Rosemarie, erasing all her anger.

Rosemarie sat at her desk for almost an hour, thinking, scheming, plotting out a devious plan.

Finally, she said half aloud,

"I will have dinner with Mr. Davidson, get his offer and absolutely fuck him! Yes, that's EXACTLY what I'm going to do!"

Rosemarie picked up the phone and dialed the District Attorney's office.

"Mr. Davidson, it's Rosemarie. When would you like to have that dinner? ...Tomorrow night would be fine. ...What time? ... Eight is perfect! No need to pick me up, I'll meet you there."

Rosemarie hung up the phone with a smile on her face. Yes sir, she was most certainly going to fuck Mr. Davidson!

Rosemarie took the next day off using the excuse of needing to take care of a personal matter. Rosemarie seldom took time off so Carla had no problem granting the request without asking any further questions. Rosemarie spent her entire day off getting ready for her "big" dinner date. She made appointments to get her hair and nails done, then went shopping for something especially "sexy" to wear to greet Mr. Davidson. Rosemarie also stopped at a specialty store to pick-up a few "special" items for the evening. By then it was almost 6 pm and Rosemarie was surprisingly calm. It was almost as if she was looking forward to her "dinner date."

As Rosemarie slipped into her new extremely "sexy" dress, she saw her reflection in the mirror and it was like looking at someone else. Her hair was up in a way the hairdresser assured her was the latest style and very complimentary to the shape of her face. The dress was midnight black with a plunging neckline. Deeply plunging!! She slid on black nylons and three-inch heels. Rosemarie took one last look in the mirror and was almost embarrassed to be going out in public dressed so provocatively. But then again, she had to do what she had to do!

Rosemarie arrived at the hotel where the restaurant was located and approached the registration clerk, carrying a designer tote bag and a small clutch.

"May I help you?" The young man behind the counter asked.

"My husband and I are having a romantic evening tonight and I'm supposed to meet him here for dinner. I just want to make sure he remembered to make the room reservation. It would be under Davidson."

Rosemarie noticed the young man was staring at her breasts, so she purposely leaned forward to accentuate her plunging neckline even more. Rosemarie was amused that she was no longer embarrassed at how she was dressed.

"Yes ma'am, he remembered."

Noticing that his name tag said James, Rosemarie suddenly came up with an added tweak to her plan.

"Is it okay if I call you Jimmy?"

"Yes, ma'am!! His face turning red as he continued staring at Rosemarie's amble bosom clearly on display.

"Jimmy, I have a little surprise for my husband later tonight. Would you be so sweet and let me go up to put this tote in our room before he gets here?"

"I guess it would be okay."

James held out the key and Rosemarie caressed his hand as she took it, causing the young man to get even redder.

Within 30 minutes, Rosemarie was back at the front desk returning the room key.

"Thank-you so very much!" She was about to leave when she turned back.

"And Jimmy, let's just keep this between us, okay? We wouldn't want to ruin the surprise."

"No, ma'am! I won't say a word! Have a nice evening!"

Rosemarie took a seat in the bar and waited anxiously for her night to begin. She saw Mr. Davidson arrive just before eight and head straight to the registration desk rather than the restaurant. Ten minutes later, he entered the bar and stopped in mid-stride when his eyes caught sight of Rosemarie, staring open-mouthed for a moment before continuing towards her. Rosemarie remained seated at the bar, her long legs crossed and her dress hiked up to her thigh.

"I had no idea all this was hidden underneath those suits you wear!"

"Thank-you."

Mr. Davidson held out his hand to lead her to their table. As Rosemarie slid off the bar stool, he stood there openly ogling her. She couldn't help but think what a disgusting pig he was. Once they were seated in their booth, Mr. Davidson ordered a bottle of Dom Perignon. Rosemarie could tell he was expecting her to make a comment on the expensive champagne but she didn't say a word about it. Instead, Rosemarie said,

"Well, I'm here. What's the offer?"

"Why be in such a hurry? Let's enjoy the evening. We can talk business later."

Rosemarie didn't press it any further. They ate dinner and made small talk with Mr. Davidson mostly talking about himself. He finished off the champagne before Rosemarie had even finished her first glass.

"Perhaps we would be more comfortable discussing the offer upstairs." Mr. Davidson suggested.

"Upstairs?" Rosemarie replied with feigned surprise.

"I took the liberty of booking a room. I thought it would be more private. "

Mr. Davidson charged the meal to the hotel room and the pair headed to the elevators, passing the registration desk where Rosemarie glimpsed "Jimmy" watching them with a knowing smile. When they reached the door to the hotel room, Rosemarie took the key card from the prosecutor.

"Allow me."

As soon as the door opened, Mr. Davidson turned toward Rosemarie in an attempt to kiss her. She quickly shoved him away.

"I thought we were going to discuss an offer for my client."

"We have plenty of time to talk business..."

"I want to get down to business now." Rosemarie replied.

"Okay, if you insist."

Mr. Davidson took off his coat and threw it over the chair.

"The offer is that he would plead to simple assault with a stipulated five-year sentence."

"That's your offer? You wasted my evening to tell me something you could have easily told me over the phone?!?"

"Okay, relax! What kind of offer were you expecting?"

"I want the case dismissed! Mr. Lamas has an airtight alibi and I believe we will win at trial."

"Then why do you care about an offer?"

"I'm concerned that when the jury sees those photos, they will want to punish someone and Mr. Lamas is all they have."

Rosemarie saw that the disgusting pig was mulling over what she just said.

"So, you want a dismissal?

"I certainly do!"

"I'll tell you what… slip out of that slinky dress, get into bed and I'll dismiss your case in the morning. How's that for an offer?"

"Let me make sure I understand you correctly. If I sleep with you, you'll dismiss my client's case?"

"Well, I wasn't thinking of actually "sleeping"."

Rosemarie wanted to slap that smug smirk right off his face!

"So do I have your latest offer right… sex for a dismissal?"

"You sure do Baby!"

"How do I know I can trust you? "What's to stop you from reneging in the morning?"

"Why would I?"

"Because you got what you wanted. What's your incentive for keeping your part of the bargain?"

"I've never gone back on my word before."

"You've done this before?"

The slime-ball began laughing.

"What? You thought you were special?"

"What's to stop me from going to the District Attorney's office tomorrow and telling him what you just proposed?"

"And who is he going to believe? You? A sleazy defense lawyer who went out to dinner with me all decked out and agreed to sleep with me for a dismissal or me, a highly respected prosecutor?"

Rosemarie just stood there staring at the so-called highly respected prosecutor.

"Now slip out of that dress!" His tone was more of an order than a request.

"You know what? I'll take my chances at trial."

"Are you kidding me?!?"

As she walked past him to leave, the angry prosecutor grabbed her by the hair.

"You're not leaving, you cold-hearted bitch!" And he spun her around so that her face was within inches of his.

"You know what we call you at the courthouse? The Ice Maiden! Maybe I'm just the one to melt you!"

"Let go of me!"

"Or what? Do you want a dismissal? Then start earning it!"

"Keep your damn dismissal!"

The prosecutor's strong hands grabbed her neck so fast Rosemarie didn't have any time to react as he began choking her.

"What? No kiss first?" Rosemarie uttered in a whisper.

"That's more like it!" The prosecutor released his hands from her around her neck and pulled Rosemarie toward him.

With her lips inches from his, Rosemarie propelled her knee hard into the prosecutor's groin. His knees buckled and he dropped to the floor in a praying position as all the color drained from his face.

"I'll expect that dismissal in the morning!"

"You bitch! You have no idea what I'm going to do to you in the morning!"

Rosemarie left the room, slamming the door behind her and went back downstairs to the bar.

Nearly an hour later, she saw Mr. Davidson come off the elevator and leave the hotel. Rosemarie waited five more minutes to make sure he didn't return before going back to the hotel room. Using the key, she kept after opening the door earlier, Rosemarie retrieved her tote bag from the closet, gathered up the camera and recording devices that she had strategically placed in the room earlier, packed them carefully in the tote and left the room with a pleased look on her face.

As Rosemarie passed the registration desk, she heard a familiar voice say,

"I hope Mr. Davidson liked his surprise."

Rosemarie flashed "Jimmy" a big smile.

Oh, Jimmy, Mr. Davidson is definitely NOT going to like his surprise Rosemarie thought to herself and she couldn't be happier!

In fact, Rosemarie kept smiling at the wonderful success of her plan for the rest of the evening and all the way to the courthouse the next day.

Chapter Ten

She placed the key in the door-lock to her apartment, hesitating a moment before entering. Abbey hated this moment of her day, coming home to the empty loneliness that consumed her living space and found herself working extremely long hours to avoid being in her apartment any longer than necessary. Abbey missed her dad terribly but no matter how hard she tried, he steadfastly refused to move to Miami. They spoke every evening and Abbey could sense his loneliness as well, yet he wouldn't give in. However, tonight she decided not to take "no" for an answer and would give her dad an ultimatum. Abbey had considered all the arguments her dad would present and had an answer prepared for anything he might say.

Yes, tonight's call would definitely be different!

Abbey set her briefcase on the coffee table before heading to the kitchen. It was already after 9pm and she knew her Dad would be home sitting in his recliner, drinking a beer, staring at the television but not really watching. Abbey hoped he had eaten supper even if it were simply microwaved as she sat staring at the phone, rehearsing in her head how she would speak to her dad this final time.

Abbey took a deep breath, told herself to stop stalling and made the call.

With surprisingly steady hands, Abbey dialed the Tennessee number.

"Hello, Sweetheart!"

Her dad always answered in the same way before even hearing her voice since she was the only call John Arnold ever received.

"Hi Dad! Have you eaten yet?"

"How was your day?" Her dad asked instead of replying to her question.

"My day went well, however there is something I want to discuss with you."

"Abigail, we've had that discussion many times before. There is nothing you could say that will make me change my mind. I am never moving to Miami!"

Abbey thought he sounded more resolute than usual.

"Dad, please listen."

"I've told you repeatedly that I am not interested in leaving my home to live with you in a tiny apartment!"

Abbey hated the way her dad referred to that

dinky old trailer as home with such pride in his voice.

"The small apartment you refused to even look at happens to be more than 3,000 square feet which is much bigger than a double-wide! It has three bedrooms and four baths."

Abbey was prepared to continue describing her apartment as she had so many times before when her dad suddenly interrupted.

"The answer is no Abigail. I have work to consider. I can't just move and leave everything behind."

This time it was Abbey who interrupted.

"Dad, you can't begin to imagine the kind of money I'm earning. I make more money in one month than you do in a year with both your jobs combined."

The silence from the other end was deafening.

"I didn't mean that like it sounded. I was just trying to point out you could finally retire and start enjoying life. You have certainly earned it."

"I'm already enjoying life. And what would I do with our home here in Memphis?"

The question gave Abbey a glimmer of hope that his resolve may be softening.

"You could sell it, rent it or just lock it up for now."

"I couldn't sell it. What if we had to come back here one day?"

Abbey wanted to tell him she would never go

back to live in the trailer under any circumstances but felt her dad didn't need to hear that right now.

"Then just lock it up Dad! Why don't you visit for a couple of weeks and see how it goes?"

"Who would watch the trailer for us?"

"Ask Ellie, from next door to keep an eye on it. Let her know we will pay her $50 every week just to check on it and keep us informed if anything needs our attention."

"I'm sorry Sweetheart. I simply can't move to Miami."

She knew her dad thought the discussion was over but Abbey was about to play her last card.

"Okay, Dad. Then I'll move back to Memphis."

Abbey waited for what seemed like an eternity for a response.

Finally, Abbey heard a heartbreaking plea uttered in a soft, faltering voice filled with emotion.

"Please don't do that Sweetheart."

"I miss you so much Dad, more than you could ever imagine. I am so lonely here. I miss our in-person conversations, our dinners together and..." Abbey's voice broke off into a crescendo of sobs.

Her dad didn't have to imagine how she felt since he felt the exact same way, probably even more so. When his wife died, all the lights in John's life went out except for the glimmering candle Abigail represented. John hung onto life knowing he had to tend to that candle. When she moved to Miami, it was as though someone had blown out the candle. John lived in utter darkness, stumbling through each day. Even so, he knew it would be an act of utter selfishness to be a part of her new life. John had tended to the candle well. Abigail graduated from law school with honors, found a fantastic job with people who appreciated all her hard work and created a wonderful life for herself. Yes, John had done a wonderful job and it was time to release Abigail from the burden of him to freely continue on her own path.

"I miss you too but I don't want you to give up on everything that you worked so hard for. Therefore, since you feel so strongly about my moving there, I'll make you a promise that I'll think it over."

"Will you really Dad? I love you so much! And you are going to love Miami! You'll see. It will be like the old times, just you and me!"

"I only said I would think it over."

Yet John couldn't help but smile at her enthusiasm. And for a brief second, he thought to himself, maybe I …

But John knew in his heart that he never could and never would.

Chapter Eleven

As Nick ascended the stairs to his office, Frank was on his way down.

"Walk me out to the car, Nick."

Once outside, Frank turned to Nick and spoke in a faint voice, almost a whisper.

"You have a plan I assume."

"I do."

"Great! I will be back around 11:30 and we'll have lunch. Did you get the photo yet?"

"Raul's picking it up as we speak."

"Then I'll have Raul meet us for lunch also. I assume you'll need him to implement your plan."

"Yes, I will."

"Okay, we'll see you at 11:30."

Nick went back inside and as he passed Abbey's office, she came running out, staring at the floor as usual.

"Here's that information you needed." Abbey whispered as she handed him a folder.

"Thanks, Abbey." Nick took the file and gave her a smile.

Nick went into his office, shut the door and began analyzing the information that Abbey had just provided.

He was researching immigration laws and visa requirements of several of the Caribbean Islands with port-of-calls for cruise lines when Frank knocked on his door. Nick always appreciated how all the members of the firm, even Frank, respected his privacy when the door to his office was closed.

"Come in, Frank."

"Are you ready for lunch Nick?"

"As soon as I finish printing this information, I'll be ready."

Nick didn't have to ask where they were going for lunch. Whenever Frank had business to discuss, whether with a client or a member of his staff, he took them to Casa Ochoa, a small Cuban style restaurant in Little Havana. Frank and the owner grew up in the neighborhood together and occasionally Frank represented an employee at the request of the owner. The place had a small private room in the back, closed off from the rest of the restaurant with no windows. It was more like a bunker than a dining room. When they arrived, the owner greeted Frank like family, as always, and asked if they would be using the private room.

Frank ordered a Hatuey, a Cuban beer once the

pride of Cuba, now brewed in Baltimore. The beer is still extremely popular and is found in its green bottle at beachside bars throughout south Florida.

Nick ordered a mineral water even though he knew Frank didn't mind his staff having a beer at lunch. Nonetheless, Nick wasn't much of a beer drinker, he preferred scotch and that definitely wasn't an acceptable drink for lunch in Frank's eyes.

Even though this was Nick's third time at Casa Ochoa, he had yet to see a menu. Food was simply brought in without anyone even ordering. Frank explained that the food was special homemade Cuban dishes and nothing more was ever said about what they were being served. Nick always enjoyed the food even though he found it a bit spicy at times.

Raul arrived simultaneously with the food as if he had been waiting in the kitchen. Raul Ruiz had worked exclusively for Frank for the past six years. It was rumored Raul once worked for the Cuban Mafia in Miami and his reputation for brutality was well known. If Frank needed something done, legal or illegal, Raul Ruiz could accomplish it. He stood about 5'9" and weighed over 200 pounds. His arms were covered with tattoos and he was clean shaven with a bald head. He appeared to be in his forties, however no one seemed to know for sure. Shortly after joining the firm, Nick had taken Carla out for drinks after work to learn what he could about Frank and the other employees. After several rounds of drinks, Carla began opening up to Nick. When the topic of Raul came around, Carla leaned over the table and whispered in Nick's ear not to ask about or even mention Raul's name. After a few more rounds of apple martinis, Nick did ask. A tipsy Carla ignored her own warning and relayed her understanding of how Raul came to work for the firm.

Apparently, Raul had been arrested, accused of a barbaric contract killing of a Haitian drug dealer trying to establish a heroin business in Little Havana. The body had been dismembered and the bloody parts mailed to members of the media with a note proclaiming Haitians were not welcome in Miami. The media ran with the story, causing quite a stir in the Haitian community. Raul's arrest was based primarily on hearsay accounts and a few shaky eyewitness identifications. He was referred to Frank for legal counsel by a small-time drug dealer Frank had once represented. By the time the trial finally came around, all the witnesses had disappeared, except one who identified Raul and claimed to have seen the murder take place. The witness, a young Haitian man believed to be the nephew of the victim, disappeared a week before trial. On the day of trial, the body of the eyewitness was dumped on the courthouse steps with both his eyes removed. The case was dismissed for lack of evidence. Several months later, Frank learned through one of his other clients, a contract was issued on Raul's life and warned Raul of the threat. It didn't take long to discover the contract was issued by the family of the dead, eyeless witness. Two days after Frank spoke to Raul, the family's house burned down with the entire family locked inside. After that, no one bothered Raul Ruiz. Eleven months later, Raul married a refugee from Cuba and shortly thereafter they had a son. Once his son was born, Raul decided to change the direction of his life to keep his son from following in his footsteps. At the same time, Frank's office needed an investigator and Raul was offered the job. Much to everyone's surprise, Raul accepted Frank's offer and has worked for the firm ever since.

Nick realized Carla was getting too drunk to continue conversing clearly and concluded the evening by sending Carla home in a cab. Neither spoke of that night or their conversation regarding the office staff, especially Raul, ever again.

"Raul!"

"Frank. Nick." With that being the only thing said to the two men, Raul sat down and began dishing up a plate of the delicious Cuban food.

"Raul, I have a job I need you to work on with Nick."

"What's the job?" Raul asked in broken English, with a mouthful of food.

His question was barely discernable. When Frank and Raul spoke alone, they spoke in Spanish, but out of courtesy to Nick, they were speaking in English.

"You need to get a client into the country undetected? Which country?" Raul asked half-joking.

"I was thinking Cuba." Frank replied.

"That will be easy. I have contacts there."

Nick wasn't sure he was following their conversation since he thought they were trying to smuggle someone into the United States. If these two were kidding around, no one was laughing.

"Couldn't we just fly the person into Cuba on a private plane and pay off the customs officers at some rinky-dink airport?" Raul asked.

"Too risky with the way the security is managed, even in small private airports. By the time the plane lands, ICE agents will be waiting." Frank answered.

"Just how important is the success of this task?" Raul questioned as he continued eating.

"Well, let's just say failing isn't an option."

Raul looked over at Nick.

"And you're trusting this important job to the kid here?"

"To him and you."

"Since when do I need ayuda?"

"I didn't say you needed help. Nick is simply devising the plan and you will carry it out. However, if I don't like the plan, then you work with Nick to improve it or devise a new one."

Raul took another look at Nick who merely raised his eyebrows.

"So, Nick, you said you had a plan?"

"I certainly do."

"Well then, let's hear it."

"First, I'll need that photo of our client."

Raul slid the photo across the table while taking another forkful from his plate.

"Next, I need to know if our client can be brought to an island in the Caribbean."

"Which island?" Frank asked with a quizzical expression.

"My thought would be Dominica. It has the least immigration restrictions and law enforcement. However, I am open to other possibilities if you know of an easier access to another island."

"I'm sure the Dominican Island arrival can easily be arranged if it is essential. How soon would you want this person there?"

"He will need to be in Roseau and meet with Raul in four days."

"Okay, Nick." Frank answered with a slight

hesitation, not following Nick's train of thought.

"Then what?"

"From Dominica, said person will board a cruise ship and eventually disembark the ship in Nassau. As I am sure you are aware, as long as a passenger has his ship boarding card, he will be allowed on and off the ship with a minimal amount of scrutiny and does not have to go through customs or immigration."

Raul had stopped eating and was now paying closer attention to Nick's plan.

"How do you propose he board the cruise ship in Dominica?" Frank asked.

"That's where Raul comes in. I have a list of cruise ships that will port in Roseau during the next week. On one of those ships, we need to find someone who looks like our client. It does not have to be an identical match, but similar. Our client will be wearing vacation clothes with a hat so similarity will be enough."

"I have a few questions." Raul interjected with a laugh.

"First, what if there is no look-alike?"

Nick responded without any hesitation. "There will be 3,000 passengers on board and at least half of them are men. When a person boards the ship, their picture is taken for a boarding card, much like a driver's license which is then put into the cruise line's boarding system. When a passenger disembarks at a port, they swipe their card to show that they left the ship. Then when the passenger reboards, they swipe their card again and a lowly, disinterested crew member barely looks at it to confirm the identification of the passenger since their goal is to keep the line moving as quickly as possible. Most of the time the crew member is watching the girls in their bikini tops board rather than concentrating on the photos."

"Like I said," Nick continued, "similarity is good enough. As the look-alike goes ashore, Raul will approach him and persuade him to give up his passport and ship boarding pass. Our client will then board the ship with the card and stay on board until disembarking in Nassau."

"And if the passenger doesn't go ashore?" Raul asked skeptically.

"I'm confident you can find a way to get him ashore Raul."

Still skeptical of the plan, Raul asked Nick how he proposed Raul persuade someone to give up their boarding card.

Nick shot Raul that universal sideway look that says 'really?'

Raul turned to Frank asking,

"Any restrictions?"

"Just try to keep the collateral damage to a

minimum." Frank responded.

Nick continued detailing the plan.

"Once in Nassau, a charter fishing boat will take the client to rendezvous with another charter who will bring him into Florida. It's a six-hour cruise from Nassau to Florida. The charter will appear to be nothing more than a fishing boat returning from a day at sea. There will be an exchange of men, so the same number return in each boat. I will provide the charter service in Florida with the name to put on the fishing license after Raul calls to let me know our man is aboard the cruise ship. Once Raul meets with the client in Dominica, he will fly to Nassau and meet the cruise ship."

Frank didn't immediately respond as he was milling over the plan searching for problems.

"This idea seems to involve a lot of people." Frank finally said.

"Not really." Nick responded defensively and continued explaining his plan.

"Other than the cruise ship passenger, it only involves the two charter boat captains. And I am certain with enough money the captains won't ask any questions about their passengers or the exchange. In any case, each captain will have the necessary documents should the Coast Guard stop them. Besides, the Coast Guard is looking for drugs, not a fisherman."

"Why not have our client stay on the cruise ship until it returns to Miami?" Raul asked.

"Because he would have to clear customs as well as immigration and the Miami terminal is extremely vigilant, even using a fingerprint scanner to verify passports." Nick patiently explained.

"Don't they check at the marina when the charter returns?" Frank wondered aloud.

"Yes, but it is very casual, especially if it is a local charter whose boat is usually docked at the marina."

Frank turned to his investigator.

"Well, Raul, what do you think?"

After a moment of retrospection, Raul finally said that he thought Nick's plan might just work.

Nick added that there would be absolutely nothing that ties any of it to them since everything thing will be set in motion through burner phones.

Frank wanted to know if Nick had a Plan B.

"Sure. We simply put our client on a commercial flight, highjack the plane, then let him jump out and parachute somewhere between Portland and Seattle, D.B. Cooper style. Hell, they'll never find our client either."

Frank laughed heartedly as Raul stared at Nick as if he were from outer space.

"Do what?"

"I'm just kidding, Raul. I don't have a Plan B.

However, if you don't think you can pull this off, I'll go to work on a new idea."

"Let's stick to Plan A. I'll make it work." Raul assured everyone.

With everyone now in agreement, the three men left the restaurant and went about putting Nick's plan in motion.

Chapter Twelve

Something kept nagging at Detective Henderson, mostly about the coolness of the attorneys with the firm. He wasn't exactly sure what it was but decided to follow up with one of the attorneys anyway. His instincts told him Rosemarie Callahan would be his best bet to get more details. The Constantine guy was too slick and Abigail Arnold was too afraid and most likely not in the loop at the firm. He also thought about the cleaning woman but figured she was an illegal migrant worker who wouldn't admit to anything that might draw attention to herself. If necessary, he could always circle back to those three later.

It was nearly 4:30 in the afternoon and he presumed Miss Callahan would be leaving work soon. Detective Henderson found the number in his notebook and gave her a call. Rosemarie was sitting at her desk deep in thought about what had happened to Frank, wondering what her future held as well as the future of the firm. She also wondered what Nick might be thinking, therefore it took her a few moments to realize that her phone was ringing. As Rosemarie picked up the phone, she looked at the caller ID. noticed it was a blocked number and contemplated not answering. However, the call could be the court calling or the prosecutor's office regarding a case since their numbers were always blocked. Rosemarie finally answered on the sixth ring.

"Hello."

"Miss Callahan? This is Detective Henderson. We met during the …"

"I know who you are." Rosemarie interjected, cutting him off. Her voice was very matter of fact. Detective Henderson thought her tone was odd and she didn't even ask what he wanted. There was just silence.

"I was wondering if you had a moment for a few more questions." He didn't have to explain what it was concerning.

"Of course." Rosemarie felt compelled to agree since she knew she didn't really have any other option.

"Since it is getting late in the day, how about we do the questioning over a few drinks?"

Rosemarie found it curious that the detective would be inviting her for drinks to discuss a homicide. However, she knew from experience it would be better to stay close to Detective Henderson so she could keep an eye on the investigation.

"How about the Hacienda? Do you need directions?"

No was Rosemarie's only response.

"Say in an hour?"

"I'll be there." Rosemarie replied, hanging up the phone without saying goodbye.

Rosemarie leaned back in her chair and wondered what additional questions Detective Henderson might have or was this just a ruse to take her out for drinks. Maybe his objective was to get a few drinks into her to hoping she would loosen up, revealing some information she might not if they were sitting across his desk at the precinct. She wondered what the detective was after. From her experience at the city attorney's office in Chicago, detectives never interviewed people without some agenda. Did Detective Henderson also call Nick or Abbey for follow-up interviews? Rosemarie didn't get the feeling he was hitting on her but believed the meeting was truly about the case. She thought about going home before the meeting with Detective Henderson to change clothes then realized she didn't have enough time. Besides, she was wearing a conservative business suit which would be more than appropriate for meeting the detective in a bar. She called for a cab to pick her up in thirty minutes and spent that time trying to figure out what questions Detective Henderson may have. While she wasn't at all nervous about meeting the detective, she did want to be prepared.

Rosemarie arrived at the Hacienda exactly one hour from the phone call. Detective Henderson was already sitting at a booth in the bar with a drink. It appeared to be a Cuba Libra. Across from the detective was a glass of white wine which she assumed was for her. Rosemarie walked over to where Detective Henderson was waiting, sliding into the booth with an air of superiority. Afterall, she was a lawyer.

"I took the liberty of ordering you a white wine. You look the type."

What a chauvinist! Without responding to his comment, Rosemarie raised her hand and waved the server to the table.

"I'll have an Irish Whiskey, neat."

Rosemarie enjoyed the shocked look on Detective Henderson's face. She made no apologies about not wanting the white wine. In fact, she thought to herself she wouldn't have accepted the glass of wine even if she did drink white wine, just to show him she's in charge of this so-called meeting. Without any pleasantries, Rosemarie looked at the chauvinistic detective and said matter-of-factly,

"What are these follow-up questions you have Detective?"

"Well, you certainly don't beat around the bush."

"I didn't come here to beat around the bush or to have drinks, I came here to answer the questions you said you had. "

"Look Rosemarie. Do you mind if I call you Rosemarie?"

She didn't respond.

Detective Henderson began again,

"Look, I'm just trying to find out who killed your boss. Where were you on the weekend of the murder?"

Rosemarie stared at Detective Henderson, realizing this was first time anyone had used the word murder associated with the death of her boss.

"So, it has been officially determined that Frank's death was not from natural causes but rather murder?"

"I didn't mean to use the word murder. I actually meant to say your boss's death." Detective Henderson lied.

"So, can you tell me where you were that weekend?"

"I was in the same place I was the last time you asked me. My location hasn't changed since we last spoke."

Rosemarie was intentionally being vague because she couldn't quite remember what she told the detective the last time she was interviewed.

"I would like to hear your answer again, just to make sure that my notes are correct."

"I'm sure your notes are correct, Detective. If you

want to know where I was that weekend, you can simply check your notes. Am I a suspect?"

"Of course not." Detective Henderson responded, lying once again.

However, Rosemarie knew he was lying, especially since she was certain that everybody that worked in the office was a suspect.

"So, what are your other questions?" Rosemarie asked, showing a bit of annoyance in her tone.

"I did a background check on you and I see you come from a houseful of cops."

Rosemarie saw no reason to respond to the detective as it wasn't an actual question.

"How close were you to your boss?" Detective Henderson asked.

"I don't understand your question."

"Then let me be more direct. Were you sleeping with Mr. de la Carta?"

"No, I was not."

"The reason I ask is that I heard you and he spent the night together once."

"Clearly, you heard wrong."

Rosemarie knew this was a tactic often used by law enforcement. They merely want to see the look on your face when they ask the question and analyze the tone in your voice when you answered. "Do you have any other questions" she asked pointedly.

"You're sure you weren't sleeping with your boss? Because if you were, it's going to come out eventually."

"There are only two people in the entire world who would know if I was sleeping with my boss. One is dead and the other just said no."

Detective Henderson was taken aback by the abrupt way Rosemarie said the word dead and decided to move on.

"Who would you suspect might be involved in Mr. de la Carta's death?"

"I have no idea."

"What about Mr. Constantine? Do you think he could be capable of murder if this is indeed a homicide case?"

Rosemarie didn't like where this was heading.

"Why don't you ask Mr. Constantine?"

"Don't worry, I will." Detective Henderson replied with a bit of frustration in his tone.

The detective could see the conversation was going nowhere and he wasn't going to get any information out of Rosemarie. Although, Detective Henderson did note how cold she was about the whole conversation. Rosemarie showed no emotion when talking about her boss or his death. It was as though she was talking about a random victim from one of her cases. Rosemarie appeared cold, distant, aloof and uncaring. It could simply be her way of coping with the loss of her boss or maybe she had just become hardened from her years at the city attorney's office. Detective Henderson waved to the server and ordered another drink for himself, noticing Rosemarie had not even touched her Irish Whiskey.

"If there is nothing else, Detective, it's been a long day." Rosemarie said pointedly as she slid out of the booth.

"You don't want to finish your drink?"

"I really don't feel like drinking, so if there is nothing else, have a good evening."

Rosemarie left Detective Henderson sitting and wondering about this cold-hearted woman while she walked out and hailed a cab.

"Where to, ma'am?"

Rosemarie gave the cabbie Nick's address. She had only been to Nick's place once before and was stunned at the magnificence of his home. Rosemarie often forgot that Nick was a millionaire in his own right. She often wondered why he was working in a small law firm in Miami instead of jet-setting around the world. Rosemarie wondered what she would do if she were a millionaire. She knew one thing for sure, she would definitely NOT be working for Francisco de la Carta in Little Havana!

Rosemarie thought about calling Nick first rather than just dropping by, however she was becoming a bit paranoid after her conversation with Detective Henderson and didn't want to risk being overheard on the phone. Besides, Rosemarie knew in all likelihood that Nick would be home as it was too early for him to have gone out. His usual routine, the best she could figure out, was going back to his place after work, changing clothes, freashening up and then going out to dinner. On the drive over, she continually looked to see if anyone was following the cab. It was tempting to ask the cab driver to take some circuitous route to Nick's but Rosemarie was concerned that might raise some suspicions in the cabbie's mind wherein he would pay closer attention to who she was and where she was going.

Nick had just stepped out of the shower and was wrapped in a towel from the waist down when the doorbell rang.

"Now who in the hell could that be?" Nick said to no one in particular.

Nick could not have been more surprised to see Rosemarie standing on his doorstep as he looked through the peephole of his front door. Before he could open the door to let her in, the doorbell rang again. Nick debated whether he should put on a pair of pants before opening the door but the look on Rosemarie's face indicated he should open the door immediately.

"I apologize for just dropping in on you like this but we need to talk!" Rosemarie said briskly walking in.

"Is something wrong Rosemarie?"

"I'm not sure Nick but like I said, we need to talk."

"Give me a minute to get dressed a little more appropriately."

After a few minutes, Nick returned wearing designer sweats and carrying two empty scotch glasses.

"Can I offer you a drink?"

"You are the second person to offer me a drink tonight but this one I'll accept."

As Nick was pouring two glasses of scotch, he kept looking at Rosemarie in the mirror above the bar. It was clear she was unsettled about something.

"So, who was the first to offer you a drink this evening?"

"Detective Henderson."

Nick nearly dropped the scotch bottle. He spun around to face Rosemarie, sloshing the scotch almost to the limit of the glass's edge. "You had a drink with Detective Henderson?" The tone in his voice portraying his disbelief.

"Why in the world would you have a drink with Detective Henderson?"

"That's a good question. He called me at the

office, said he had a few more questions he wanted to ask and suggested we meet for a drink. I thought it might be better to have the conversation over a drink in a bar than over a desk at police headquarters."

"Well, the conversation couldn't have been very long." Nick said rhetorically.

"You were still at the office when I left and that was barely two hours ago."

"I'm worried, Nick. I think Detective Henderson suspects someone from the office of killing Frank."

"Killing Frank? Since when has this become a homicide? I thought the initial report from the coroner's office indicated death by natural causes."

"Detective Henderson's instincts are telling him something different He's calling it a murder."

Nick took long sip of his drink.

"So, who does he think is responsible" Nick asked.

"He didn't say but I have the distinct feeling that he thinks it is one of us and most likely, me."

"Why would he even think it's you or one of us?" Nick asked in a concerned voice.

"It was the way the good detective looked at me when he asked me once again where I was on the weekend of Frank's death."

"What did you tell him?"

"I told him he could look at his notes because it was the exact same place I told him when he first interviewed me. He also asked me if I thought anyone else in the firm could have done it, like you."

"Seriously?" Nick said, finishing his drink and heading to the bar.

"I'm dead serious. He was very pointed in some of his questions, including asking me if I've ever slept with Frank. He indicated he had some information that we had spent a night together."

Nick turned to look at Rosemarie as he was pouring his second drink.

"You didn't, did you?"

Rosemarie looked at Nick with shooting daggers.

"Of course not, Nick! How could you even ask me that?"

"Well, Henderson must have heard it from someone to even ask the question." Nick replied defensively.

Rosemarie stood up from the couch and walked toward the bar, finishing her first drink.

"That's just the way cops are. They ask questions in order to get a reaction. I don't believe for one minute he heard that from anybody and it certainly isn't true. Nick, I think he is going to be talking to you also."

"So let him, I have nothing to hide. He can ask me all the questions he wants to ask me.'" Nick continued speaking with less than a confident voice.

"Did Henderson give you any indication of what evidence he had that suggested it was a homicide, Rosemarie?"

"None whatsoever. Detective Henderson even retracted his use of the word murder. He said he meant to say death."

"I'm sure he thinks every death that he is involved with is a homicide or he wouldn't be involved."

"Nick, it sounds so crazy. Do you think somebody really killed Frank?"

"It wouldn't surprise me one bit considering the clientele we deal with. There are people that Frank has as clients who wouldn't hesitate to kill somebody, even him."

"Like whom?" Rosemarie asked with more surprise than she meant to convey.

"As if you don't know which of our clients would kill without batting an eye."

"Do you think we should tell Detective Henderson about some of those clients. Maybe then he'll look at one of them, instead of us." Rosemarie asked with no conviction.

"He's not looking at me."

"Nick, I'm worried. I don't think it's a good idea to have him or any other law enforcement agency looking into our law practice or our clients."

"Rosemarie, you need to stay calm. They have no

evidence of a homicide, they have no reason to believe you, me or any else from the firm had anything to do with his death. If they want to look at our clients, let them look. We have nothing to hide. We are lawyers. We represent people, all types of people, even criminals have the right to legal counsel. We have absolutely nothing to worry about. Right now, we need to put Frank's death behind us and get this firm back to operating as usual. We'll call a meeting of all the staff to let them know that I will be taking over leadership of the firm. And to stay in business, we must keep as many of our clients as we can, especially the ones that were close to Frank and constitute much of the firm's income. We're probably going to need to expand our clientele and perhaps look at some areas of law other than criminal defense."

Rosemarie thought about what Nick was saying.

"So, do you intend to say on at the firm, Nick?"

"Of course I do."

"Why, Nick? Why would you stay? You don't need the money and you certainly don't need the aggravation."

"It's a long story, Rosemarie and one I don't want to explain to you right now. Nonetheless, I intend to stay on and grow the firm. And even though I'm not Cuban, I honestly believe I can earn the trust of the people that Frank dealt with. Rosemarie, I hope you will stay as well. You are an excellent lawyer and a tremendous asset to the firm, not to mention I enjoy working with you immensely. We would make such a great team."

Rosemarie had not thought that far ahead. The first thing that came to her mind was how flattered she was that Nick thought so highly of her. The second thing that came to mind is how he was immediately taking charge, confidently knowing that he was the best choice to take over as the head of the firm. It seemed to Rosemarie that this was something Nick had thought about long before this evening.

Rosemarie was beginning to feel extremely anxious as she hadn't really thought about what was going to happen in her future. She just stood there with a blank look on her face. Suddenly, Nick walked over to Rosemarie, pulled her close and looked into her eyes. His face was no more than six inches from hers.

"Rosemarie, listen to me. This is all going to work out fine as long as we keep it together. By the way, have you had anything to eat since lunch?"

"I haven't even thought about eating."

"What do you say I take you out to dinner? I know a nice restaurant with a private booth where we can continue discussing the future over dinner."

"You don't have a date tonight?" Rosemarie asked lightening the mood.

"Don't worry about my plans, they are always flexible. Right now, this is the most important thing for both of us. I'll finish getting dressed and then we'll go have dinner somewhere quiet."

A few minutes later Nick came back into the living room dressed in one of the expensive suits he always wore.

"Okay, I'm ready. Let's go eat."

Nick took Rosemarie by the arm and walked her out, locking the door behind him. As they reached the street, a cab was already waiting. Rosemarie wondered if he always had a cab waiting or if he had called one from the bedroom. As they got into the cab, Nick gave the driver the name of the restaurant without asking Rosemarie if she approved. Nick was clearly in charge.

Chapter Thirteen

Raul was standing at the gates near the loading area for the cruise ship, looking around the terminal, checking out all the tourists as they approached the check-in area. Raul wasn't at all sure this plan hatched by Francisco's boy would work. The kid, as he referred to Nick, made it sound so easy in his presentation over lunch, yet so much could go so wrong. For starters, there was no guarantee that he could even find a lookalike boarding one of the many ships departing for Dominica. Secondly, Raul would have to ensure that the lookalike debarked at Roseau. After that, the plan did get a little easier. Raul was sure he could persuade the man, whoever he was, to part with his documents. The one thing the kid was correct about, reboarding the ship would be easy for their client. Raul began formulating his own plan for enticing the vacationer to relinquish his documents as he watched hundreds of people checking in, paying especially close attention to the male passengers, occasionally taking another look at the photo of the client to refresh his mental picture for comparison. Raul focused on faces as he knew the hair could be covered with a hat, if necessary. Sunglasses would also help. Raul stayed until the last of the last of the passengers had checked in and left without a single possibility. His skepticism of the kid's plan was growing.

The following day, Raul arrived back at the terminal for his last chance of finding a match. This was the last cruise ship leaving to port in Dominica this week. Raul had to find someone today or start developing a new plan.

Raul had decided last night, after a wasted day, that maybe he was being too particular, expecting to find the perfect match rather than a general resemblance. Even with his new mindset, whenever Raul would spot a profile of a man he thought would work, as he approached and saw the entire face, he realized the mouth and/or eyes were all wrong. As the day dragged on, Raul was getting increasingly discouraged, when suddenly he saw the perfect choice. It was as though someone had sent a person from a Hollywood casting studio. The man could easily be their client's twin. He was perfect, except for one major problem. The lookalike was traveling with a female companion.

It never dawned on him there would be a

woman in the equation. This changed everything. This was a complication. A complication he didn't like, a complication he hadn't planned on. As Raul stood there dumbstruck, the couple walked past and headed toward the line to check in. At the counter, they would be processed, room assigned, keys given and a photo taken for their boarding pass. Raul knew he needed to get their room number and name. He waited for them to leave the counter and hurried to intercept them before they headed up the ship's ramp to board. Raul pulled out his own passport and stopped the couple as they approached the gate.

"Excuse me, sir." Raul took the man's arm gently but firmly.

"I believe you picked up my passport by mistake at the check-in counter."

"I don't think so." the man responded, looking surprised.

"I am almost positive it was you, sir. This one isn't mine." Raul said holding up his own passport. "I'm certain you have mine."

"Honey, just look at your passport to make sure" the young lady instructed her companion. The busty blonde female wasn't wearing a wedding ring, although the gentleman was and she looked to be at least 20 years his junior.

"Fine!" The man responded while showing his displeasure at the intrusion. He took his passport from a pocket in his cargo shorts and opened it.

"Sorry, this is my passport!" The man said with a certain amount of sarcasm.

"May I see for myself?" Raul asked.

The man showed the photo page to Raul without relinquishing control of the document. Raul immediately memorized the name on the passport.

"I am so sorry. I was positive you had my passport. I feel like a total fool." Raul said, feigning embarrassment.

"Please allow me to apologize by sending a bottle of Dom Perignon to your room." Raul deliberately mentioned the name of that particular champagne so as to impress the young lady. Fortunately, the ploy worked.

"That won't be necessary." The man replied, still irritated at Raul's "mistake."

"Honey, the man is just trying to apologize," she cooed as she took her companion's arm and pulled it against her chest.

"You know how I love champagne."

"Okay." And he gave Raul their room number.

"My apologies again. I hope you have a great cruise. Maybe we'll run into each on board."

The lookalike placed his passport back in

its designated pocket, put his arm around his girlfriend's waist and went aboard without any further pleasantries. First step done Raul thought, as he headed to his car. Next, he called Francisco's office and spoke with Nick, giving him the name their client would use chartering the fishing boat and obtaining the fishing license. Nick was duly impressed with the investigator's work.

Before leaving the parking lot at the cruise terminal, Raul had a sudden thought and went back inside the terminal to find the excursion kiosk set up for people to purchase shore excursions at each port. There were several couples ahead of Raul at the kiosk, so while he waited in line, he read the options from a brochure listing each port and what was available. He looked at the excursions for Dominica and immediately ruled out such athletic endeavors as zip line rides and hiking. He was certain his mark wasn't the type to engage in anything physical. Snorkeling seemed more the man's style Raul thought with a chuckle.

"How may I help you enjoy your vacation to the fullest?" the kiosk attendant inquired.

"I have a friend aboard and would like to surprise him with a shore excursion in Roseau."

"What a nice gesture. Have you selected an activity?"

Raul smiled and thought to himself only cruise people talk like that. "Yes, I have. My friend really enjoys snorkeling, so I selected that option, departing the ship at 9am and returning at 1pm."

"That's an excellent choice."

The kiosk attendant then asked for the name of the individual and their room number. Raul provided both and was assured by the attendant that the gift would be delivered to their room after departure. As Raul was leaving the kiosk, the attendant called out to him.

"Excuse me, sir, what name would you like to be included as the giver of this gift?"

Raul thought for a minute and turned back to the attendant.

"Put compliments of your travel agency."

The attendant looked quizzically at Raul but didn't ask any further questions before wishing him a good day.

Chapter Fourteen

John Arnold sat in the rental car across the street from the law offices of Mr. Francisco de la Carta mustering the courage to confront the attorney who stole his daughter. On the 15-hour drive from Memphis, nearly 1,000 miles, he had rehearsed over and over what he would say to the man who had enticed his daughter, the only person left in his life, the only reason he kept living, to move from their home and abandon her father when he needed her most. John would plead with him to let his daughter come home. He would explain to Mr. de la Carta how much he needed her. He would try to reason with the man, explaining there were thousands of lawyers in the world but that he only had one daughter. While John sat there feeling sick to his stomach, thoughts were rushing through his mind. Suddenly, he was beginning to doubt the wisdom of this whole idea. Why should some lawyer care about a lonely old man wallowing away in sorrow, living in a trailer park in Tennessee? Why did he think he'd be able to argue with a man who argues for a living?

"This is a stupid idea. What was I thinking?" John wondered aloud.

And in that instant, John Arnold made up his mind to leave, realizing this was a selfish and completely foolish act on his part. Why would a loving father want to ruin his daughter's life? He should never have driven to Miami. As John reached down to insert the key into the ignition, his hands trembled almost beyond control. Nonetheless, he buckled his seat belt and was about to put the car into gear, when suddenly he froze. All at once he felt as though he had been punched in the stomach. Seemly out of nowhere, his daughter had just appeared on the steps of the law office. John instinctively slumped down in his seat so as not to be seen. My God, he hadn't even considered she might actually be there. How could he not have thought of that? He couldn't let her see him! How could he rationally explain what he was doing in Miami? John Arnold had done a lot of stupid things in his life, however this may have been the worst of them all! He needed to leave but his body wouldn't cooperate. John just sat there as though he would be invisible if he remained motionless. He was thankful he had rented a car in Memphis and not driven down in his recognizable truck. He tried to glance over to see which direction his daughter was heading without moving his head. Out of the corner of his eye he could see she was walking with another woman and turning in the opposite direction of where he sat frozen. John couldn't help but notice how happy Abigail looked. He had always hoped somewhere deep in the recesses of his heart that she would not like living in Miami working for a large law firm and would eventually come home. But as time went on, John knew that was not going to happen, which is why he decided to act so desperately. Something he now regretted, yet he couldn't bring himself to drive away. As his daughter faded out of sight, John reached down and turned off the car, noticing his hands had stopped trembling. Even though John had just seen how happy Abigail was, he now knew for certain that he had to go through with his original plan because needed her home. He couldn't stand the loneliness any longer and the emptiness of the trailer. After pushing the release on his seatbelt, John placed his hand on the door handle but could not bring himself to open the door. He sat for what seemed like an eternity, motionless, with his hand on the door handle. The next thing John remembered was walking across the street and up the steps to the front door of the law firm.

As he entered the building, John saw what he

assumed was a secretary sitting at the front desk. He had made an appointment for 6pm using a fictitious name, assuming that by then the offices would have been empty, yet he saw several people milling around. Now he worried that Abigail may come back to the office. What if she wasn't even going home? Maybe she was just taking a break and would return soon. John Arnold wasn't sure he could stand up much longer as he felt his legs getting weak. Once again, he chastised himself for making what was perhaps the worse decision of his life. Suddenly, John heard a voice in the distance.

"May I help you sir?"

John turned around and looked at the receptionist, saw that her lips were moving and realized she was talking to him.

"Sir, is there something I can do for you?" she asked again.

John tried to answer but no words were coming forth. He could see the secretary's look change from inquisitive to concern.

Conjuring up all the energy he could, he whispered,

"I have a 6 o'clock appointment to see Mr. de la Carta."

"Oh, yes, you must be Mr. Smith."

John had forgotten the name that he used to make the appointment but Smith would work.

"Yes, ma'am. I'm here to see Mr. de la Carta."

"I'll let him know you are here."

John stood frozen in his tracks, knowing if he sat down, he may never be able to get back up. He watched as the receptionist went upstairs. Now was his chance to run, before the receptionist returned he could be gone and Abigail would never know he had even been there. John, aka Mr. Smith, could just disappear, but his feet refused to move.

Descending halfway down the stairs, the receptionist stopped and motioned for Mr. Smith to follow her back upstairs to Mr. de la Carta's office.

"Mr. de la Carta will see you now, Mr. Smith."

John slowly turned towards the stairs and began to ascend the stairs like a man climbing a ladder to the gallows. He was ushered into Frank's office. The receptionist left, closing the door behind her. Mr. Arnold felt as though someone had just slammed a cell door locking him inside.

"Please have a seat, Mr. Smith." Mr. de la Carta offered.

John took a moment trying to assess the man standing before him. He didn't look like the devil, he seemed nice enough for someone who stole his daughter. John had to remain strong in his resolve to plead with the attorney and not allow himself to like this man, reminding himself that this was not his friend but rather his enemy.

"How can I help you, Mr. Smith?" Mr. de la Carta began.

"Actually, my name is not Mr. Smith, sir. My name is John Arnold, I'm Abigail Arnold's father."

John noticed the look of confusion on the attorney's face.

"Well, Mr. Arnold, what brings you to my office?"

All the preparation John had made on his drive from Memphis was suddenly forgotten. For hours he had gone over one scenario after another of how this would go. Without any warning, without any forethought, John Arnold screamed at the startled attorney standing in front of him, "I WANT MY DAUGHTER BACK!"

Frank stood speechless, staring at the lunatic before him.

"Does Abigail know you are here, Mr. Arnold?"

"No, she doesn't." His voice calming down.

"I'm not certain what you mean by wanting your daughter back.'"

"I mean just that, I want my daughter back! I want her to come home with me to Tennessee, I want her out of Miami and I want her out of this law firm. I need my daughter."

John's voice was beginning to tremble. He had promised himself that he would not resort to tears, that he would not beg this man but would try to reason with him in a logical manner. Now he wasn't sure he was going to be able to do that since the more he spoke, the more emotional he became.

"Mr. de la Carta, you don't need my daughter as much as I do. You may not know that I lost my wife a few years ago and now Abigail is all I have to hold me together. We were content living in Memphis and she was happy taking care of me. I need her, sir. I need her to come home immediately and be with me."

"Well, Mr. Arnold." Frank began.

"This is somewhat of an unusual request. I can't say I have ever dealt with this situation before. Have you spoken to Abigail about returning to Memphis?"

"No, you don't understand. She can't know I was here, she can't ever know I even spoke to you."

"Well, how do you suggest we deal with the situation?"

"You need to fire her, you need to tell her she is not needed here anymore."

"Well, Mr. Arnold, that would be less than sincere, wouldn't it? Abigail is more than welcome here, in fact, she has done an excellent job working for us. Not to mention, the great progress she has made in becoming more open in her personal relationships with other staff members since she has been here. We value her very much in this firm and there is no way I would fire her."

"But you must! Don't you understand that is the only way she'll come back home?"

"Mr. Arnold, I don't have to do anything and I certainly am not going to fire your daughter so that she can come back home and live in a trailer to take care of you. Your daughter went to law school and graduated top in her class. She's extremely bright and a gifted writer. I can't believe that you would want to take her back to Memphis, put her in your trailer and have her take care of you rather than practice law."

"Abigail can practice law in Memphis, she doesn't have to practice law in Miami."

"It's my understanding she tried to get a job near home and there were no offers. In fact, I understand she sent out resumes to firms across the country and I was the only one that responded. If it is so important to be with your daughter, why don't you move to Miami? Hasn't Abigail even offered to move you here numerous times, yet you steadfastly refused, never even coming to visit?"

"I can't ask her to come home, Mr. de la Carta, Abigail would resent me forever."

"And rightly so. This may be the most selfish thing I've ever seen a father do regarding a daughter. How could you put your need for a companion above your daughter's well-being and happiness? You're right not to let her know you were here. You're also right to believe that if she were forced to go back to Memphis, she would resent you. I can't even believe you're actually here. Perhaps we should call your daughter and have her come back to the office so the three of us can discuss this."

"No, I don't want you calling her or ever mentioning this to her. This is between you and me."

"This is not between you and me. This has nothing to do with me. This is between you and your daughter. If you want your daughter to come home, talk to her about it. There is no way that I am going to fire Abigail and put her in a position where she must return home because you are lonesome. I just won't do that. I think too much of your daughter. Apparently, more than you do."

John didn't know how to respond. This was the last thing he expected to hear from this lawyer. He couldn't believe Mr. de la Carta could not see his point of view. That he could not understand how a father needed his daughter.

"Do you have children Mr. de la Carta?"

"That's none of your business. This isn't about me or my children, if I have any, or how I would act as a father. I'm not going to tell you again, Mr. Arnold, I am not going to fire your daughter. I am not going to aid you in any way in this selfish request. If you want Abigail to come home, talk to her, not me."

"I'm begging you, Mr. de la Carta, please help me get Abigail to come home."

"Mr. Arnold, I think it is best you leave now."

"Not until you tell me that you'll keep this meeting between us."

"I can't promise you that, Mr. Arnold. I need you to leave my office now!"

John could feel his anger boiling up inside. The hair on the back of his neck was standing on end. He did not have to try to hate this man, he did. But John also now realized coming to see Mr. de la Carta was a huge mistake.

Mr. de la Carta walked over and opened his office door.

"Carla, could you come up here, please."

"Yes, Mr. de la Carta."

"Please escort Mr. Arnold out of the building."

"Yes, of course."

John stood for a moment wondering what he should do. He looked at Carla and back at Frank.

"Mr. Arnold, I think it's best you leave now!"

The attorney's voice was strong and authoritative. It seemed to catch John off guard. A few seconds passed before John reluctantly followed Carla down the stairs and out the front door.

Carla returned to Frank's office with an inquisitive look.

"What was that all about, Frank?"

"Do you know who that was, Carla?"

"Not really. You called him Mr. Arnold, but I thought his name was Smith."

"That was Abigail Arnold's father."

"Was he looking for Abbey?"

"No, quite the opposite."

And for the next ten minutes, Frank explained to Carla exactly what Mr. Arnold had wanted.

"You have got to be kidding!" Carla responded in astonishment.

"As unbelievable as it sounds, that's what he wanted me to do, fire Abbey!"

"That is the most selfish thing I have ever heard!"

"That's exactly what I told him."

"So how did you leave it?"

"I told him that I would not fire his daughter, that if he wanted her to come home, he should talk to her directly. Mr. Arnold was petrified that I might tell her that he was here and begged me not to say anything."

"Did you agree not to say anything?"

"No, I told him I couldn't make that promise. While I'm not going to run to Abbey and tell her that her father was here with an idiotic plan to get his daughter to return home but if the subject ever comes up, I certainly am not going to lie to her. It's just so unbelievable that he would even come here and ask me to do that."

"What do you think he'll do now?"

"Hopefully, he'll return to Memphis and let it go."

Carla turned to Frank before leaving his office to ask if he needed her to stay any longer since Mr. Arnold was his last appointment for the day.

"No Carla, thank-you."

"Are you leaving now also?"

"No, I'm going to stay and do a little more work."

"Okay, have a nice evening."

"I will. Thank-you again, Carla."

Chapter Fifteen

Angelo was still annoyed by the intrusion of the man wanting to see his passport as he and Emily headed to their state room. Angelo Bucci was a first-generation Italian American. Both his parents were from Italy and had settled in the Midwest, a few years before Angelo was born. Not having much of a head for formal schooling, Angelo dropped out at the age of fourteen and began working at a construction company. By the time he was 25, he had started his own small handyman service. Angelo eventually built his own construction company, Bucci Construction, employing over 35 people. Although he was now highly successful and financially set, Angelo would always be Angelo Bucci, the handyman, as he wasn't very polished, nor had he mastered any social graces.

Four years ago, Angelo hired Emily Peterson as his personal assistant. Everyone in the construction company knew the only reason Emily was hired was because of her looks. She was given the title of Personal Assistant to Angelo and the entire construction company knew what that really meant since even though Emily came to the office every day, made appointments for Angelo and handled his schedule, she had no actual employment skills. But Angelo didn't seem to care. As long as Emily kept herself in shape and dressed like a hooker, he was happy.

Once a year, there was a construction convention in Miami and Angelo always attended. Angelo has been married to an Italian woman for more years than he cared to remember. His wife was a typical Italian housewife, loving to cook, clean and take care of the children. Over the years she had gained a significant amount of weight and now weighed almost as much as Angelo. Everyone liked Mrs. Bucci, even though they only saw her during the holidays at company functions. Although Angelo was happy with his plain, plump Italian wife, when he went to the yearly convention in Miami, Emily was the one on his arm. No one in the company ever questioned why Emily took her vacation at the same time as the construction convention every year. Angelo had already explained to the entire staff that since Emily was his personal assistant, there was no reason for her to be at work while he attended the convention and insisted she take her annual vacation during the time he was in Miami. However, for the past four years, Angelo never attended the seminar in Miami, instead boarding a cruise ship heading to the Caribbean with Emily. Being full of energy and unbridled enthusiasm, Emily reached the stateroom way ahead of Angelo. She could not contain her excitement as she threw open the stateroom door and ran to the balcony. They always had an outside room, with a small balcony, midship, on the 4th deck. As he occasionally experienced motion sickness on ships, Angelo went on cruises mainly to please Emily. He always made sure to book a stateroom in the middle of the ship as there was less motion than in the bow or stern. The one thing Angelo did like about a cruise is the privacy. He did not have to worry about running into anybody he knew while on a cruise ship. Emily loved going on the cruises because she knew without Angelo, she would never be able to take one. During the year between cruises, there was no outside relationship with Angelo. It was all business, although the rest of the company would never believe that. Angelo would never run the risk of going anywhere with Emily in his hometown where someone might see them together. As for Emily, she was quite satisfied with their arrangement since she had a respectable job that paid well while not asking too much work of her and once a year, she got to take a cruise in the Caribbean. Who could ask for more than that?

When Angelo reached the stateroom, Emily was

leaning over the railing breathing in the fresh ocean air. It always made Angelo nervous how Emily would bend almost in half across the railing. He had no idea how she didn't fall onto the lifeboats down below. Angelo entered the stateroom shutting the door behind him and sat down at the small desk. Emily ran back into the stateroom and threw her arms around Angelo almost knocking him off the chair. She began to unbutton her blouse as she knew what the first thing Angelo wanted to do. It was the same way on every cruise. Therefore, Emily was taken aback when Angelo reached up, grabbed her hand and stopped her.

"We need to wait a minute."

"Why, Angelo? Is something wrong?"

"No, it's just that the bags haven't arrived yet and the bellman will be at our door shortly. I would rather wait until our bags have been delivered."

Emily looked at him strangely and wondered if something really was wrong until she remembered it always took Angelo most of the first day to unwind and realize they were safe from being caught together.

While Emily was reading all the literature left in their suite, there was a knock on the door. Before Angelo could stand up, Emily had the door opened and was surprised to see it was not the bellman with their bags but the Concierge.

"Excuse me for interrupting" The Concierge said in a most polite tone, handing Emily an envelope.

"What is this?" she excitedly asked.

Without answering, the Concierge discreetly left. Emily was tearing open the envelope as she walked back inside. Angelo looked at her with some skepticism.

"What is it, Emily?" he snapped.

Emily looked up at Angelo and said, "It's a free shore excursion."

Angelo jumped out of the chair and grabbed the envelope from Emily's hands.

"From whom?"

"It says it's from your travel agent."

Emily could see Angelo sigh with a bit of relief. Before either of them could determine what the shore excursion was and on which island, there was another knock on the door. This time it was their luggage as expected. While Emily was opening the suitcases, Angel placed a Do Not Disturb sign on their stateroom door. Emily knew what that meant. She resumed unbuttoning her blouse as Angelo got undressed. To Angelo, foreplay was nothing more than removing his clothes. Within seconds he was on top of Emily on the bed and in only a few seconds more, it was over. Emily had gotten used to Angelo's idea that sex was satisfying himself without any romantic involvement. Whether Emily had enjoyed the brief moment the two had sex did not concern Angelo. Afterall, this wasn't about her, this was about Angelo. Emily was simply happy that he was satisfied and continued to take her on the cruises. While Emily put away their clothes, Angelo took a shower and now their vacation officially began.

Three days later, their ship reached port at Roseau, on the island of Dominica. It was a beautiful day in the high 80's and even though it was only 8:30 in the morning, Emily was already in her bikini.

"Hurry up Angelo, we don't want to be late! This is the day we are going on the free snorkeling excursion your travel agent gave us, remember? I can't wait to get to the beach. It is going to be so much fun! I just love to snorkel."

On the other hand, Angelo did not like to snorkel. In fact, Angelo didn't even like the beach. However, what Angelo did like was sitting in a chair on the beach having a drink while Emily flaunted her incredible body across the sand to reach the snorkeling area with everybody looking. He was immensely proud of the fact that Emily was with him. Although Angelo knew what people were thinking regarding the couple's huge age difference, he didn't care. All that matter was that he was the one with Emily. A sexy girl who was very affectionate in public, which is one of the main reasons they never did anything back home together since Emily is never able to contain her enthusiastic displays of affection for Angelo. But being in the Caribbean was like being in a different world and Angelo could be a carefree version of himself. On the cruises, Angelo could have a week of fantasy that most men can only dream about. A week where he could be somebody else, with a beautiful somebody else and not look over his shoulder. As Angelo came out of the bathroom, he stared at Emily, standing there in her vibrant pink bikini which barely covered her top and did not cover her backside at all. She truly was beautiful.

"I'm just about ready. Don't worry, we're not going to be late. We don't have to be down there until 9 o'clock."

It seemed like it took Angelo forever to put on his bathing suit and shirt. Finally, Angelo put on the last piece of clothing, his Panama hat. Whenever they were on vacation, Angelo wore the Panama hat wherever they went. The other passengers and even most of the locals began to know Angelo by his hat. Although Angelo preferred to believe that they didn't really know him by his hat, but rather by his extremely sexy companion. The couple took the elevator down to the level where they disembarked and walked ashore. Emily was looking around for the spot where the excursion bus would pick them up for the snorkeling excursion when she saw a chauffeur standing next to a Lincoln Town car.

"Look, there's a man over there with your name on a sign."

Angelo's head snapped to the left to see where Emily was pointing so fast, he almost broke his neck.

"Maybe your travel agent arranged for us to be taken to the beach in a private car."

Even though Angelo was a bit leery, that did make sense. Why else would this man have his name on a sign? The pair walked over to where the chauffeur was waiting with the town car door open.

"Are you Mr. Angelo Bucci?" The chauffeur asked with a very polite heavily accented voice.

"I am."

"Excellent. I've been hired to pick you up and take you to the beach."

"Will anybody else be joining us?" Angelo inquired.

"No, sir. Your travel agency arranged for a private car to take you and your companion to the beach, then back again at your convenience."

Being picked up in a private chauffeured-driven car had never happened in the previous years that Angelo and Emily had cruised together. Perhaps the travel agency was finally appreciative of all the business Angelo gave them. He had repeatedly used the same agency as they always demonstrated a high degree of discreetness.

"Come on, Angelo, let's go!" Emily said excitedly, pulling on his hand.

Angelo obliged Emily and the two of them got in the back of the town car.

"This is going to be so much fun! I can hardly wait to get into the water!" Emily exclaimed, holding Angelo's arm tightly against her chest.

Angelo was still a little leery about the whole private car situation and kept noticeably quiet. He saw the driver repeatedly looking at them in the rearview mirror. As they drove, Angelo noticed that they seemed to be getting further and further away from the beach. A few more miles went by before Angelo finally spoke up

"Are you sure you know which beach we're going to?"

"Yes, Mr. Bucci, I know exactly where we are going. Do not worry, I know a short cut. I've lived on this island my whole life, so I know the best routes to avoid all the traffic and get you to your beach as quickly as possible."

Angelo felt a little better but was still somewhat guarded.

"How long will the ride take?"

"Thirty more minutes and we will be there."

Emily was happily looking at the scenery and enjoying the lush green vegetation without a care in the world. Angelo was watching the driver. He noticed that there hadn't been another vehicle for the past ten minutes and the vegetation seemed to be getting denser. Angelo couldn't imagine a beach anywhere near this location. He was about to say something when the driver pulled the car over to the side of the road. Before Angelo could ask why they were stopping, the rear doors flew open with two men grabbing Angelo from the car, while another man grabbed Emily from the other side. Yanked forcibly from the town car, the shocked couple were dragged into the dense vegetation with Emily screaming hysterically the entire time.

"What the hell's going on?" Angelo asked in a loud demanding voice.

The man who was tightly holding Emily warned her to stop screaming or he'd make her stop, even though he had been instructed not to harm her or leave any physical bruising since she would be going back to the ship. Although Emily was terrified, she heeded the warning and stopped screaming.

Out of nowhere, appeared yet another man. The first thing Emily thought when she saw the man was what a striking resemblance he had to Angelo. The man walked over to Emily and in a very calm voice instructed her to continue to be quiet.

"Nothing is going to happen to you. You are perfectly safe, I assure you. No one wants to hurt you, so just do what I ask and in a few minutes you'll be told exactly what's going on. Can you do that for me?"

Gripped with fear, Emily couldn't find her voice, so she just shook her head up and down in an affirmative motion.

"What's this all about?" Angelo asked once more.

"You will go with these men, while I speak to your girlfriend."

Angelo disappeared with the two men even deeper into the forest. Within a few seconds, Emily could no longer see Angelo and began visibly trembling in fear.

The man spoke to her again.

"There is no reason for you to be afraid. I can see you are quite frightened, however, like I said before, nothing is going to happen to you."

"Where are you taking Angelo?" Emily asked, finally able to speak.

"Angelo will be fine. He will be joining you again later."

"I don't understand. What is this all about? Why are you doing this?"

"Okay, I will now explain what is happening but you need to listen very carefully to what I say since that will make a difference as to whether you live or die."

Emily felt her knees go weak. She could hardly

stand and if not for the fact she was being supported by her captor, Emily was sure she would have fallen to the ground.

"Okay, here is what is going to happen next. You and I are going back on the cruise ship together."

"What about Angelo?"

"Angelo is going to stay here with my men."

"Why? I still don't understand what's going on."

"Let me finish. Angelo will be flown to the Bahamas."

"Flown?"

"Because I will be taking Angelo's place on the cruise ship. We will get off the cruise ship in the Bahamas, then you and Angelo will be back together once more. I will be gone and you will never hear from any of us again."

"Why are you doing all this? I'm not understanding what you're saying."

"There's nothing not to understand!" The man shouted in frustration.

Emily became even more frightened. The face of the man whose calm voice had now turned to anger had a look that would scare anyone.

"Please just explain it to me again."

"It's quite simple. I will now be Angelo. We will get back on the cruise ship and go to Nassau. Once we arrive in Nassau, you and I will get off the cruise ship together. I will then leave and you and Angelo will be back on the cruise ship alone to finish your vacation. Now do you understand what I'm saying?"

"No, I don't."

Realizing Emily was too frightened to ever understand what he was trying to explain, the man decided to use a different approach.

"Never mind, you don't have to understand what I'm saying, you just have to do whatever I tell you. But let me make one thing perfectly clear, if anyone discovers that I am not Angelo or that we are not actually together, Angelo will die. I assure you he will never leave the Caribbean alive."

Tears were forming in Emily's eyes. She didn't know whether she should believe what the man was saying, whether or not she would ever see Angelo again or even what would happen to her if she went on the ship with this man.

"Why are you doing this?"

"It's quite simple. I need to get from here to Nassau and the only way I'm going to be able to do that is to board the cruise ship with you. Do you understand that much?"

"Yes." Emily quietly responded, too scared to say no again.

"Just remember, if you tell anybody or try to get away from me at any time between here and Nassau, Angelo is a dead man."

Tears were now flowing freely from Emily's eyes. This could not be happening to her. It was like a nightmare except that she was wide awake.

"We will enjoy the cruise and Angelo will not be harmed. He will be treated well as long as you do what you are told. But make no mistake, I will not hesitate to kill Angelo if necessary. If you do everything exactly as I say, I will contact my men when I reach Nassau and have them safely return Angelo to you so you can finish the cruise together as planned. Now, are you ready to return to the ship with me?"

Once again, Emily could only shake her head affirmatively.

The man then walked into the forest in the same direction the other two men had taken Angelo. Ten minutes later, Emily saw what she thought was Angelo coming back to the car but as the person got closer, she realized it wasn't Angelo at all. It was the man returning, only now he was wearing Angelo's clothes, his signature Panama hat and sunglasses. While she knew it wasn't Angelo, Emily could definitely see how other people would think it was. The resemblance was uncanny. Even so, Emily still did not comprehend what was going on.

"Emily, we are now going to go to the beach where you will enjoy a lovely day of swimming and snorkeling, while I sit at the bar. And if I have any indication that you are not cooperating fully, rest assured, you will not like the consequences."

"After all of this, I don't feel like going to the beach anymore. Can we please just go back to the ship instead?" Emily pleaded.

"No! We'll go back to the ship when it's the actual time to return from the excursion. So, for now, we're going to the beach as planned. And I better not see anything except you enjoying your day at the beach. No tears, no trembling, no scared looks or Angelo is a dead man! With that said, he then turned to speak to the person that had taken Emily out of the car and the three of them re-entered the vehicle, heading to the beach.

Emily spent the next three hours swimming and snorkeling, finding the water a welcome relief. The man sat at the bar wearing Angelo's Panama hat and sunglasses, enjoying a drink while watching Emily frolic in the waves. When it was time to leave, the man tipped one of the servers and asked him if he could retrieve his wife from the surf. Emily took a few running steps toward the outdoor bar and the man sitting under the thatched roof, wearing the Panama hat before she suddenly remembered it wasn't Angelo. Her running turned to walking and each step was slower than the one before until she finally reached the man posing as Angelo.

"Have a seat, Emily. We're going to have a drink before we leave."

"What should I call you? I don't even know your name."

"You'll call me Angelo, of course."

The man had her drink two strong drinks in rapid succession with Emily immediately feeling the effects. Having gotten Emily drunk enough, the couple got in the town car and went back to the cruise ship. It was almost one in the afternoon and passengers were returning from their morning excursions. Several groups of people were leaving the ship to catch the afternoon outings as the morning excursioners were reboarding.

When they reached the gang plank, the man put his arm around Emily and told her to act as though she was a little drunk. Emily had no problem with that as she was starting to really feel the effects of the strong drinks the man had given her. He then had Emily take off her blouse so she was only wearing her bikini top. The man helped her up the gang plank and as they reached the top, he slid their ID cards through the monitor but did not take off the hat or sunglasses as he pretended to assist Emily. As hoped, the shipmate paid more attention to Emily's breasts than he did to the pictures on the monitor.

"Sorry about my wife, she had a little too much sun and alcohol."

"No worries, it happens to everyone. Hope you enjoyed your day on the beach."

"We loved it!" The man said walking through the metal detector and up to the stateroom.

So far, so good. Javier was securely on the ship.

Chapter Sixteen

Getting on the ship was easier than he had thought. Javier had to admit that he had serious doubts about the plan but since there was no Plan B, it was a huge relief that everything went so smoothly. As they walked down the narrow corridors toward their stateroom, Emily was hanging onto Javier's arm for balance as well as out of sheer terror. She was shaking and her legs felt like jelly. Emily assumed once they reached the stateroom he would have no more need for her, and in all likelihood, would kill her. As they passed other passengers on the way to the stateroom, she thought about screaming, hoping someone would help her. Emily couldn't explain why she didn't. Perhaps it was because of Angelo and her fear that they would kill him, but was she really willing to die so he would be safe? And there was no assurance he would be safe in any event. With all these thoughts running through her head, she remained silent.

Javier inserted the key in the stateroom door

and pushed it open, letting Emily enter first. He placed a Do Not Disturb sign on the outer handle and closed the door. Javier finally let go of Emily's arm and she sat quietly on the edge of the bed while he searched the entire cabin. Javier opened every drawer, riffled through the clothing, unzipped the suitcases, he even searched the bathroom medicine cabinet. Emily had no idea what he was looking for and wondered if that was what this was all about. Did Angelo have something that she didn't know about and this man wanted it? After what seemed like an eternity, her captor grabbed the chair from the desk, pulling it to the edge of the bed where Emily was sitting in fear. Sitting in the chair, Javier began speaking in a quiet, non-threatening tone.

"Let me explain how this is going to work once again, Emily. We will be reaching the Bahamas in two days, so for the next two days we will act as though we are a loving couple. I have no intention of harming you nor will I take advantage of you in any way while we are together, so long as you do everything I say. We will enjoy each other's company over the next few days and at all times you will stay in my presence. At no time are you to leave this cabin without me. If you will do that, everything will be fine. Do you understand?"

Emily simply shook her head.

"Why don't you take a shower and get cleaned up while I order room service." Emily began to feel a little more at ease and her shaking started subsiding. She went into the shower, turned on the water, sat on the shower floor and cried.

Over dinner and a bottle of wine, Emily asked Javier what he planned to do with her.

"I told you, nothing will happen to you so long as you behave according to the plan."

Javier poured them each another glass of wine. During dinner, he asked Emily about her background. Emily explained that she had dropped out of high school when she was fifteen and when she got a job at sixteen working in a fast-food restaurant, her father made Emily give her entire paycheck to him each week. She never had any money of her own even though she worked full time. Her dad was an alcoholic but never abused her, at least not physically. When she was 18, she left home with a boy she had met working at the restaurant. They lived together for about a year until she came home from work one day and he was gone. From that point on, Emily bounced in and out of relationships and held only menial jobs since she had no education or specific job skills. While working as a cocktail waitress, Emily had the good fortune of meeting Angelo Bucci. For some reason, he took an immediate liking to her and offered her a job as his assistant. Emily had no idea why Angelo was so taken with her the first time they met and was a little leery about being someone's personal assistant since she had no idea what that entailed. However, whatever it was, it had to be better than being a cocktail waitress. Emily went on talking about herself for the next hour while Javier leaned back, sipped his wine and said very little. Emily had no idea why she was opening up to this man. Was it the wine, the fear or possibly a little bit of both? After dinner and another glass of wine, Emily felt herself falling asleep. The two single beds had been pushed together to make one double bed and Emily wondered if Javier would separate the two beds. Javier took Emily's hand and led her into the bathroom, told her he was going to take a shower and instructed her not to leave the bathroom. When they retired for the evening, Javier placed Emily's wrist against his wrist, wrapped a small plastic security tie around the joined hands and pulled it tight. With Emily secured to his side, Javier fell asleep. Emily followed suit shortly thereafter.

For the next two days Javier and Emily behaved as though they were a loving couple enjoying the cruise. Occasionally, Javier let Emily to lay by the pool to get a little sun. He always sat wearing his hat and glasses at the bar a few feet away from Emily, never taking his eyes off her. They enjoyed the restaurants on the ship and even took in a show one night. One day as he was sitting at the bar looking over at Emily sunning herself, Javier thought that under different circumstances, he could actually learn to like this girl. It was a shame she had such a rough background, no children, both parents now deceased, but for the plan, it couldn't be better. It was sheer luck that no one would notice she was missing for a long time, if ever.

It was their last night before arriving in Nassau and Emily realized if Javier was going to do anything to her, tonight would be the night. Yet, for some reason, she wasn't scared. They had a nice dinner at the restaurant and finished a bottle of wine. Back in the stateroom, Javier opened the bottle of champagne that he had ordered earlier and had on ice. After a glass of champagne, Javier thoughts started turning towards sex with Emily. Emily was also feeling the effects of the champagne mixed with all the wine and slowly started walking towards Javier. Maybe if she had sex with him, he won't kill her. Besides, if they found her body, it would have some of his DNA. Emily found herself relaxing and even wanting to please Javier as she stood in front of him as he sat on the bed. She reached up, stroked her hair and then rubbed her cheek with the back of Javier's hand. Emily was staring into Javier's eyes and couldn't help but notice how they seemed so empty, so distant. Javier asked her to undress. It was more of a request than an order and Emily complied.

"Slower" he instructed her.

As she undressed, she tried to turn the lights off, but Javier insisted they remain on. It had never been an issue before but suddenly Emily felt self-conscious about her body. There was just something about the way he was looking at her. As she slid off her panties, a small scar was revealed near the side of her hairline. Her hand instinctively covered the small flaw as she walked closer towards Javier. He reached out, removed her hand and began gently tracing the outline of the scar with his finger. Javier was so gentle, almost childlike. He pulled her toward him, bent down and softly kissed the imperfection. She wasn't sure how to interpret his actions. So muscular, so strong, yet so gentle. Who was this man? What were his intentions? Why had he intervened in her life?

Emily was so lost in her thoughts she hadn't realized that Javier had rolled her onto the bed and was now on top of her. He entered her, slowly at first, then faster and harder. With each stroke, he became more animalistic. It was as though he was metamorphosing right before her eyes. He spoke no words, just grunted with each thrust, like an animal. He was sweating profusely. His eyes were wide opened and she could tell his mind was somewhere else. Emily wondered what his mind saw that drove him into this frenzy. Then, with no warning, Javier just stopped and pushed her off him as he sat up. He had not climaxed. Without a word, Javier took her hand and led her to the shower. As small as the shower was in the stateroom, he was able to step in and pull her in behind him. They both managed to shower, however, there was no display of affection or intimacy. It was just a shower. Emily was suddenly afraid, very afraid! She didn't know why but something told her this evening was not going to end well and deliberately did not clean herself below the waist, hoping to save any remnants of his DNA. Why she thought of this, she had no idea. As the shower engulfed her body, Emily wondered if he was going to kill her right then and there, letting the blood flow down the drain. She started shaking in fear just as the water stopped. Javier stepped out onto the bathmat, grabbed a towel, wrapped it around his waist and left the bathroom, all without a word. What was going on? What did he want? Emily's thoughts were interrupted by Javier's voice.

"Would you like another glass of champagne?"

Again, a real question and not a command.

"That would be nice." Emily responded.

Emily wrapped herself in a towel and stood in front of the closet trying to decide what to wear. She didn't know if she should wear something sexy to stay in his favor or something that would not excite him. As Emily reached for a mini-length shift, her eyes fell on Angelo's clothes. She just stood there staring. What had they done with him? Was he dead? Would she ever see him again? Would she ever see anyone again? Emily dropped the towel with her back to Javier and pulled the shift over her head. She brushed her hair but elected not to put on any make-up. As she turned around, Emily saw Javier sitting on the balcony of their room reading a book. He looked so normal. So relaxed. Emily wondered if Javier would even notice if she slipped out the door and went for help. Instead, Emily stepped out onto the balcony and, for a reason she could not explain, bent down and kissed him on the cheek. Javier looked up at Emily with those blank eyes.

"How about we go up on deck and get some air. On such a beautiful night, it would be a shame to stay cooped up in the cabin."

Javier stood up and without waiting for Emily to respond, took her gently by the hand and together they headed for the deck.

It was almost three in the morning and Emily saw no other passengers on the deck. Javier was leaning against the deck's railing and seemed to be staring off into space. She wondered what was going through his mind.

Javier turned to face Emily, reached up with a hand on each side of her head, bent down and kissed her. Emily was taken by total surprise and returned the kiss with a great deal of relief. In the next instant, Emily was flying through the air, heading toward the dark ocean below and Javier was calmly returning to the stateroom.

The following morning, Javier called room service to order breakfast for two. While waiting for the steward, he went over and pulled back the covers on both sides of the bed. Javier went into the bathroom and turned on the shower just as the steward arrived with breakfast. While the steward was arranging the plates in the cabin, Javier yelled into the bathroom for Emily to hurry up so her breakfast doesn't get cold and then winked at the steward. Later that morning, Javier put on the Panama hat, sunglasses and disembarked the ship sliding Angelo's passenger I.D. through the machine as he exited. And that was the last time anyone ever saw Angelo Bucci.

Chapter Seventeen

As planned, Javier blended in nicely with the rest of the passengers who disembarked from the ship in Nassau walking toward the tourist shopping district. The next step was to find a fishing boat to take Javier out to rendezvous with the boat Frank was sending to pick him up. He decided to take the city bus rather than risk a taxicab where the driver may remember him. Having boarded one of the local buses, Javier was glad to see it was full, with a good blend of both tourists and locals so that he wouldn't be conspicuous on the bus. The first bus stop was a few blocks from the fishing marina where several of the passengers, including Javier, got off. Javier walked slowly to the marina looking for a boat that was apart from the main group of boats. At one end of the marina, Javier spotted what he thought would be the perfect boat. There was only one person working with the fishing nets and he appeared to be the captain of the boat. The man looked like a native Bahamian, weathered and dark complected from years in the sun, presumably in his late fifties. It was a little after ten in the morning and Javier was anxious to get off the island as soon as possible.

Javier didn't know much about boats but estimated that this one was about a 40-footer. It was outrigged with several fishing poles and looked well kept. Javier wasn't sure how far out to sea he would have to go to meet the boat sent by Frank, since all he had was the coordinates. Hopefully, this boat would have the fuel capacity to get him where he needed to be.

"Sir, are you the captain of this yacht?" Javier yelled out to the man on the boat.

The captain looked up with a wry smile and said, "I'm the captain of this here fishing boat. I don't think you'd call it a yacht. You looking to go out fishing, Mr.?"

Javier continued approaching the vessel and the captain stepped off, extending his hand.

"They call me Captain Jack."

Javier shook Captain Jack's hand without offering his name.

"I'd like to go for a ride. Are you up for that?"

"What do you mean for a "ride"? You just want to go out on the water for a while?"

"Exactly."

"How long are you thinking about?"

"I'm not sure but not long enough to get seasick. I've got some friends who are organizing a party on a large boat and I don't want to be in the middle of the ocean with my friends watching me throw up."

The captain let out a little chuckle while looking Javier up and down.

"I'm thinking that if we went out for a couple of hours and you gave me a tour of the nearby islands, I'd get a feel for how well I can handle the sea."

"When were you thinking of going?" Captain Jack asked.

"Right now."

"Well…" Captain Jack responded hesitantly.

"What's the matter? Do you have another passenger you're waiting on?"

"No, it's not that. It's just that a boat usually isn't taken out impulsively."

"Hey, I'm an impulsive kind of guy. What do you say we take off for a couple of hours so I can test my sea legs?"

Without giving Captain Jack a chance to respond, Javier reached into his pocket and took out ten hundred dollar bills.

"Will this cover the trip?" Javier asked as he handed the money over to Captain Jack.

"It certainly will! By the way, I didn't catch your name."

Javier looked at him for a minute, turned to get on the boat and said,

"I didn't throw it."

"I should contact the dock master to let him know we're going out."

"Is that really necessary?" Javier asked.

"It's not officially required but we usually let them know when we're leaving."

"What do you say we keep this between you and me since we're only going to be gone for a couple of hours. C'mon, let's get this boat moving!"

Captain Jack was a bit taken aback by Javier's request and was beginning to worry. This man was certainly a strange individual but even so, he did pay a thousand dollars for a simple boat ride.

"Alright then, let's shove off."

As they were making their way out to sea, Captain Jack tried to engage Javier in a little small talk but Javier wasn't interested.

"Where you from, Mister?"

"If it's all the same to you, Captain Jack, I just want to concentrate on not getting seasick, so I'd appreciate a little quiet time."

"Have it your way. Any place in particular you want to see?"

"Actually, there is." Javier reached in his pocket and pulled out the coordinates.

"I want you to take me to this spot."

Javier handed Captain Jack the piece of paper.

"That certainly is out a ways."

"Do you have enough fuel to get me out there?"

"Oh sure, there's plenty of fuel to get you there. But I thought you were just checking out the nearby area."

"I am. However, the friends that I told you about earlier are having a party on a yacht at that particular spot. If I knew for sure that I wouldn't get seasick, I would be on the yacht with them."

Captain Jack looked at Javier with skepticism.

"I tell you what, Captain Jack, how about another five hundred to help cover the fuel?"

"That won't be necessary. The thousand is plenty to cover the fuel."

"Well, I'd feel better if I gave you a little more."

Captain Jack wasn't one to argue about an extra five hundred dollars and took the money Javier was now waving in the air.

The rest of the nearly three-hour trip passed in silence as Captain Jack concentrated on running the boat and Javier was lost in thought about what he was going to do with Frank when they met. Frank had become a problem that Javier now had to deal with. The silence was finally broken when Captain Jack pulled back on the throttle and hollered over to Javier that they were almost to the coordinates and no one was in sight.

Javier stood up with concern.

"Do you have any binoculars aboard?"

"They're down below. You'll see them hanging near the hatch."

Javier stepped down the three steps to the lower deck, grabbed the binoculars and came back up. After scanning the horizon for about two minutes, he spotted a boat.

"That may be the boat off to your right, Captain Jack."

"Gottcha!" Captain Jack responded as he turned the boat slightly and headed off toward the unknown boat in the distance. As the captain picked up the microphone from the radio to signal the other boat about their approach, Javier politely took the microphone from his hand.

"I'm positive that's the boat. We don't need to radio ahead."

"How can you be so sure?"

"I recognize the boat."

Within a matter of minutes, the two boats were alongside one another. Javier didn't recognize the captain of the other boat nor the male passenger but before he could say anything, the man hollered over,

"Frank sent us."

"Is that you, O'Shaughnessy?" Captain Jack yelled over.

"Yes. Is that you Captain Jack?"

"You know this guy?" Javier asked, looking at Captain Jack quizzically.

"Oh sure, we've known each other for years. O'Shaughnessy's like a fixture in these waters."

"I'll be right there! I just have to get something from down below."

Javier turned and went down into the lower deck. A few seconds later he yelled up to the captain to come down and give him a hand.

Captain Jack couldn't imagine what Javier needed a hand with since he didn't board with anything but headed down anyway. Once the captain reached the last step into the galley, he was suddenly struck in the head with something hard and went down on one knee. As he looked up, Captain Jack saw a big metal object heading for his head again but before he could move out of the way, he felt another blow, lost consciousness and never felt the repeated blows. Javier took the flare gun that he had found during the trip, walked to the top of the stairs and fired into the galley below. The intense heat of the flare ignited the cabin. He then reloaded the flare gun and after boarding the O'Shaughnessy boat, Javier fired the last flare into the boat near the engine housing, tossing the gun onto the burning boat. O'Shaughnessy never said a word as he pulled his boat away.

Javier turned to the captain of the new boat,

"So, your name is O'Shaughnessy?"

"It is."

Javier then turned to the man standing at the rear of the boat staring wide-eyed at the burning boat.

"And you are?"

The man didn't respond, he just kept staring at the burning boat.

"Hey, you! What's your name?"

"What happened to the man on the other boat?" The man finally managed to utter.

Javier walked over, put his face inches from the man's face and yelled,

"What's your name?"

"Nick. I work for Frank de la Carta."

"And what do you do for Frank?"

"I'm a lawyer."

"Really? Frank sent a lawyer to pick me up?"

"He said that he didn't trust anybody else. Frank wanted to make sure nothing went wrong."

"Well, Frank must have an awful lot of faith in you, Nick if he sent a lawyer to pick me up."

O'Shaughnessy turned the boat around and headed back to Florida.

Nick sat quietly in total disbelief over what he had just witnessed. He couldn't believe that the captain of the other boat had been killed by Javier, the man he had just smuggled into the United States. Would O'Shaughnessy, or even Nick, suffer the same fate? Who is this guy? And how is Frank mixed up with him? Nick kept thinking about the other boat and how O'Shaughnessy never blinked. It was as though he had done this before.

Javier came and sat down next to Nick, who was still deep in thought.

"So how long have you been working for Frank?"

Nick just stared at him. He couldn't find the words to respond.

"Take it easy, kid. If you work for Frank, you know that there is going to be messy things happening. Hasn't he filled you in on who I am?"

"No sir, he hasn't. Frank simply said you were a friend and I was to make sure you got to Miami safely."

"I suppose you might say I'm a friend, a friend Frank probably wishes he didn't have."

"Nonetheless, before we dock, there is something we need to discuss."

"Like what?"

"Just tell me that you'll vouch for O'Shaughnessy, that he's not going to go to the authorities or to tell anybody about this boat trip. Frank vouched for you so that means if I can't trust you or you go sideways, I take it out on Frank. I like your balls but I'm telling you right now, I won't hesitate to take you out if your man O'Shaughnessy does anything to jeopardize my safety or my life, do you understand that?"

Nick knew that Javier meant every word that he said, but Nick wasn't about to let him kill O'Shaughnessy.

"I'll vouch for O'Shaughnessy."

"Are you sure you want to do that, kid, I mean, Nick?"

Nick was beginning to feel more emboldened.

"Yeah, I do."

"What's the story about this O'Shaughnessy anyway, Nick? Why is he such good friends with Frank?"

"Apparently back in the day O'Shaughnessy was running Cubans in his boat. One night the Coast Guard pulled him over when he had a boatload full of Cubans. Frank heard about it, contacted O'Shaughnessy and told him he would represent him. O'Shaughnessy explained he didn't have any money for a lawyer but Frank felt an obligation to help the guy because he was bringing over Cubans. He told him he'd take the case for nothing but O'Shaughnessy would owe him. From what I heard, one of the Cubans in the boat agreed to say that they were in a disabled boat when O'Shaughnessy pulled up alongside to make sure everyone was okay. The Cuban testified that he had a gun, pulled it on

O'Shaughnessy and made him take everyone aboard. When the Cuban saw the Coast Guard coming, he threw the gun into the ocean.

"So why would one of the Cubans say that?"

"It's my understanding that the Cuban's family was paid fifty thousand dollars and in return he was given a jail sentence of four years. When the Cuban got out, it turns out his wife took the money and split. Frank made arrangements for him to stay in the United States as a refugee. Ever since then, O'Shaughnessy has always been available for anything Frank needed. That's why he is doing this, and that's why you're not going to hurt him."

"Nope, I'm not going to hurt O'Shaughnessy because you vouched for him. Hope you know what you're doing."

O'Shaughnessy pulled into the marina and docked the boat. Javier approached O'Shaughnessy, with Nick right next to him. He wasn't going to leave Javier alone with O'Shaughnessy for one second. Nick extended his hand to O'Shaughnessy and thanked him for the favor. O'Shaughnessy didn't reply. Nick wondered if O'Shaughnessy was worried about meeting the same fate as Captain Jack. Javier stepped up on the dock without saying anything to O'Shaughnessy. Nick looked back and O'Shaughnessy gave Nick a nod of thanks.

As they were heading to the parking lot, Javier stopped, looked around and turned to Nick with a slight smile.

"It's been a long time since I've been in the United States. It feels great to be back."

Chapter Eighteen

Detective Henderson was at his desk working on a fresh case involving the murder of a prostitute when his captain called him into the office.

"What's up, Captain?"

"Where are you on that attorney's death?"

"de la Carta? That is on hold for now. I have a few more leads to follow up on, why?"

"The department is getting a lot of inquiries from the Cuban community and we need to know whether the guy died of natural causes or not."

"At the moment, it seems that his death was from natural causes." Detective Henderson replied hesitantly.

"Something tells me you're not sure."

"Just a gut instinct, Captain."

"We need to close this case, Henderson! If there is no evidence pointing to anything other than natural causes, close it! I'll expect your report in the morning."

"Captain, could you give me a little more time, say a couple of weeks?"

"Why?"

"I have a strong feeling that something's not right with this case."

"Look, I'm getting a lot of pressure."

"I get it, but wouldn't it be better to exhaust all possibilities, so we know for sure? It'll show the Cuban community that we care when one of their own dies."

"Listen Henderson, I don't want you to turn this case into a homicide if it's not one. Especially if it is not one you can solve. That really would not go over well with the Cuban community, not very well at all!"

"I realize that. I'm just asking for a couple of weeks."

"No promises on two weeks Henderson but I will give you a few more days. Be sure to keep me posted."

Detective Henderson closed the file he was working on and placed it in the pending folder. It could wait. He picked up the phone and called his partner.

"What are you working on, Joe?"

"Running down that lead on the pimp."

"Let it go for now. The captain wants us to close out the de la Carta case."

"Go ahead and prepare the report, I'll sign off on it."

"Not so fast. I'm not convinced it isn't a homicide."

"Don't we have enough real homicides without you manufacturing one?"

"I can't put my finger on it but it just doesn't seem like an open and shut case."

"Okay, what do you want to do?"

"Meet me at de la Carta's office. I want to talk to that office manager. I believe her name was Carla."

"Okay, see you there."

Both detectives arrived at the law office at the same time.

"Do you have anything in particular you're looking for?" Detective Garcia asked.

"Not really. There's just something about this case." Detective Henderson replied.

Carla heard the front door open and looked down the stairs, immediately recognizing the two detectives. Detective Henderson noticed everything seemed normal, considering they had just lost their boss.

"May I help you?" the receptionist was asking when she was interrupted by Carla, who had bounded down the stairs.

"Detectives, how may I help you?" Carla inquired.

"Actually, you're the one we wanted to speak with. Carla, correct?" Detective Henderson asked.

"Yes, that's right. How can I help you?"

"Is there some place we can talk privately?"

Carla escorted the detectives to the conference room, closing the door behind them.

"I know I've asked you this before Carla but are there any of Mr. de la Carta's clients who may have been upset with him?" asked Detective Henderson.

"Like I said before, no one that I can think of."

"I'd like to go back over the Friday night before the murder."

"Murder! Do you really think it was a murder? Who would do that? Why do you think it's a murder?"

"You'll have to excuse my partner," Detective Garcia interjected.

"We are homicide detectives and sometimes we use the term inappropriately." Detective Garcia explained, shooting a disapproving look at his partner.

"Sorry, I meant to say the Friday before his death."

"I'm sure I told you everything."

"I'd like to go over it again, if you don't mind."

"Okay."

"You said it was about five in the afternoon when you last saw him, is that correct?"

"No, I was mistaken about the time. I was so shaken that day I wasn't sure of anything."

"Have you had more time to think about that evening since we last spoke?"

"Actually, I have. Frank had a client coming in around 6pm and I was still at the office when the client arrived. According to the appointment calendar, it was a Mr. Smith. Although, I didn't set the appointment, the receptionist did."

"Had you seen him before?"

"No, but I later found out his name wasn't Smith."

The two detectives exchanged glances, rolling their eyes.

"Did you find out his real name?" Detective Henderson asked.

"Yes."

"Well, what was it?"

"Arnold, John Arnold."

"Any relation to the attorney Arnold who works here?" Detective Garcia inquired.

"Her father."

"Do you know why he used the name Smith?"

"Yes."

"Why?" Detective Henderson asked, his impatience growing with Carla's curt answers.

"He didn't want his daughter to know he was here."

"How do you know that?"

"After he left, Frank told me who he was but not to tell Abbey since Frank had promised Mr. Arnold that he wouldn't let her find out he had been here."

"What did he want?"

"Frank didn't say but I could hear them arguing."

"About what?"

"I don't know, but Mr. Arnold was very upset and kept yelling at Frank."

"Was Mr. de la Carta yelling?"

"No, just Mr. Arnold."

"How long were they arguing?"

"About twenty minutes or so. Then Frank opened his door and asked me to show him out."

"How did Mr. Arnold seem to you?"

"Very upset, really upset. He was shaking and extremely red in the face."

"Did Mr. Arnold have any injuries, such as a black eye, cut lip, bloody nose, anything like that?"

"Not that I noticed."

"What did you do after you showed Mr. Arnold out?" Detective Henderson asked.

"I came back upstairs."

"Was anyone else here?"

"No, everyone had left. In fact, Abbey had left just a few minutes before her dad came in."

"Do you know if Miss Arnold saw her dad?"

"I don't know but I don't think so because Frank wouldn't have said not to tell Abbey her dad had been here."

"Carla, after you showed Mr. Arnold out, did you lock the door?" Detective Garcia inquired, now picking up the questioning.

"I'm not sure when I locked the door but I

know it was definitely locked when I left for the day."

"What exactly did you do after you showed Mr. Arnold out?"

"I went upstairs to ask Frank if there was anything else he needed. He replied no and wished me a good weekend."

"How did Mr. de la Carta look?" Detective Henderson was back to asking the questions.

"Fine."

"Did you notice any injuries?"

"No, like I just said, he looked fine."

"How long were you upstairs before you left?"

"Five, maybe ten minutes. I said goodnight, cleared off my desk, grabbed my purse and left."

"And you're sure you locked the door before you left?"

"Positive."

"And you don't know why Mr. Arnold was here?"

"I have no idea."

"Well, that's all for now, unless you have any further questions Detective Garcia."

"None that I can think of at this time." Detective Garcia responded.

"Thank you for your time, Carla."

As the two detectives were heading towards the stairs, Detective Henderson suddenly stopped and turned back to Carla.

"Actually, there is one more thing I'd like to ask. What is going to happen to the firm now that Mr. de la Carta is gone?"

"Mr. Constantine is taking over the firm."

"Who?" Detective Henderson asked with surprise.

"Mr. Constantine, Nick Constantine. He's our law firm's senior attorney."

"So, what do you think?" Detective Henderson asked his partner once they had reached the parking lot.

"I'm not sure, but I'm beginning to see your point. I think it's time to interview Mr. Arnold."

Chapter Nineteen

As they were leaving the marina in Nick's Mercedes, Javier asked Nick if he knew where the restaurant Café Ochoa was. Javier wasn't surprised when Nick said he knew the restaurant well. Javier chuckled to himself. Of course, Nick would know the restaurant, especially since Javier knew that's where Frank went whenever business needed to be discussed in private. And it was the same place Javier often took Frank when they first began doing business together.

On the drive over to the restaurant, neither of the men said a word. Javier was deep in thought about how he was going to handle Frank and Nick was deep in thought about how he was going to handle his feelings about the dead boat captain. For the first time in Nick's life, he felt scared. Nick wondered how he ever got involved with this whole situation. Working for Frank had seemed so harmless, even though on occasion he was asked to do things that were slightly in the grey area of the law. But nothing like murder! Nick had never even known a man as ruthless as Javier. He couldn't wait to get to the restaurant and drop Javier off. Nick also wondered what Javier was thinking as they rode in silence.

Upon arriving at the restaurant, Javier sat for a moment before reaching for the door handle, then turned to Nick with a look on his face that made the hair on the back of Nick's neck stand up.

"Turn the car off Nick. I'd like you to come in with me."

"I'd like to Javier, but I really need to get back to the office."

"That wasn't an invitation, Nick. Turn the car off and come into the restaurant now!" Javier commanded.

Nick knew not to argue and turned off the car.

The two of them made their way to the table at the back of the restaurant, the same table where Frank had taken Nick to discuss picking up Javier. At the table, three men of apparent Hispanic background were already seated. As Javier approached, they all stood up and one by one, shook Javier's hand while giving him a hug, the kind of hug a subordinate gives to his boss. It was clear that these men worked for Javier.

"It's great to see you, boss." One of the men said, confirming Nick's observation.

"Gentlemen, I'd like you to meet somebody. "This is Nick, one of the young lawyers that works for Frank. He's going to be our new legal counsel here in Miami."

Nick stared at Javier in disbelief. He didn't want to work for Javier. He never wanted to see Javier again after this day. Not to mention, nothing was ever discussed with Javier or Frank about Nick becoming his counsel. And if Nick was going to be the new local counsel, what was going to happen to Frank? Nick wanted to say no thank you, turn and head for the door but he knew he couldn't. For the next ten minutes, Javier was the only one who spoke. He asked the three men if they had acquired the things he needed. One of the three men reached across the table and handed Javier a set of car keys. Another one of the three men reached across the table and handed Javier a pistol. Javier then turned to Nick.

"Nick, I want you to remember who these three people are. They will be your contacts here in Miami when you take over the law firm."

"But Javier," Nick began but was abruptly interrupted.

"Nick, this is not open for discussion. You will be taking over the law firm. I like you, kid. I think the plan you had for getting me into the United States was pure genius and outside the normal thinking. Also, there aren't many men who would have stood up to me to save the life of that Irishman, especially after seeing firsthand what I'm capable of. That took balls and I admire that. That's also the only reason why you and the Irishman are still alive. I respect that you stood up to me. But know one thing for sure, Nick, do not mistake the decision I made as a sign of weakness. When I leave here, I'm going to meet with Frank and smooth everything over for the transition. Starting Monday, you will be the new head of the firm. You can keep any of the employees that you already have or you can get all new employees, it makes no difference to me."

And without giving Nick any time to respond, Javier began to explain the arrangement.

"The arrangement you and I have will be the same arrangement I had with Frank. You will receive $100,000 per month, in cash, to manage my affairs. You can run your law firm and represent anybody else you like, any way you like, but my business comes first. When you get a call that I need representation for somebody, you are to oversee the situation. And when I say you are to oversee that, I mean YOU. I don't know how much Frank told you about my operation but this is how it works."

For the next three hours, Javier explained to Nick exactly how his operation worked. What he expected of Nick, the line of communication between Javier and Nick, as well as the role each of these three individuals at the table would play in any given situation. Nick sat speechless. He felt trapped. Finally, Nick turned to Javier asking,

"I thought you had a permanent arrangement with Frank. I understood you to be close friends with him."

"I did have an arrangement with Frank but now I have an arrangement with you."

"What about Frank?"

"That's not your concern, Nick." And with that said, Nick was dismissed.

Javier spent that evening and most of the next day managing certain affairs that needed his personal attention while he was in Miami. He needed to put his house in order. It was not easy running an operation of this size from outside the United States. He had to let people know that he was still in charge. Or, as he liked to say, put the fear of Javier in them. Especially since he didn't know how long it would be before he would be returning to the United States once this trip was over.

After taking care of business, Javier knew it was time to pay a visit to Frank. There was no need to call ahead, he knew Frank would be waiting.

Frank sat in his house as he had for the last three days and waited. He knew Javier would come to the house when he was ready. The thing that bothered Frank the most is that he didn't know why Javier had come to the United States. He thought everything was going fine and hoped his trip did not mean Javier was unhappy with him. Nonetheless, Frank knew this wasn't a social visit.

Very few people had ever been to Frank's house, which he preferred to call a villa. To him, the villa was his sanctuary, a place to relax, unwind and isolate himself from his daily work. Javier was the rare exception. Frank had known Javier since childhood. Before leaving for college, Frank had worked for Javier, arranging the logistics of his pick-ups and deliveries. As he sat there waiting, Frank's mind drifted back to how he had begun to work for Javier. When Frank was just out of high school, his father had a heart attack and needed a transplant as soon as possible. Unfortunately, his father couldn't afford to go to a private physician and pay what it took to be placed higher on the list of waiting recipients, therefore he was put on the waiting list at the university hospital where uninsured and indigents were treated. Frank and his family were told there was about a 5% chance a match would be found before he died. Frank wasn't about to let that happen. After hearing the dire news, Frank made a vow to himself that he would do whatever it took to get his father a new heart. The next day he went to meet the only man he knew who could help, Javier Cortez. Javier was a legend in the neighborhood. While he was known as the leader of a ruthless drug organization, it was rumored that he had also helped many people in the community. Javier used his "good deeds" as a type of insurance policy. Rather than try to keep himself safe through intimidation in his sphere of influence, he did it through acts of charity. While everyone knew what kind of man Javier truly was, no one would ever think of cooperating with the authorities against him. Javier paid those who worked for him well and took care of the families of those who were killed or arrested. Families were actually proud to say their sons worked for El Santo, as Javier was often referred to.

Before going to see Javier, Frank had heard so many rumors about the horrible things he had done as leader of the drug cartel, he couldn't believe it was the same person he knew from childhood. Frank closed his eyes, remembering the conversation that he and Javier had the day he went to ask him to save his father.

"I understand you are looking for me."

"I am, sir."

"What can I do for you, Francisco? And don't call me sir, call me Javier."

"Yes sir, I mean, Javier."

Frank was trembling but his resolve was clear. He

needed Javier's help, drug lord or not because without his help, his father would soon die.

"I'm sorry to bother you but my father is dying."

"I'm sorry to hear that. How can I be of service?"

"My father needs a heart transplant. However, we don't have any money to elevate his standing on the waiting list of a private hospital. And even though my father is on the waiting list at University Hospital, we have been told there is almost no chance they will find a heart in time."

"And what do you think I can do for you?" Javier asked.

"I don't know but you're the only hope I have."

Javier liked having people come to him for favors since that is how he kept control of his neighborhood and the allegiance of the people living there.

"What's your father's name?"

"Are you going to help us?"

"I'll look into it."

"I need someone who will do more than just look into it. If you won't help us, I'm going to have to find someone else who will."

"And who would that be?"

"I don't know but there must be someone who will help us. I can't just stand by and let my father die."

Javier heard the desperation in Frank's voice and

knew he would do anything to help save his father. Javier also knew that if he helped Frank, he would shift that loyalty to him forever. Javier looked into Frank's eyes and with a soft, soothing voice said,

"I'll look into it."

And suddenly, a wave of calmness washed over Frank. With those simple words, Frank knew everything was going to be all right. He believed Javier would find a way to save his father. What price Frank would have to pay for that favor, he didn't know, nor did he care. He would pay any price if it would save his father. Frank gave Javier his father's full name, and the number of the hospital room before leaving with the feeling of relief that his father's life would be saved.

Two days later, Frank received a call from the hospital. While still on the phone, Frank began to cry as the hospital administrator told him that someone donated a heart specifically for his father and it was a match. They were preparing him now for surgery. Frank hung up the phone, fell to his knees silently thanking Javier and God, in that order. Without ever being told, he knew Javier had made it happen. Exactly how, Frank didn't know and he didn't ask. The only thing that mattered was that his father was going to live.

The heart transplant was a success and after two months recovering in the hospital, Frank's father was able to come home to the family. Frank never told a soul that he had spoken to Javier but rumors began to spread throughout the community. It was said that Javier had paid to find a man who would be a match for Frank's father and then purchased the heart while the man was still alive, telling the man that if he was willing to give up his heart, Javier would take care of the man's family for the rest of their lives. They would never have a single worry in the world and he would always watch over them. However, if he wasn't willing to do that, then he would be killed anyway, his heart would still be taken and no compensation would be given to his family. No one knew for sure who the man was but there was a lot of speculation, especially since one of the families living in the neighborhood suddenly seemed to be living well beyond their means and there was no husband in the picture. Of course, no one knew for sure and no one would ever ask. It simply added to the mystique of Javier Cortez.

A couple of months later there was a knock on his door and when Frank answered, a young man was standing there. He said that Javier would like to see him. Frank knew this was the day to pay the piper, so asking no questions, he silently followed the young man to Javier's.

"How is your father doing? I understand your father received that heart transplant after all."

Frank didn't know how to respond but as soon as he began to say something, Javier motioned for him to be quiet.

"There's nothing to be said Francisco. And it will never be a topic of conversation again."

Frank immediately understood.

"The reason I asked you to come by today is that I have a small job that I need done and I thought you would be the perfect person to do it."

"What type of work?" Frank asked, knowing it didn't really matter.

"I need someone smart who can do some paperwork that involves keeping track of orders, shipments, bills and payments. It would be an office job that you can do around your school schedule."

"I don't have a school schedule, so I would be able to work full time." Frank replied.

Javier extended his hand and Frank shook it. He knew at once he was making a deal with the devil. But Frank he didn't care.

For the next three years, Frank worked diligently for Javier. He proved to be a great asset to the organization. He set up systems for tracking shipments, keeping track of who owed money and in general, managing the day-to-day planning of Javier's large empire. Frank was good at his job and it did not go unnoticed by Javier. Javier's organization employed hundreds of people but Frank was a stand-out. There was something different and special about him. He didn't use drugs, he was smart, clean-cut and approached his job as though it was a legitimate organization. Frank didn't care that Javier was a drug dealer or involved in human smuggling and he made sure to separate himself from what the products were that he was tracking and shipping. It was the only way he could justify to himself the work he was doing.

Frank continued going over in his mind all the events that had led up to this moment, including the evening when Javier showed up at the office unannounced. Javier had invited him to dinner at Café Ochoa. It was a restaurant Frank knew that Javier used to do business. He joined Javier without asking any questions. Frank never asked questions. He just did what he was told. After ordering dinner, Javier began a conversation that would change Frank's life forever.

"I have a proposition for you, Francisco." Javier began.

"I've watched you now for nearly three years, you're extremely smart and uniquely different than the other people I have working for me."

Frank wondered where this conversation was going.

"I would like to make you an offer that I hope you'll accept. I want to send you to college and then to law school. I will cover all your expenses, you will continue to earn the same salary you're earning now and when you graduate from law school, I will set you up in your own practice where you will do any legal work required by me or my associates whenever necessary. In addition, I will pay you a monthly stipend to keep you on retainer as long as you are always available for all my legal needs."

Frank didn't know what to say. A chance to go to college AND law school? To get out of this end of the business? To leave the poverty of the neighborhood? Frank looked up at Javier with a bit of bewilderment.

"I would like that Javier but what if I don't graduate or can't pass the bar exam? What if I don't become a lawyer? What happens then?"

"Well, we'll just have to make sure that you do graduate. I believe in you and know that you will work hard to do just that. I figure that you becoming a lawyer will benefit both of us in the future. So, what do you say, Francisco? Do want to give it a try?"

Frank looked at Javier without responding. Javier stuck out his hand and once again Frank shook the hand of the devil.

Word spread throughout the neighborhood that Frank was going to college. Everyone in the community was excited that one of theirs was escaping the neighborhood. It didn't even matter that

Frank was going to college compliments of Javier Cortez. It only mattered that he was going. Frank made it through college in three years, graduating with honors. He was accepted into law school and three years later, Frank had his license to practice law in the state of Florida. And as promised, Frank received a monthly salary from Javier with all expenses paid, leaving Frank to graduate law school without any debt. Also as promised, Javier set Frank up in practice and began delivering a retainer of $100,000 per month, beginning the first month of his practice. Even if Frank never had another client, it wouldn't have mattered since he was paid more than enough by Javier to be his lawyer. However, Frank preferred to grow his law firm and soon had a thriving practice.

"Hello, Frank." the voice shook Frank out of his reminiscing.

As he looked up, he saw Javier Cortez standing in front of him.

"Javier! How did you get in here?"

Chapter Twenty

"That's how you greet me after all these years, Francisco, how did you get in here?"

Frank stood up from behind his desk, walked up to the man he hadn't seen in years and stuck out his hand but Javier didn't take it.

Javier always knew a day would come when Frank would get too big and feel he no longer needed Javier. It made Javier sad and his voice reflected that sadness.

"You want a drink, Javier?" Frank was not feeling good about this visit.

"Do you still have some of that expensive scotch?"

"I do." Frank poured two glasses of scotch, a little more in his own glass than in Javier's.

After taking a sip, Javier looked at Frank.

"Francisco," he began.

Javier still called Frank Francisco whenever they talked privately.

"I think the time has come for a change. Francisco, I need you to step down as my personal lawyer and allow someone else to step in. Frank looked stunned. He never believed for one minute that Javier would ever replace him. Afterall, they had a special bond that went back to childhood. Frank had always done whatever Javier wanted and had always been there for him. Frank didn't understand what could have brought about Javier's wanting to end their long-standing agreement.

"Francisco, I think you have forgotten how we started, what we owe one another."

"I haven't forgotten, Javier, not for one minute."

"Well, it seems to me that you have. You are no longer tending to business. You are delegating the responsibility to other lawyers, you are not personally appearing in court on my behalf according to our agreement and you're not getting the results that you once did."

"Are you talking about this last case?"

"I'm talking about many of the last cases, Francisco, with the loss of this last case being the worst. Instead of managing it yourself, you sent that girl to handle the case. She not only lost the trial but my nephew went to prison for ten years. Do you have any idea what that cost me?"

"Rosemarie happens to be an excellent lawyer and it wasn't her fault. If your nephew wasn't such a moron to load the illegals himself, they wouldn't have been able to identify him. Furthermore, you had assured me that none of them would be able to identify him."

"Only because I didn't know he personally loaded them against protocol. If I had known, there would not have been any witnesses."

"That's what this is about after all these years? One case?"

"No, not just one case, Francisco! It's your whole attitude of how you are managing my affairs. I think you have completely forgotten that you owe me."

"Javier, our deal was that I would handle your legal matters and that is exactly what I do. Not to mention that you haven't paid me in over ten months! That's a million dollars Javier!"

"So now you think I owe you a million dollars?"

"Yes, I do!" Frank said with a certain amount of defiance.

"I've been managing your legal affairs all this time even though the payments have stopped Javier. And who do you think is going to take over this firm? Have you thought that through?"

"I have, Francisco. I have already spoken to Nick, the young man you sent to pick me up on the boat."

"Nick Constantine? You're having Nick take over this firm? He's barely out of law school."

"He reminds me of you, Francisco, when you were

young. He has a lot of nerve and I think he'll do what it takes to make sure my affairs are managed properly."

"I've always taken care to make sure your affairs were managed properly."

"Not lately."

"Is that why the payments stopped?

"Exactly! It just took me a little while to figure out how I was going to handle the situation. We go back a long way, Francisco and it makes me sad that you have forgotten how we started."

"Don't go there, Javier! I have never forgotten what you did for me and my family and I will always be grateful! I would do anything for you but things have changed."

"Nothing has changed, Francisco, except you. You've changed. You have become more complacent."

"Javier, think about what you're doing. We can work out any problems."

"I already took care of the problems Francisco. Now I need you to step down. I know you couldn't possibly have spent all the money I've paid you over the years so you should be fine financially."

Frank knew there was no sense in arguing with Javier. He had seen that look of resolve on Javier's face many times over the years.

"So that's it, Javier, after all these years?"

"That's it. Don't make it any harder than it needs

to be, Francisco. It's nothing personal, it's strictly business. I can't afford to have you handling my affairs any longer."

"What about the million dollars you owe me?"

"Again, I ask you, do you really think I owe you a million dollars, Francisco?"

"I worked for ten months per our agreement and didn't receive a single payment. So yes, I think you owe me the one million dollars."

"And you think one million dollars is really fair?"

"Yes."

"Alright, Francisco, if you think that's fair, I'll have it delivered tomorrow."

"Just like that, Javier, no negotiations?"

"No, Francisco, if you think that's fair, I won't insult you with a lesser amount. You'll have your one million dollars."

Javier stood up and headed for the door.

"I can show myself out."

Frank watched his friend walk out the door without their traditional handshake, leaving him with an uneasy feeling.

Chapter Twenty-one

Although it had only been a few days since Frank's death, things seemed to be running smoothly under Nick's control. While there was no official changing of the guard, Nick was assumed to be the de facto leader of the firm and was doing the best he could to maintain the status quo. The staff of attorneys continued to work on their assigned cases, court appearances were kept and the investigation of Frank's death was still ongoing. Nick had moved into Frank's upstairs office with Carla staying on as his assistant.

As Nick was looking through the massive mound of files stacked on his desk, his office door suddenly flew open and Carla rushed in.

"Nick, you need to help Abbey right now. Something's seriously wrong."

Without hesitation, Nick followed Carla to Abbey's office. As he entered Abbey's office, Nick saw Abbey curled up in the corner, sobbing hysterically. Nick walked over and knelt down beside her.

"Abbey, what's wrong?"

Abbey was sobbing too hard to answer Nick.

Nick grabbed both her arms and turned Abbey towards him.

"Abbey, answer me. What is the matter?"

Clearly in a state of hysteria and unable to even comprehend that Nick and Carla were in the room with her, Abbey continued to lay on the floor of her office, uncontrollably sobbing.

Nick turned to Carla and asked if she knew what had happened.

"I have no idea. All I know is that Abbey received a phone a call and when I walked past her office a few minutes later, Abbey was lying on the floor in a fetal position, sobbing."

Nick looked down, saw that the phone receiver was lying next to Abbey and when he picked it up, realized that someone was still on the line.

"Who is this?" Nick demanded.

"This is Mr. Arnold's next-door neighbor in Memphis." The woman on the phone replied, without offering her name.

"Were you the one just talking to Abigail Arnold?"

"Yes, I called her with some news about her father."

"What news?" Nick asked in the same demanding tone.

"Her father is dead." The woman replied coldheartedly.

Nick stood there for a moment, completely stunned. He knew what a close relationship Abbey had with her father, that Abbey was all that Mr. Arnold cared about in the entire world and vice-versa. At times, it seemed to Nick, that all these two had were each other.

Nick whispered in Carla's ear that Abbey's father was dead.

Just as stunned as Nick at hearing the sad news and knowing how devasting the death would be on Abbey, Carla sat down next to her and held Abbey's limp body, trying to comfort her.

"I am so sorry, Abbey. Is there anything we can do?"

There was no response from Abbey.

After a few more minutes, Abbey sobs quieted and Carla was able to get an emotionally drained Abbey off the floor and over to a small sofa in the corner of Abbey's office. Once she was on the sofa, Abbey stopped crying but sat motionless, blankly staring into space.

"Nick, you better call Dr. Harrison and have him come here as quickly as possible."

Dr. Harrison is the doctor the law firm used on occasion when things needed to be taken care of discreetly.

After putting Mr. Arnold's neighbor on hold, Nick called Dr. Harrison and asked that the doctor come to the law office as soon as possible without giving too many details. Dr. Harrison told Nick he would be there within twenty minutes.

While waiting for the doctor's arrival, Nick had resumed talking to Mr. Arnold's neighbor. During the terse conversation, he found out that Mr. Arnold had committed suicide, taking a gun to his right temple, pulling the trigger and dying instantly. There was a suicide note left in the trailer. Nick also found out they did not discover the body right away. Mr. Arnold's body was only discovered after the neighbor, who noticed Mr. Arnold's truck had not been moved in several days and seeing no activity inside the trailer, called the police.

Nick ended the call just as Dr. Harrison was arriving. After quickly assessing the situation, the doctor gave Abbey a mild sedative to help her rest.

Shortly after Dr. Harrison left, Rosemarie returned from court and noticed Nick and Carla sitting in Abbey's office.

"What's going on?" Rosemarie asked.

"Abbey just received some news from home." Nick somberly replied.

"What kind of news?"

"Abbey's father is dead." Carla said quietly.

"Was he involved in an accident?"

"No, it was a suicide." Carla replied and then sadly left Abbey's office.

Just as stunned as Nick and Carla, Rosemarie could find no words.

"Rosemarie, I think you should stay with Abbey tonight. I'm worried about her frame of mind. As you can well imagine, Abbey was completely devasted when she heard the news and became quite hysterical. Dr. Harrison came to the office and gave her a sedative but when it wears off, she probably shouldn't be alone.

"I agree. I'll take her to my place." Rosemarie responded.

"No, it might be better if you take her to her apartment. I think it will be more comforting for her to be home than if she awakes someplace else. Do you have any court appearances tomorrow?"

"No, none at all."

Nick didn't have to ask if Abbey had any appearances pending since she never went to court.

Rosemarie decided to quickly run home and pick up a few things she needed for her overnight stay at Abbey's apartment while Abbey was sleeping. However, before leaving, Rosemarie turned back to Nick.

"I wonder if she wants to go to Memphis and take care of any arrangements."

"I hadn't thought of that. Just in case she does, let me have your schedule for the next few days and I'll cover for you so you can go with her."

"Thanks, Nick. I have a pretty light week, therefore it should be relatively easy."

Later that day when the sedative had worn off and Abbey awoke from a fitful sleep, Rosemarie sat and listened to Abbey talk about her childhood until early the next morning. She talked about the death of her mother and how Abbey and her father held each other together. Throughout the day and long night, Abbey went through all the stages of grief. Finally ending in the disbelief that her father would ever do something so awful as committing suicide.

"Rosemarie, this is all my fault. If it weren't for me, he would still be alive."

"Abbey, you can't think like that."

"I should never have left him. If I had just stayed in Memphis…"

"And do what, Abbey? You couldn't spend your whole life just taking care of your father."

"Yes, I could. That was my job as his only daughter. Once I left, he was all alone. I should have known this would happen."

"How could you have known, Abbey?"

"After my mother died, there were times when my father said that I was the only thing that kept him alive. And what do I do? I just walk out of his life in some selfish move to Miami."

"Abbey, there's nothing selfish about what you did. He encouraged you to go to law school. He encouraged you to look for jobs. He even encouraged you to take this job."

"Now I can see that he didn't mean it. He had secretly hoped I would stay with him and get a job in Memphis."

"But there weren't any jobs in Memphis."

"Then I should have found a different type of job. I should never have left him, Rosemarie. I should never have left him. This really is all my fault."

"Abbey, stop that." Rosemarie said in a firm voice before continuing,

"You know as well as I do no one is responsible for someone else's actions. He took this action on his own and whatever his reasons were, they were his reasons and there are no assurances that those reasons would be any different if you had stayed in Memphis."

Realizing that the morning was slipping away, Rosemarie decided she better find out if Abbey intended to return to Memphis to take care of any arrangements that might need to be made.

"Abbey, if you want to go to Memphis today, Nick has agreed to cover my schedule so I can go with you."

Abbey turned and looked at Rosemarie. At the very thought of going back to Memphis, Abbey began to cry, so Rosemarie simply held her hand while the two of them sat on the couch.

"Abbey, you know you have to go back to Memphis. You have to make the arrangements for your father and his belongings." Rosemarie finally said softly.

"Yes, I know. But I don't want to think about it anymore today. We'll go in the morning."

The next morning on the flight to Memphis, Abbey barely spoke. She sat staring out the window thinking about how things were so different since her mother had passed away. And now her father was suddenly gone. At the airport in Memphis, Rosemarie rented a car and then drove directly to the coroner's office. Before leaving Miami, Rosemarie had called the Memphis Coroner's office to make arrangements for Abbey to see her father. Mr. Arnold's body had already been positively identified by the next-door neighbor but Abbey wanted to see her father one last time. Rosemarie had tried to talk her out of it, telling Abbey that is not how she wanted to remember her father, lying on a cold, steel table in the morgue, but Abbey insisted. She needed closure. Knowing that to be true, no matter what the circumstances are, Rosemarie went ahead and made the appointment with the coroner's office on Abbey's behalf.

When they arrived at the morgue, Abbey remained

quietly in the seat with her seatbelt secured snugly around her. Rosemarie sat patiently waiting, knowing Abbey would get out of the car when she was ready. They sat in silence for nearly 30 minutes before Abbey could undo her seatbelt and reach for the door handle. As they walked into the coroner's office, Abbey held firmly to Rosemarie's arm to steady herself. Once inside the morgue, the attendant also tried to dissuade Abbey from seeing her father. He explained in the most tactful terms possible that the death was a gunshot wound to the head. Rosemarie knew what he was so delicately trying to say but there was no stopping Abbey from seeing her father. As they got closer to the body lying under the sheet, Rosemarie felt Abbey's weight growing on her arm and was afraid that Abbey might not be able to stand once she saw her father. And Rosemarie was right. Once the attendant pulled back the sheet, Abbey took one look at her father and fainted.

Fortunately, the attendant was prepared for Abbey's reaction and caught her before she hit the floor. Holding some smelling salts under nose, the attendant brought Abbey around and helped her to a nearby chair.

"I'm so sorry for your loss." The attendant told Abbey.

Abbey didn't answer.

A few minutes later, Rosemarie asked Abbey if she felt strong enough to walk. Without saying a word, Abbey stood up, took a hold of Rosemarie's arm once again and they headed to the car.

When they reached the car, Rosemarie asked Abbey if she'd like to go to her father's trailer.

"No, I wouldn't. I'd like to go downtown to the police department and speak with the detectives who looked into my father's death. I'd also like you to call Mrs. Cauchi, the neighbor who found my dad and ask her to join us at the police department."

"Of course." Rosemarie responded, wondering why Abbey wanted Mrs. Cauchi to meet them at the police station and what she wanted to talk to the detectives about.

Rosemarie and Abbey were already at the police station and speaking with the homicide detective when the neighbor, Mrs. Cauchi, arrived.

Detective Williams was explaining his findings to Abbey. He was polite and soft-spoken, making it quite apparent he had dealt with family members who had lost loved ones many times before.

"I don't believe this was a suicide." Abbey said to Detective Williams with a great deal of conviction.

"I know it's hard to comprehend, especially in suicides, but I assure you, Miss Arnold, that is exactly what it was." Detective Williams answered.

"What makes you so sure? You didn't know my father! You don't know the kind of man he was or even what he was or wasn't capable of doing! Why do you believe this is a suicide so positively?"

The detective opened his file and pulled out a piece of paper. Very gently, he slid the paper over to Abbey. She looked down and immediately recognized her father's handwriting. Rosemarie glanced over and saw that it appeared to be a suicide note. Abbey looked at the note and as she read the last thing her father ever wrote, tears fell from her eyes onto the paper.

Sweetheart,

As you read this, I hope you can find it in your heart to forgive me. Please know I love you so much and what I did, I did out of love. I couldn't just let him take you away from me without at least making an effort to stop him. Now I know how wrong I was. I realize this is the coward's way out but I knew I couldn't bear to face you once you found out what I did. Please try to understand what I did was due to my unbearable loneliness and need for you to be with me. Please forgive me.

Dad.

It was a brief note and to the point. Abbey just held the note, staring at it with tears rolling down her face. Finally, Abbey looked up at Detective Williams and in a soft, almost inaudible voice, thanked him. As she turned around, she saw Mrs. Cauchi, her father's next-door neighbor, who walked up and without saying a word, hugged her.

"Thank you for meeting me here, Mrs. Cauchi."

"Of course, Abbey. If there is anything I can do, anything at all, please you let me know."

"Actually, there is something you can do for me, Mrs. Cauchi. I would like you to make the arrangements for my father's funeral because I don't think I can handle it."

"Of course I will."

"I'll make sure that you are paid for your time and all the other expenses will be handled by me."

"Don't worry about any of that right now."

"Also, Mrs. Cauchi, I want you to have my father's trailer, including all its' contents. Anything that you don't want, please donate it to charity. I don't want to go back to the trailer and I don't want anything that is inside it except for our family photos. If you wouldn't mind, please box them up and hold them for me."

"Abbey, that's very kind of you but I don't think I can afford to buy the trailer."

"Mrs. Cauchi, I'm not selling the trailer, I'm giving it to you along with all its' contents."

"But Abbey…"

"There's no point in arguing Mrs. Cauchi, my mind is made up. I can't think of anybody I would rather give it to than you. You have always been a good friend to my father as well as to my mother when she was alive. I know in my heart that they would like you to have the trailer. I will have all the necessary paperwork drawn up by my law firm and sent it to you once I return to Miami."

"Okay, Abbey, if that is what you want. Thank-you for your kind generosity. I feel deeply blessed."

After given her a long hug, Mrs. Cauchi asked Abbey if she had given any thought to how she wanted her father's funeral arrangements to be made.

"I would like him cremated."

"Are you sure?"

"I'm positive."

"And the ashes?"

"I don't care. They can do whatever they want with the ashes."

Rosemarie saw that Abbey was now angry, knowing with sudden certainty that her father had left her all alone by his own hand.

As they were heading out the door toward the car, Rosemarie told Abbey to wait for her in the car as she had forgotten something. Rosemarie went running back inside and grabbed Mrs. Cauchi's arm as she was leaving.

"Mrs. Cauchi, please don't get rid of Mr. Arnold's ashes. Right now, Abbey is angry at her father for what he did but I know the time will come when she will want them. Would you please keep her father's ashes with the box of photos for now?"

"Of course, I will. That's not a problem at all. No matter how long it takes, when Abbey is finally ready, his ashes as well as all their family photos will be waiting for her."

Chapter Twenty-two

Detective Henderson knew he was running out of time. It had been two days since his captain had given him the ultimatum to close the case if no evidence of a homicide was found. If nothing new developed in the next twenty-four hours, the detective knew his chances for proving de la Carta's death was a homicide would be over and someone had gotten away with murder.

His thoughts kept circling back to John Arnold, Abigail Arnold's father. Why had he come to Miami to speak to de la Carta under an alias? What had the two gentlemen argued about? Detective Henderson couldn't shake the feeling that there was more to Mr. Arnold's mysterious visit than just a heated argument.

The detective's thoughts were interrupted by his Captain's voice.

"Henderson, in my office. Now!"

As soon as the detective entered the captain's office, he knew his twenty-fours had just flown out the window.

"Yes, Captain?"

"Shut the door, Henderson and then tell me you have something new on that dead lawyer from Little Havana."

"Nothing yet sir but…"

The captain didn't let the detective finish his sentence.

"Henderson, I gave you a couple of extra days, against my better judgement, to find any evidence that the death was a homicide, however since it seems you weren't able to do that, I'm closing the case under natural causes."

"Captain, before you do that, there is one lead I would like to follow up on. There is something strange about a visit to de la Carta by a Mr. John Arnold, the father of one of the firm's attorneys. All I'm asking for is a little more time to interview Mr. Arnold. And if nothing comes of the interview, I'll concede that the case should be closed without any further argument."

"Where is this Mr. Arnold?"

"Memphis."

"Memphis! Let me see if I'm understanding this correctly, Henderson. You actually want me to authorize funds to fly you to Memphis, Tennessee to interview somebody concerning a death that appears to be from natural causes? Do I have that right?"

"Yes."

"Are you out of your mind??!!"

"Maybe. But my instincts are telling me that Mr. Arnold might hold the key to this entire case since, other than the office manager, he was the last one to see de la Carta alive.

"Look Henderson, you're one of my best detectives and over the years that we've worked together, I've learned that your instincts are seldom wrong, however, in this case you have nothing to go on, no evidence, nothing! Even the medical examiner is willing to sign off that the death was due to natural causes. Let's just close it out and be done."

"I can't let the case go that easily, Captain. If it was a murder, it's our job to find the murderer, no matter what it takes!"

"On the other hand, Henderson, if there is no murder, there is no reason to invent one."

"Captain, I just need a round-trip ticket to Memphis so I can speak to this Mr. Arnold regarding his covert Miami visit on the day de la Carta died. Just let me interview him and I'll be satisfied, regardless how it ends up."

"I must be crazy to even be listening to you, Henderson."

"Is that a yes?"

"On one condition."

"Anything!"

"I don't want it known that you're investigating somebody in Memphis, Tennessee, who may or may not have murdered a prominent lawyer from the Cuban community. Is that clear?"

"You got it, Captain."

As Detective Henderson was exiting the captain's office, he turned to say thank-you.

"Don't thank me Henderson. Just get this done and have a report on my desk tomorrow, one way or another."

"Will do, Captain."

Walking past his desk, Detective Henderson approached his partner.

"Joe, I'm following up on a lead so I will be out of the office for the rest of the day. See you tomorrow."

"Where are you going? Do you need a back-up?"

"No, I'm good. It's just an interview."

"For which case?"

"I have to get going. I'll fill you in when I get back."

Within twenty minutes, Detective Henderson was heading to the airport. On the way, he called de la Carta's office manager, Carla to obtain the address of Mr. Arnold. The detective wasn't sure what exactly he was going to ask Mr. Arnold but he hoped to at least get an explanation regarding the man's curious trip to Miami and the argument he had with de la Carta.

Upon arrival at the Memphis airport, preferring to rent a car instead of taking a cab, the detective went straight to the car rental counter where he received the keys to a compact sedan as well as a map of the Memphis area and directions to the trailer park where Mr. Arnold resided.

Detective Henderson had no trouble finding the trailer park and was soon pulling up to Mr. Arnold's home, such as it was.

As the detective started to knock on Mr. Arnold's door, a woman walked up behind him.

"May I help you?"

"I'm looking for Mr. John Arnold. Do you happen to know if he is home?"

The woman replied that she was Mr. Arnold's neighbor, Mrs. Cauchi and asked who he was.

The detective introduced himself as Detective Henderson from the Miami Police Department.

"And what would a detective from Miami want with Mr. Arnold?" Mrs. Cauchi inquired with a certain amount of authority.

"I just want to ask him a few questions regarding an investigation I'm conducting in Miami."

"Well, I'm afraid you're too late to be asking Mr. Arnold anything."

"What do you mean?"

"Mr. Arnold is dead. He committed suicide."

"What?! When?" Detective Henderson asked incredulously.

"You would have to ask the coroner to be certain but I believe it was just a few days ago."

Detective Henderson was completely stunned.

"Do you have any details?"

"Again, you'd have to ask the coroner." Mrs. Cauchi replied with growing annoyance.

"Thank-you for your time, Mrs. Cauchi. Oh, by the way, do you happen to know the directions to the coroner's office?"

Her patience with the detective wearing thin, Mrs. Cauchi answered him with a terse no, making it quite clear that she was done answering any more of his questions.

Looking at the Memphis area map, Detective Henderson reasoned the coroner's office would be near the center of town and headed in that direction. His hunch was right and he soon found himself at the county morgue, which was conveniently located next to police headquarters. The detective suddenly decided he would prefer to speak directly to someone in the Memphis Police Department rather than the coroner, since the coroner would have limited information regarding Mr. Arnold.

Detective Henderson introduced himself to the desk sergeant, asking who he could speak to about the death of a Mr. John Arnold. The Desk Sergeant directed him to the Information Desk.

Introducing himself to the woman behind the desk, Detective Henderson asked if there was a police file on the death of Mr. John Arnold that he could look at.

"Let me check for you, Detective."

The woman left her desk, returning shortly with the name of the detective who investigated the case.

"Detective Williams is the person you will want to speak with."

"Is he available now?"

"I'm not sure but I'll ring his office for you."

On the second ring, Detective Peter Williams answered, indicating to the woman that even though it was on such short notice, he would be able to see Detective Henderson now. The woman hung up and escorted Detective Henderson down the hall to Detective Williams office.

"I understand you're here from Miami needing some information regarding the death of Mr. John Arnold, Detective Henderson." Detective Williams said while shaking hands and motioning for the Miami detective to take a seat.

"Yes, I'm investigating a potential homicide case that Mr. Arnold may or may not have been involved in." Detective Henderson replied.

"Potential homicide?"

"Well, at the moment, the cause of death hasn't been determined. The medical examiner is leaning towards natural causes, however there is still an awful lot of unanswered questions."

"And you say Mr. Arnold may have been involved? What would make you think that?"

"It turns out his daughter, Abigail Arnold worked for the victim, Mr. Francisco de la Carta and apparently Mr. Arnold had visited him just hours before the death was discovered. The two gentlemen had an intense argument resulting in Mr. Arnold being escorted out of the building. Mr. Arnold could very well be one of the last persons to see Mr. de la Carta alive. I came to Memphis hoping to ask him a few questions regarding his trip to Miami."

"I'll grab his file and maybe we can get you some answers even though Mr. Arnold is now deceased."

In a few minutes, Detective Williams returned with the file detailing the events of Mr. Arnold's death.

"Unfortunately, it looks like there's not much here, Detective. We were called to Mr. Arnold's home because the next-door neighbor, Mrs. Cauchi hadn't seen any activity for a couple of days, which she said was highly unusual. When we entered the residence, we found Mr. Arnold dead on the floor, having died instantly from a gunshot wound to his head. The gun was lying next to him. When it was dusted for fingerprints, the only prints found were Mr. Arnold's. A suicide note was also found at the scene. I'm sorry, it appears this was an open and shut case, so you may not be getting any helpful answers after all."

"Would you mind showing me the suicide note, Detective?"

"Not at all."

Detective Williams handed the Miami detective the note. As Detective Henderson began reading, it was hard to hide his elation. Not only was it a suicide note, it was also a confession to the murder of Mr. Francisco de la Carta!

"Could you make me a copy of this note?"

"Of course."

Five minutes later, Detective Williams returned with a copy of the suicide note. Thanking the Memphis detective for his assistance, the two detectives shook hands and Detective Henderson quickly headed to the Memphis airport.

On the drive to the airport, Detective Henderson was basking in the glow that he finally had the proof that this case was a homicide just as he had thought all along.

"I knew it! My instincts are seldom wrong!" The detective said out loud.

He could hardly wait to get back to Miami

and show the note to his captain. Not only did he have concrete proof that the de la Carta case was a homicide, he also had the name of the murderer. And the cherry on top is that killer committed suicide so now the case could be cleanly closed. No lingering investigations, no trial and no bad publicity for the Miami Police Department, everything was all wrapped up nicely with a neat little bow.

The one small detail that Detective Williams didn't share with the Miami detective was that Mr. Arnold's daughter, Abigail, had been to the Memphis Police Department as well and she also had a copy of the suicide note.

During his flight back to Miami, Detective Henderson re-read the note once again. It was very clear that Mr. Arnold was admitting to his daughter that he had killed her boss. But how? There were no marks, no bruises, no cuts, no blood, no gunshot wound, absolutely no signs of a violent death anywhere on de la Carta's body. Obviously, Mr. Arnold had a gun, so why didn't he use it? And if he were going to Miami to kill de la Carta, why would he make an appointment? It didn't make any sense. Why would Mr. Arnold bother to make an appointment, show up at de la Carta's office, letting someone see him there and then kill the man? Why not wait until de la Carta leaves for the day and ambush him outside of the office so no one would know he had even been there?

Unfortunately, Detective Henderson began to realize that Mr. Arnold's suicide created more questions than answers.

Chapter Twenty-three

On their flight back from Memphis, Abbey and Rosemarie sat in first class next to one another. Abbey sat quietly staring out the window without saying a word. Rosemarie knew that there was nothing she could say to help console Abbey in the loss of her beloved father. Rosemarie sat through Abbey's silence thinking about the suicide note Abbey's father had left behind. Even though Abbey hadn't told Rosemarie that her father's suicide note also included a confession to killing Frank, she did tell Rosemarie that her father had apologized for what he had done. Rosemarie wondered if he was referring to the suicide or something else. Reaching across the armrest, Rosemarie put her hand on Abbey's arm.

"Are you okay?"

Abbey didn't respond. She just kept staring out the window. It was only a two-hour flight to Miami but it seemed like it took forever. As they were beginning their descent into Miami, Abbey turned to Rosemarie.

"Rosemarie, why would he do it?" Abbey asked, her voice pleading for an answer.

During her years as a prosecutor, Rosemarie had dealt with victims of all types of crimes, so she was used to seeing heartache in unanswered questions. However, this situation was different. Abbey wasn't just her co-worker but a dear friend as well. And sadly, Rosemarie had no answers to offer her friend. She worried about what Abbey would do when they arrived home, how she would deal with the death of her father while living all alone in her apartment. Rosemarie wondered if Abbey would be strong enough to continue working at the firm. Yet, Rosemarie felt Abbey would at least try to stay with the firm. Afterall, while they were in Memphis, Abbey had given her father's trailer to the neighbor, Mrs. Cauchi and told her to take care of all the funeral arrangements, making it quite clear that Abbey had no intention of returning to Memphis.

Rosemarie had made prior arrangements with Nick to have him pick them up at the airport. As Nick was walking towards the two women, Rosemarie shot him a look that conveyed he shouldn't say a word to Abbey. Nick saw the look and knew immediately what it meant. So, without a word, they all got in Nick's car and exited the airport. Rosemarie leaned forward from the back seat and whispered to Nick,

"My place."

"No, Rosemarie, I would like to go home." Abbey interjected.

"I think it would be better if you stay with me tonight, Abbey."

"I appreciate your kindness Rosemarie but I need some time to think. I need to be alone."

"Please stay at my house just for the night then, Abbey."

"I'll be okay. Don't worry, Rosemarie, I'm not going to do anything foolish. I just want to try to make some sort of sense out of what happened."

"Abbey, you do know it wasn't your fault, right?"

Abbey didn't respond.

Rosemarie's concern for her friend was growing.

"Well, what if I stayed with you then?"

"Really, Rosemarie, I simply need some time alone. I'm going to be fine. You don't have to worry about me. I will see you at work tomorrow morning."

"Abbey, I think you should take some time off."

"Time off is exactly what I don't need right now. I need to stay busy and keep focused on my work. I will be in the office tomorrow, however tonight, I want to be alone."

"Okay, Abbey, if that's what you feel you need to do, we'll drop you off at your house and see you in the morning."

Abbey gave her concerned friend a heartfelt thank you, sat back in the seat and returned to silently staring out the window.

That night, Abigail Arnold sat alone in her apartment searching her troubled mind for answers. What could she have done differently? What drove her father to such despair? Her father had killed her boss and Abbey knew it was because he couldn't cope with her absence. He knew she would never return to Memphis and despite repeatedly begging him to move to Miami, she knew he never would. Therefore, led by some misguided idea, her father must have thought if he eliminated Frank, she would have no other option but to return home. If only he had spoken with her. If he had only been open about his feelings, she would have raced home. While she enjoyed her life in Miami and was glad to be away from Memphis, her father was more important to her than anything else in the world. If she had known he was in such a mental state, she would not have thought twice about leaving Miami and returning home to take care of her father. But he never gave her that chance. As she sat in the dark, thoughts rushing through her head, she began to get angry. Angry at him for being so selfish and even more angry at herself for being equally selfish. However, what completely puzzled Abbey was the fact that her father could do something like that. Not the suicide so much as she had constantly worried about that when her mother passed away because her father had gone into such a deep, dark depression but rather the murder. In Abbey's entire life, no matter what, her father had never, ever shown a streak of violence. He was a kind, gentle man that would do anything for his family. She would never in her wildest imagination have thought that murder would be one of the things he was capable of doing. Abbey loved her father and realized what she had to do now. There was no way that she was going to allow her father to be remembered as a man who killed someone. That just wasn't who he was. She was not going to let his memory be tarnished by one insane act of violence in a misguided act of love for her. That is definitely NOT how John Arnold was going to be remembered. Content in knowing what she needed to do, a sudden calmness came over Abbey and she fell into a fitful sleep on the couch.

The next morning, instead of heading to work, Abigail Arnold walked into police headquarters and asked to speak to Detective Henderson. The detective had just arrived at the office and hadn't had an opportunity to talk to his captain yet about the trip to Memphis. The receptionist buzzed Detective Henderson and informed him there was someone there to see him, someone by the name of Abigail Arnold. Detective Henderson immediately went to the front desk and greeted Abbey.

"Miss Arnold, this is an unexpected surprise."

"Wouldn't any surprise be unexpected, Detective? Nonetheless, do you have a minute to talk?"

"Of course." Detective Henderson directed Abbey back to his office.

Once they were both seated, Detective Henderson asked Abbey how he could be of assistance.

"I'm here to confess to a murder."

The detective stared at Abbey in total disbelief. Is this entire family homicidal?

He wasn't sure whether he should immediately handcuff her or let her continue speaking. He was afraid if he took any type of aggressive action, she might ask for a lawyer. Or recant her confession. And since the detective didn't even know what murder she was confessing to, he decide it would be best to stay calm until he could figure out exactly what Miss Arnold was talking about.

"Did I hear you correctly, Miss Arnold? You said you want to confess to a murder? Whose murder would that be?"

"I killed my boss, Frank de la Carta."

Detective Henderson suddenly went from disbelief to total confusion.

"Miss Arnold, before you say another word, I need to advise you of your constitutional rights."

"I'm a lawyer, Detective. I know my constitutional rights."

"Nonetheless, Miss Arnold, I would feel more comfortable if you allowed me to advise you of your rights."

Without waiting for a response, Detective Henderson proceeded to explain Abbey's constitutional rights as required by law. When he finished, he looked directly at Abbey.

"Do you understand these rights, Miss Arnold?"

"Of course I understand these rights."

"Alright then, let's start at the beginning. You say you killed Mr. de la Carta?"

"That's correct."

"And when did this happen?"

Abbey thought for a moment.

"Over the weekend, prior to the Monday he was found."

"I see. And how did you kill him?"

Suddenly, Abbey realized she hadn't thought this entirely through, especially since she didn't even know how Frank had died.

Detective Henderson knew immediately Abbey's confession to killing de la Carta wasn't true. He didn't know why she was admitting to a murder she didn't commit, except maybe to protect her father's memory or through some state of confusion. He wasn't sure.

"Miss Arnold, you still haven't answered my question. How did you kill Mr. de la Carta?"

"I would rather not say."

"Is that because you don't know?"

"I killed Mr. de la Carta and that is all I have to say."

Abbey did not know that Detective Henderson had a copy of the suicide note and the detective didn't know Abbey had a copy also, thus creating a rather unique dilemma for both parties in the room.

"Miss Arnold, I think before you say another word, you should have a lawyer present."

"I don't need a lawyer. I killed Mr. de la Carta, so arrest me, Detective."

"Well, if you're going to insist that you killed Mr. de la Carta, I will eventually arrest you but not until I investigate your allegations further. I need something more than just your word to corroborate the fact that you killed him."

Abbey just stared at the detective.

"Please wait here for a moment, Miss Arnold. I'll be right back."

Detective Henderson opened the drawer of his desk, took out a file and walked over to his partner's desk, laying the file in front of him. He leaned over and spoke in a hushed tone.

"Joe, I need you to get a hold of Nick Constantine."

"Who?" Detective Garcia asked.

"Nick Constantine. He's one of the lawyers that worked for de la Carta."

"The dead guy?"

"Yes. I need you to tell Mr. Constantine that we've got Abigail Arnold here at the precinct and I need him to come down immediately."

"What's going on?"

"Please, just do it. I'll explain everything later. Right now, get a hold of this Constantine and be sure to tell him that we have Miss Arnold here to ensure that he will come down here."

"Do we have Miss Arnold here?"

"Yes, we certainly do and she's confessing to murdering de la Carta."

"What?!?"

"Miss Arnold is insisting that she killed de la Carta but I don't believe her."

"She willingly comes in to confess, yet you don't believe her? How are you going to explain that to the Captain?"

"There's more to the story. I just haven't had a chance to fill you in on what I learned in Memphis. But get this, I have a copy of a suicide note written by Mr. Arnold also confessing to the murder of de la Carta."

"Are you kidding me?!"

"No, I'm not. Now call Constantine and get him down here pronto!"

"Will do."

Nick was in his office when Detective Garcia called. He slammed the phone down and as he was heading down the stairs, he ran into Rosemarie.

"You're not going to believe this."

"What's wrong, Nick? You look like you just saw a ghost."

"Worse than that, I just got a call from Detective Garcia."

"One of the detectives investigating Frank's death?"

"Yes."

"What did he want?"

"He wants me to come down to the precinct."

"For what? Hasn't he asked you enough questions?"

"Oh, it's not about me."

"Then why would he want you to come down to the precinct?"

"Because they have Abbey and she is confessing to the murder of Frank."

Rosemarie had to grab the handrail on the stairs to stop from falling.

"What?!"

"You heard me. Abbey is sitting in Detective Henderson's office right now confessing to the murder of Frank."

"So, why would Detective Garcia call you?"

"I don't think they believe her, but for whatever reason, Detective Garcia asked me to come down to the precinct immediately."

"Let me grab my purse and I'll go with you."

"No, I think it's better if I go alone. This is probably going to be more of a lawyer-client conversation than a friendly chat."

"You don't believe for one minute she killed Frank, do you Nick?

"No, I don't."

Rosemarie hadn't had time to tell Nick much about the trip to Memphis, let alone mentioning the suicide note.

"There's something you should know before you go down there, Nick."

"Rosemarie, I don't have time. I need to get down there to see Abbey before she says something that we can't undo."

"I understand but I need to tell you..."

Nick stopped Rosemarie mid-sentence as he hurriedly grabbed his car keys.

"Fill me in when I get back. Right now, I need

to get down to the precinct. I can't let Abbey sit there with that slimeball Henderson confessing to something we both know she didn't do."

And with that said, Nick was out the door and on his way to rescue Abbey.

Chapter Twenty-four

"**D**etective Henderson – where is he?" Nick bellowed as he strode into the precinct.

Without responding, the desk sergeant picked up a phone and presumably dialed Detective Henderson.

"I have a Mr....?" The sergeant paused, looking at Nick.

"Constantine, Nick Constantine."

"A Mr. Constantine here at the front desk. He says you wanted to see him."

"He'll be right out." The statement being made with no pleasantries.

In less than a minute, the familiar detective was standing in front of him.

"Thanks for coming down, Counselor. We seem to have a unique situation on our hands. Your associate, Abigail Arnold, waltzed in here and confessed to killing your boss. Normally, I would be delighted to have a killer confess to a murder. I could close the case, send it to the DA for prosecution and move on to my next case. But believe it or not, I'm not in the habit of arresting people for murder who didn't commit a murder, especially if they are covering for someone else and I strongly believe that is what she is doing."

"Can I see her?" Nick interrupted.

"In a minute. I believe she is trying to protect her father." Continued Detective Henderson.

"You do know her father is dead, don't you?" Nick was getting more agitated by the minute.

"Yes, I do know, Counselor. Mr. Arnold killed himself, leaving a suicide note for his daughter, confessing to killing de la Carta."

"So why is Abbey confessing?" Nick asked.

"Beats me. Maybe she wants to protect his name or maybe he killed the guy because of his daughter and she feels guilty. I don't know why she's confessing but I don't believe she did it, which is why I had Detective Garcia ask you to come down to the precinct. I want you to find out what is really go on with Miss Arnold since she refuses to recant her bogus confession."

"Well, where is she?" Nick demanded.

"Follow me."

Abbey was sitting in the holding cell on a metal bench.

"What is Nick doing here?" Abbey demanded.

"I had him come down because you need a lawyer."

"I don't want a lawyer. You can leave Nick, I did it."

Nick glanced over at Detective Henderson.

"May we have a minute?"

"We don't need a minute." Abbey declared loudly.

Detective Henderson shot Nick a look and left anyway.

"Abbey, what are you doing? What is this all about?" Nick asked in a professional voice.

"Nick," Abbey began now in a calm, matter-of-fact tone.

" Thank-you for you coming down here but I don't need you. I just want to get this over with."

"I'm not leaving until you explain to me what this all about."

"I don't need to explain anything. I killed him and that's that. Now, please leave."

Abbey turned from Nick and called for the guard. There actually were no guards in the holding cell area, however upon hearing Abbey's cries for a guard, Detection Henderson returned to see what was happening.

"Detective, you have an obligation to arrest me, so what are you waiting for?"

"Every time there is a murder in this town, dozens of crackpots call us to claim responsibility. It's my job to determine the real killer from the crackpots. I don't believe you did this and unless you can convince me otherwise right now, you're free to leave."

"I did it. I confessed. What more do you want?"

"If you tell me why you did it, I might reconsider."

"Abbey, please don't say another word." Nick pleaded.

Completely ignoring Nick, Abbey continued.

"I don't need a reason. Motive is not an element of the crime."

Detective Henderson turned to Nick with a look that said see what I've been dealing with.

"Okay, Miss Arnold, here's the deal." Detective Henderson said sharply as he was beginning to lose his patience.

"Tell me HOW you killed de la Carta and I'll book you on a murder charge. Go ahead, tell me how you did it."

Detective Henderson really hoped she could answer the question because no one had yet figured out how de la Carta had died. No one was really sure he was even murdered, in spite of the note left by her father.

"I don't have to tell you how I did it." Abbey yelled in frustration.

Detective Henderson turned to Nick.

"Take her home, Counselor."

"No, please, I really did it." Abbey said pleadingly to the detective.

As Abbey and Nick walked down the hall to leave, Detective Henderson could still hear Abbey proclaiming her right to be arrested as a confessed killer.

"Good luck, Counselor." The detective muttered under his breath.

Chapter Twenty-five

"We've been partners a long time, Bob and I don't believe I've ever seen you refuse to take a confession from a murder suspect."

"I just don't believe her, Joe."

"What if you're wrong? Shouldn't you at least have taken her confession, especially before calling her lawyer? How are you going to explain this to the captain? You know that he's going to go ballistic, right?"

"I'll chalk it up to another kook trying to take credit for something they didn't do just to get their five minutes of fame."

"You're going with that?! Really?" Detective Garcia replied incredulously.

"Joe, you know every time there is a high-profile case plastered all over the news, the phone starts ringing off the hook with people claiming responsibility. We end up interviewing dozens of people who are nothing but crackpots looking to get on the evening news."

"So, you think this Abigail Arnold is a crackpot?"

"No, I don't think she is but I also don't think she did it. The woman couldn't even tell me how she did it. Actually, Miss Arnold had no details whatsoever regarding de la Carta's death, which is exactly why we don't release the details to the public, so we can weed out all the false confessions."

"Bob, this case makes no sense. We have a dead lawyer, no cause of death, no reason to believe it's a homicide, a dead guy who leaves a suicide note which seems to include an admission to killing the lawyer and the dead guy's daughter, a lawyer in de la Carta's firm who confesses to killing her boss but can't tell us how, not to mention, there's no apparent motive for anyone to kill de la Carta, except he's a lawyer. Why don't we just close this case, instead of trying to turn it into a homicide? The coroner already signed off on the death certificate."

"Yeah, showing the cause of death as undetermined." Detective Henderson interjected.

"Undetermined! Can you believe that, Joe? In this day and age, we can't figure out how a guy dies?"

"Beats me. All I know is when the coroner gives us a death certificate, declaring the death a homicide, we try to solve it, not the other way around. What's with you and this case anyway, Bob?"

"I can't explain it. All I know is that my gut

instinct is telling me something's just not right about this case. We have to be missing something."

"Like maybe it's just a death from natural causes and not a homicide?"

Detective Garcia knew his partner well enough to know this conversation was going nowhere.

"Okay, so how do you want to handle it?"

Before Detective Henderson could answer, the phone rang.

"Detective Garcia. What? Where? We'll be right there."

Turning to his partner, the detective tells him that they have an actual homicide to investigate.

"Where?"

"Over on Calle Ocho, near Domino Park.

"Isn't that the street where de la Carta's office is located?"

"Not only is it the same street, the body was actually dumped on the front steps of the office building."

Detective Henderson just stared at his partner in disbelief.

"You've got to be kidding."

"No, I'm not. But do me a favor, if someone wants to confess when we get there, please let them."

"I will." Detective Henderson replied.

Then quickly added,

"But only if they really did it."

The two detectives pulled up to the law office building and as they got out of the car, noticed several people wearing FBI jackets standing near the body of the victim.

"Why is the FBI here?" Detective Henderson whispered to his partner.

"Damned if I know. And it isn't just the FBI. It looks like everybody's been invited to the party including DEA and Homeland Security." Detective Garcia whispered back.

Detectives Henderson and Garcia approached one of the FBI agents and introduced themselves.

"Detectives Henderson and Garcia, Miami DADE P.D."

"Svenson, FBI."

"What's going on? Why all the interest in a dead body? We were told this was a routine homicide case."

Detective Henderson inquired without really expecting an answer since Federal agents were notorious for not sharing information with local police departments. However, much to their surprise, the two Miami police detectives did get an answer.

Once they were told that the victim had just been identified as Javier Cortez, the two detectives immediately knew what all the fuss was about. Javier Cortez was one of the world's most wanted criminals for a large variety of crimes ranging from drug dealing to murder and everything in between. You name the crime and he's done it. Javier Cortez operated a large criminal enterprise on almost every continent, thus making his murder anything but a routine homicide case. It was no longer a mystery as to why all the top government security agencies were involved.

Detective Henderson thanked the FBI agent for the information and the two detectives left the scene.

As they got into their car, Detective Henderson said to his partner,

"This is huge and certainly NOT a coincidence!!"

Chapter Twenty-six

"Where are you taking me?" Abbey asked in a soft, barely audible voice. "This isn't the way to my place."

"We're going to my condo. Rosemarie is going to meet us there." Nick responded in a tone that left no room for argument.

Abbey didn't even try to respond.

The rest of the drive to Nick's condo was draped in complete silence. They soon arrived at a gated condominium complex that looked more like a resort than a residence.

After parking in his assigned space in the underground parking area, Nick escorted emotionally drained Abbey to the private elevator leading to his condo.

Once the elevator doors opened, they were standing inside Nick's condo. Abbey just stood in the entryway, not sure what to do next.

"Have a seat." Nick directed Abbey with an arm motion toward the sofa. Abbey obediently sat down on the velvety soft sofa.

When Rosemarie arrived just a few minutes later, Nick was already pouring three glasses of a vintage merlot for everyone.

Rosemarie took two of the glasses and sat down next to Abbey, handing her a glass of the delicious wine. Nick removed his tie and undid the top two buttons of his shirt before sitting down in a large, leather armchair located next to the sofa.

Nick raised his glass to make a toast.

"Here's to one hell of a day!" Nick's tone more disgusted than jovial.

He took a long sip from his glass, savored the flavor for a moment and then looked at Abbey who sat holding her glass and shaking miserably.

"So, tell us Abbey, what is this fake confession really all about? We know you didn't do it so why are you trying to take the blame for Frank's murder?"

There was no response from Abbey.

"Rosemarie and I just want to understand...."

At this point, Rosemarie decided to take over as Nick was making it sound like an interrogation rather than two friends simply trying to help.

"Abbey, what Nick is trying to say is that we're your friends and we're here for you. Whatever it is, we want to help. We've all been through a lot lately but we have stuck together. Please Abbey, let us help you."

Abbey saw the concerned look on her friend's face and tears began to fall. Rosemarie took the wine glass from Abbey's hand for fear she was going to spill it and set it on the table. She slid next to Abbey and put her arm around her shoulder. Suddenly, Abbey began to cry, softly at first and then growing into loud, uncontrollable sobs. Rosemarie held her friend against her chest, trying silently to console her. Nick had no idea what he should do so he poured himself another glass of wine, stared at the two women across from him, waiting and hoping for some answers. They didn't come. For thirty minutes, Rosemarie held her trembling, sobbing, scared friend until Abbey, completely spent, fell asleep in her arms like a small child would.

"Help me get her into the guest room, Nick."

Nick gently picked up the sleeping Abbey and carried her to the bedroom. He laid her on top of the covers where Rosemarie removed Abbey's shoes, then covered her with the blanket that was folded across the foot of the bed. Nick and Rosemarie returned to the living room, closing the bedroom door behind them.

"Now what?" Nick asked Rosemarie.

Rosemarie picked up her wine glass and took a sip before answering Nick.

"I don't know about tomorrow but tonight Abbey needs to stay here so she's not alone."

"Why here? Why not with you at your house?"

Rosemary sensed a tenseness in his voice.

"Because she needs to have complete rest right now. And when she does wake up, we need to be here for her."

"**We** need to be here?"

"Well, at least one of us should be is what I meant, however since she is staying here, I think 'we' is a better idea."

"Agreed! Let's order dinner, have some wine and try to figure out what we're going to do next."

Rosemarie finished what was left in her glass and poured herself another one as Nick called his favorite nearby Chinese restaurant and ordered for both of them without any input from Rosemarie.

"I'm going to change. If you want to get more comfortable for the evening also, I have some sweats you could borrow, of course they may be a little big on you." Nick offered with a slight chuckle.

Rosemarie followed Nick into the master suite and surprised herself at how comfortable she was going into his bedroom. She liked Nick a lot and how there was never any sexual tension between them. Nick always treated her with respect as well as an equal.

Nick slipped off his trousers, hanging them in the closet by the cuffs. He exchanged his dress shirt for a tee and then opened several built-in drawers in the walk-in closet.

"Any particular color of sweats?"

Rosemary walked into the closet and faced what must have been at least fifteen sets of designer sweats. Nick reached around her, pulled out a pair of grey sweatpants with blue stripes and slid them on over his briefs.

"Mind if I wear these?" Rosemarie asked, picking a set of powder blue with white trim.

"Anything you want is fine." Nick replied without even looking.

Rosemarie slipped out of her skirt and pulled the pants on over her thong. She was watching Nick to see how he would react. He didn't seem to notice.

"Do you have another t-shirt? It's a little warm for a sweatshirt."

"Sure do. Help yourself." Nick pointed to an array of casual tees hanging in the closet.

Who hangs up their tee shirts? Rosemarie thought to herself. She grabbed one with a "Save the Planet" logo, stripped off her blouse and hesitated just a moment before removing her bra and pulling on the shirt. This time Nick did notice. And Rosemarie left the walk-in closet smiling.

Back in the living room, the pair discussed some cases they were working on at the office while waiting for dinner to arrive. The topic of Abbey Arnold never arose.

When the food arrived, Nick answered the door and was greeted by an older Asian man.

"I added something special for you, Mr. Constantine."

"Thank you, Chen." Nick tipped him with a twenty.

"You're too kind, Mr. Constantine. Please enjoy."

Nick carried the bags into the kitchen, emptied each small container onto individual plates, brought them to the dining room table, set out cloth napkins, dimmed the lights and opened another bottle of wine. This was a side of Nick that Rosemarie had never seen before and she liked it.

Chapter Twenty-seven

Despite Frank's practice of the Santerían "religion," a Mass for Francisco Alfonso de la Carta, was being held at St. Michael's, the Archangel Catholic Church on Flagler Street. It was a huge church, yet it didn't begin to hold all those who turned out to pay their respects. The death of the well-known attorney had been highly publicized and followed by all the media, including LaNacion Cubana, an online newspaper based in Little Havana and written in both English and Spanish. The in-depth article recently posted online by LaNacion Cubana about the revered lawyer's funeral most assuredly contributed to the large turnout.

Nick, Rosemarie, Abbey along with the rest of the firm, filled up the front pew followed by what appeared to be colleagues of Frank's. Nick recognized several judges from both the state and federal courts, as well as numerous court staff. That didn't surprise Nick. However, he was surprised by the hundreds of locals who were in attendance.

Nick never fully realized how many lives Frank had touched during the years he had practiced in the closely knit community. It appeared that everyone who lived or had once lived in Little Havana were present. Past and present clients were also in attendance, some Nick recognized, some he didn't. As he sat quietly surveying the crowd, whenever his eyes fell on a familiar face, they seemed to be looking back at him with such a deep sadness. There was also a look of emptiness, a look that begged for answers as the mourners silently wondered what was going to happen next. Who will represent them now, not just in court but in their community? Who will protect them from the police or from being harassed? Who will they go to solve their problems? Nick was overcome with emotion and suddenly felt a heavy weight fall on him as though the collective burdens of all these people had just dropped on him.

Rosemarie looked at Nick sitting next to her and whispered,

"Are you okay?"

Rosemarie's voice snapped Nick back to the moment.

"What are we supposed to do now? Who is going to look out for these people?" Nick whispered back.

Rosemarie reached over, took his hand and with a gentle squeeze, replied,

"We are."

At that very moment, all her own questions were answered. Her uncertain future had just been clarified. Rosemarie knew by the look in Nick's eyes, the look on his face, that together they would take over the firm and continue the work of this revered man in the community – Francisco Alfonso de la Carta.

Rosemarie continued to hold Nick's hand as he sat quietly listening to one speaker after another pay glowing tributes to the man they so loved who lay before them and instinctively knew she would be forever connected to Nick Constantine.

Nick had been asked to be the final speaker to pay tribute to Frank but he declined due to the way he really felt and the many grudges he held. Nick could argue a case before juries with eloquence but he couldn't stand before this congregation of admirers of Frank, pretending to be one of them.

With the priest's final blessing, the crowd began to file out of St. Michael's and into their vehicles. Nick later learned it was the longest funeral procession anyone could remember. As the motorcade, with everything from limos to low riders, proceeded west to Flagler Street to Ponce de Leon Boulevard, traffic was stopped in every direction. Even as the procession reached southwest 18th Street, more than a mile away, cars were still leaving the church. When they approached

Graceland Memorial Park North on Southwest 8th Street, where Frank was to be interred, Abbey, who was riding in the lead limo with Nick and Rosemarie, wondered aloud where everyone would park.

"And where will everyone stand?" Abbey asked Rosemarie.

"What?"

"Where will everyone stand?" Abbey repeated.

Rosemarie sighed as she put her arm around Abbey.

"Abbey, you don't need to worry about where people will stand."

Nick showed a slight smile, thinking how that was so like Abbey to worry about the practical.

"I wouldn't want them to trample over the other graves."

Nick thought Abbey was going to start crying over the thought.

"Someone from the funeral home has it under control and will make sure everyone is respectful of the graveyard." he assured her.

"I hope so."

As they walked toward the lawn crypt where Frank would be laid to rest, they passed by a variety of columbariums of those who had been cremated. There were beautiful exclusive gardens offering unique, privately edged family columbariums, which included a private patio with benches. Nick even saw a cremation bench in the shape of a Chevrolet Chevelle, a bench in the shape of a seat from a cattle wagon, a Victorian bench as well as several benches commemorating a branch of the service.

Frank was being laid to rest in a long crypt, which is similar to an in-ground burial plot, but with a burial chamber like those in a mausoleum. As Abbey stood watching the ceremony, keeping one eye on the crowd to make sure they were respectful, she was startled by a bird flying past her head. In a whisper, Rosemarie explained to Abbey that the ceremony was referred to as the "flight home ceremony," which includes the symbolic release of a dove representing the deceased's flight home. Abbey wondered if the dove would come back.

As the three lawyers rode the four miles back to the office together in the limo, Rosemarie could tell something was bothering Nick. She sat staring at him not exactly knowing how to break the silence, hoping Nick would eventually say something to end the deafening silence. Finally, Rosemarie couldn't take it any longer.

"Nick, what's wrong?"

"What do you mean?"

"Nick, something is obviously bothering you. You haven't said a word since we left the cemetery."

"Did you notice anyone at the funeral who

seemed out of place?" Nick asked, in response to Rosemarie's question.

"What do you mean by 'out of place'?"

"You know, like they weren't there for the funeral but for some other reason."

"I'm not sure I follow you."

"I noticed some people staring at us, only us and not paying any attention to the services."

"Why would they be staring at us?"

"I don't know."

"Did you recognize them?"

"No. I just know they weren't there for the funeral, I can feel it."

"Nick, is there something going on that I don't know about? You know you can tell me anything."

"There's nothing to tell you. Why are you asking?"

"Because you haven't really been yourself since that trip you took for Frank."

"What do you mean, I haven't been myself?" Nick's voice was now raised and growing louder with every question.

"I'm sorry Nick, I didn't mean anything. I just noticed..."

"Noticed what?" Nearly shouting as he interrupted Rosemarie mid-sentence.

"Nothing, Nick, forget it. I'm sorry I said anything." Rosemarie was now feeling very uneasy, almost scared.

Nick noticed the scared look on Rosemarie's face and it made him feel sick. His only real friend, someone he truly trusted and deeply liked, was looking at him in fear. How had it come to this? His whole life seemed to be reeling out of control. How did he let all this happen?

"I'm sorry, Rosemarie. I'm just a little tense, with the funeral and all that's happened. I am deeply sorry."

Nick reached over and gently squeezed her hand. That was all it took for Rosemarie to feel better.

"Nick, I'm here for you, no matter what."

Nick so desperately wanted to tell her everything. But how could he? What would Rosemarie think of him if she knew everything? How would she react? He didn't want to lose her. Nick needed Rosemarie in his life for many reasons but especially because she keeps him grounded. Holding Rosemarie's hand helped Nick feel better also. The couple sat in silence holding hands for the rest of the drive to the office, so lost in thought that they had completely forgotten about a very quiet Abbey sitting in the limo with them.

As the limo neared their office, Nick suddenly bolted upright, letting go of Rosemarie's hand.

"They're here."

"Who?"

"The people from the funeral that were staring at us."

Looking out the window, Rosemarie saw three men standing on the sidewalk leading up to the front door of the office. Three scary looking men in their late 20's, one wearing a suit and two wearing jeans with bulky jackets, standing on each side of the suited man, like bodyguards. The gold chains hanging from their necks and the dark sunglasses were hard to miss. They reminded her of the people she used to prosecute back in her days working as a City Attorney.

The limo stopped with Rosemarie wondering if they should exit the limo or tell the driver to take them somewhere else. However, Nick had already opened the door and was stepping out of the vehicle. Rosemarie and Abbey followed.

As Nick approached the visitors, Rosemarie could see Nick's posture change.

"Can I help you?" Nick asked with an assertive tone in his voice.

"We would like a moment of your time." the suited man answered with a heavy Hispanic accent.

"I'm sorry but the firm is closed today. If you'd like to make an appointment, feel free to call the office on Monday."

Nick handed the man his card and turned to enter the building.

"I don't think you understand, we need to talk now!"

The man's tone now conveyed a demand, not a request. The three men followed Nick to the door with Rosemarie and Abbey staying a safe distance behind.

"It would be to your benefit to hear what I have to say."

Nick didn't respond but allowed the men to follow him into the building and into the conference room.

Not hearing any objections, Rosemarie followed the men into the conference room while Abbey went quietly to her workspace as usual.

Chapter Twenty-eight

A s the little group entered the conference room, the presumed man in charge spoke in a harsh voice to Nick, all the while glaring at Rosemarie.

"I think this conversation is best between just us, without the chick."

"Miss Callahan is my partner, so whatever you have to say to me, you can also say it to her."

"Do you know who I am?"

The question was directed at Nick.

"I have no idea. Perhaps you would like to explain just who you are and what you think is so important that you can't wait for an appointment like everyone else."

Rosemarie was surprised by Nick's aggressively firm tone which showed no signs of intimidation.

"I'm going to be your best client, Counselor."

"We're not taking on any new clients right now, so if there is nothing else, I have other things to deal with." Nick stated firmly, rising from his chair.

"Sit down, Counselor. I'm not through." The man's tone was now demanding.

Nick remained standing.

"I said sit down!"

Rosemarie sat silently remembering her days as a prosecutor, dealing with thugs like this guy and she knew the only thing they respected was someone who stood up to them, who didn't show fear, who didn't back down. She also knew they weren't going to harm Nick since they were obviously here because they needed him for something. Although Rosemarie had no clue what that something was, she was determined to find out right now.

"If you have something to say, let's hear it." Rosemarie asserted in her strong prosecutor voice, breaking the silence.

Nick was still standing.

"Well?" Nick's tone still aggressive.

"Have a seat, Counselor, please." The man said a little more politely and a bit conciliatory.

Nick begrudgingly sat back down.

"My name is Tito Mendez and I used to work for Javier Cortez. I believe you know who that is Counselor."

Nick didn't respond.

"Now that Cortez is no longer with us, I will be taking over his operation and I would like to continue using this firm in all our legal matters even though de la Carta is no longer in charge. And since you seem to have taken over, I decided we should meet, especially as we have both worked with Mr. Cortez. It takes big cojones to collaborate with a man that ruthless Mr. Constantine and I admire you for that!"

Rosemarie was confused and had trouble following the dialogue being delivered by Mendez.

"We're two of a kind, you and me."

"I'm nothing like you and I have no idea what you are talking about."

"Then how do you know you're not like me, Counselor?"

Nick didn't respond, believing the question was rhetorical.

"Here's the deal. I will pay your firm one million per year in cash for you to be available when needed. That's the same amount Cortez paid to de la Carta. In return, any time one of our trucks are stopped, you will represent the driver, who will be in possession of a Bill of Lading and the trailer door will be sealed, making it quite simple to get any charges dropped. Also, we will want the cab back. I don't care about the trailer. Now it may be that none of our trucks are ever stopped but you will get the money just the same. In addition, we occasionally have a need for representation for a member of my company for various infractions. You must be available to oversee that as well but you will be paid separately for those cases. Your primary job in those matters is to make sure there is no cooperation and that you will handle these cases personally, not pass them off to some other member of your firm. I'm not asking you to do anything illegal, just represent my company like any other client."

"Why us?" Rosemarie asked.

"I think your boyfriend understands why."

Neither Rosemarie nor Nick felt the need to correct the 'boyfriend' reference since in the overall scheme of things, that seemed to be the very least of their problems.

"And if I'm not interested?" Nick asked, his voice not quite so strong.

"That's not an option, Counselor and you know it. So enjoy the rest of your day and maybe, just maybe, we won't need your services. But, if we do, it's good to know we'll have the best legal representation money can buy." Tito Mendez then stood, motioned to the two men who had been standing behind him the entire time and the three left the law office, leaving Rosemarie and Nick staring at one another.

"Nick, what's going on?"

"I think it's time we have a talk but definitely not here since I don't know who else might decide to stop by. Let's go to my place."

As they were leaving the conference room, they saw a duffel bag on the floor by where the two men had been standing. Nick approached the bag with caution and slowly slid the zipper back. Inside the bag was money, a lot of money. Nick wasn't sure exactly how much but he was willing to bet it was at least one million dollars. There was also a phone in the bag. Nick picked up the cell phone, turned it on and noticed there was one number already programmed into the phone. Nick knew without dialing the number who would be on the other end of the call. As they were about to leave the office with duffel bag in hand, Nick saw two men exit a vehicle, which appeared to be an unmarked police cruiser and approach the office.

"Detective Henderson, just what I need right now." Nick mumbled audibly.

"Are you kidding me?!" Rosemarie asked incredulously.

"Quick, take the duffel bag and put it in the other room out of sight."

Nick opened the door and took a step outside, not wanting the detective to enter.

"Hello, Mr. Constantine. We need to talk." Detective Henderson said with authority.

"Now is not a good time, Detective. I was just leaving. It's been a long and trying day. Maybe another time."

"I think now would be a very good time." Detective Henderson replied in a firm tone.

Nonetheless, Nick didn't back down.

"Not now, Detective, not today."

The detective stood his ground.

"You don't fool me, Counselor! Just as I drove up, guess who I saw leaving?"

Nick didn't respond.

"Tito Mendez and his thugs, that's who. So, what's your relationship with Mendez?"

Again, Nick didn't respond.

"You don't need to explain because I'll tell you what I think. After seeing Mendez drive away from here, it suddenly all makes sense. You and Mendez decided it was time for a change in the hierarchy. We've been watching Mendez for some time but could never quite figure out who he was working for, that is until Javier Cortez shows up dead on your doorstop and in the next moment, Mendez appears at your office. Mendez has always wanted to take over the drug trade in Little Havana, so he decided to make his move. Meanwhile you had ambitions to take over the law firm from de la Carta, so you made a deal with the devil. You kill de la Carta, Mendez kills Cortez, dumping him on your doorstep to let you know it's done, sealing the deal."

Nick stood stoically, listening to this absurd scenario.

"So now I know who killed Cortez, who killed de la Carta and the reason for both murders. The only thing I haven't figured out is exactly how you killed de la Carta, but it is only a matter of time before I do. And when that happens, I'll be back with a warrant for your arrest."

Detective Henderson was staring at Nick, looking for some reaction that would confirm his hypothesis.

"Now, let me tell you something, Detective. You don't know what the hell you're talking about. I didn't kill Frank and I don't know who did. This fantasy scenario of yours is just that, a fantasy. So, I suggest you do your job and go look for the person who actually did kill my boss. Quit wasting my time telling me your absurd theories, I have things to do."

Nick shut the door without waiting for a response.

Detective Henderson turned to his partner.

"Did you noticed he didn't even ask who Mendez was or deny he was here? He also didn't deny he knew Mendez murdered Cortez. I'm telling you I've got this right and I'm going to prove it."

As Nick watched the two detectives drive away, he felt Rosemarie standing behind him. He turned around and knew by the look on her face that she had heard the detective's wild accusations.

"I didn't kill Frank. You need to believe me Rosemarie, I didn't kill him."

Rosemarie grabbed Nick, pulling him to her in a tight embrace and whispered,

"I believe you Nick with all my heart."

"Thank-you Rosemarie." Was all Nick could manage to say.

It meant everything to him that she believed in him. Nick took a step back and stared into Rosemarie's eyes, sensing she was about to cry.

"Now, let's go to my place and I'll explain everything."

As Nick opened the door to leave, he stopped, turned to Rosemarie to instruct her to grab the bag and with that done, they left.

Chapter Twenty-nine

The next day, Detective Henderson told his partner, Detective Garcia, that he wanted to go back to de la Carta's law firm and re-interview some of the employees, including a few of the attorneys, just in case he missed something the first time around. Detective Garcia couldn't believe his partner was still obsessed with this case.

"Why are you bothering? The case is closed as far as everyone is concerned."

"It's not closed to me. Until it is declared either a suicide or death by natural causes, I am treating it as an open case. I just want to follow up on a few theories I have."

Detective Garcia rolled his eyes, knowing there was no use arguing when his partner was this determined to do something and reluctantly agreed to accompany him back to the law office. As the two detectives were approaching the law office, Detective Henderson noticed a change in the landscaping. The gardener was planting some new scrubs along the front of the office where beautiful blue flowers had been growing on his last visit. The detective distinctly remembered the flowers because he loved their vibrant shade of blue, even speaking with the gardener about them at the time. Detective Henderson couldn't imagine why they would replace such beautiful flowers.

Detective Henderson turned to his partner and told him that he'd meet him inside in a few minutes as he wanted to discuss something with the gardener first.

"Excuse me sir, I'm Detective Henderson, Miami P.D."

The gardener looked up at the detective and not being legally registered to work in the United States, wasn't sure if he should run or not. Ultimately, the gardener decided that Detective Henderson didn't look like Immigration and felt it would be okay to speak to him.

"Do you speak English?"

"Poquito."

"What happened to the blue flowers that were growing here?"

"Como?"

"Flores?" Detective Henderson said, attempting to communicate with the confused gardener using the little bit of Spanish he had picked up living in Miami.

The gardener began rapidly speaking in Spanish.

Detective Henderson quickly realized that his limited knowledge of the Spanish language was not going to be very helpful in questioning the gardener. The detective held up his hand indicating to the gardener to stop for a minute while he went to get someone to help interpret. Detective Henderson stepped into the law office and asked the receptionist if she spoke Spanish. The receptionist recognized the detective from his previous visit to the firm when he was investigating her boss's death.

"Yes." The receptionist briefly and somewhat tersely replied.

"Would you mind interpreting for me?"

The receptionist stood up from her desk and followed the detective outside, sensing the question was more of an order than a request and saying no would not be an option.

Once outside, Detective Henderson saw that the gardener was standing perfectly still and in the exact spot where he left him. It was as though the gardener was frozen in place.

"I need to ask the gardener a few questions but unfortunately my Spanish is worse than his English." Detective Henderson said in a failed attempt to lighten the mood.

"Would you ask him what happened to the blue flowers."

"The what?"

"The blue flowers. The vibrant blue flowers that were growing along the front of the building."

The receptionist gave the detective a quizzical look but nonetheless asked the question to the gardener in Spanish. After a brief interchange with the gardener, the receptionist turned to Detective Henderson.

"The gardener said he pulled them out of the ground, put them in a bag and put the bag in the garbage. And he assures you that the bag was securely tied."

"Why would I care if the bag was securely tied?" Detective Henderson inquired.

"Por que?" The receptionist asked the gardener in Spanish.

After another brief exchange, the receptionist explained that the gardener realized the flowers were very poisonous and could make a person very sick, so he pulled them all out and safely got rid of them.

"How sick?"

"The gardener said very sick.'

"Are the flowers poisonous enough to kill someone?"

Another exchange in Spanish.

"He said probably if you ate them but not just by touching them."

"Ask him the name of the blue flower."

"Do you think the flowers were used to kill Mr.

de la Carta?" The receptionist asked the detective, her demeanor thawing just a bit.

"As far as I'm concerned, your boss did not die of natural causes. I believe that something or someone killed him and my investigation into this case will not be closed until I get some answers. Now please, ask him the name of the blue flower."

When the receptionist asked the gardener for the name of poisonous blue flower, Detective Henderson saw a dramatic change in the gardener's posture and expression. Suddenly, he was rattling off Spanish at a rapid clip in an elevated voice.

"Is there a problem?" Detective Henderson asked.

"The gardener just keeps saying that he made sure the flowers were in a bag, securely tied and placed in the trash."

"Tell him I'm not blaming him for anything. I just need the name of the blue flower."

"Como se llama de la flores azul?" The receptionist asked the gardener once again.

This time the gardener's response was slower and less agitated.

"He is not sure of the proper name but knows it as 'Blue Death'."

"Does he know where you can buy these flowers?"

Before the receptionist could interpret the gardener's response, Detective Henderson interrupted her.

"Thank-you but I understand the word 'no'."

"Gracias." Detective Henderson said directly to the gardener as he dismissed him.

"Thanks for your assistance." The detective said to the receptionist as they headed into the office. Without responding, the receptionist sat down at her desk and resumed working.

After an hour of interviewing the office staff as well as several of the attorneys and finding no new information or leads since their last visit, the two detectives headed back to the precinct. Once they were in the car, Detective Henderson filled his partner in on the discussion with the gardener about the poisonous blue flowers.

"And that is why we're stopping at the closest nursery. We're going to learn all we can about this flower called Blue Death."

Chapter Thirty

The detective's internet search for nearby nurseries showed that there were two nurseries in their vicinity. Since one of the nurseries was less than a mile away from their current location, Detective Henderson decided to stop there before returning to the precinct. At the nursery, the two detectives showed their credentials and explained to the proprietor that they were looking for a certain flower but the only information they had was that it was nicknamed Blue Death. The nursery owner wasn't familiar with the nickname but now being curious himself, looked it up for the two detectives.

"I found it! The flower is listed under its' species name of Aconitum but is more commonly called Aconite. The description says it is also known as Devil's Helmet and Queen of Poisons as well as several other nicknames, including Blue Death. It states that all parts of the flower are poisonous but especially the root. The root is so toxic that just half a tablespoon of extraction from it placed in a bottle of liquor, such as whiskey or Tequila, would be enough to kill an exceptionally large man and yet go undetected. Aconite is said to be the perfect poison to mask a murder."

"BINGO!" Detective Henderson yelled, startling the nursery owner as well as Detective Garcia.

"That's it! That's how de la Carta was killed, with Aconite, the perfect murder weapon!"

Detective Henderson asked the nursery owner to look up who sells aconite in the Miami area and found there were only two nurseries that stocked the deadly blue flower. Detective Henderson profusely thanked the owner as he and Detective Garcia left.

"I take it we're stopping at the two nurseries before checking in." Detective Garcia stated to his partner.

"Yep."

The two detectives struck out at the first nursery which sold Aconite, however, at the second nursery, Detective Henderson was elated to discover that there were several pots of the flower in stock.

Detective Henderson asked for one of the smaller potted Aconite but the owner was reluctant to voluntarily part with any, even the smallest one, claiming the flower was rare and therefore very valuable. The owner expected the detectives to pay for the Aconite, just like everyone else.

Detective Henderson politely explained that if the owner didn't want to volunteer the Aconite to help in a homicide investigation, he would presume the owner was involved in a murder and would seize all his precious flowers as potential murder weapons. The owner promptly decided to cooperate with the detectives, meticulously wrapping up the Aconite and warning them how poisonous it was, even to the touch.

Detective Henderson then asked to see the sales records for the last five years. Although reluctant, the owner complied. The records showed several sales for the poisonous flower, all in cash and with no names or addresses. There were some deliveries but none to de la Carta's office. The two detectives couldn't believe you weren't required to keep better records when dealing with something this deadly.

Nonetheless, Detective Henderson was now certain it was the gardener at the law office who poisoned de la Carta and he was determined to prove it.

After leaving the nursery, the detectives went directly to the forensic lab to explain Detective Henderson's theory regarding the poisonous blue flower.

Detective Garcia could see it was going to be quite a while before they returned to the precinct as originally intended.

"I need you to test the blood sample from the de la Carta murder for a poison from this flower."

"What the type of flower is this? I've never seen one this shade of blue before." The lab tech said quizzically.

"It's called Aconitum or more commonly, Aconite."

Fortunately, the lab still had blood samples from the de la Carta case preserved since the investigation was still ongoing. The lab tech left to enter the necessary information into his system and a few minutes later returned with the results.

"Sorry, I can't help you detectives. This substance can only be detected with extremely sophisticated toxicology analysis using equipment we don't have here. We would have to send the sample to the DEA or FBI lab and ask them to do the analysis."

"Well then, send it there!" Detective Henderson said loudly, his patience running short.

"I'll need authorization first." The lab tech replied.

"Then, get it!" Detective Henderson snapped as the two detectives left the lab.

"Now what?" Detective Garcia asked his partner.

"Nothing, we're calling it a day. However, in the morning I'm speaking with the Captain to get permission to track down the killer, who by now has undoubtedly fled to Cuba."

"You're crazy. The captain will never approve that, never!"

"We'll see."

First thing the next morning, Detective Henderson was in the Captain's office making his case, such as it was.

"Captain, I've finally figured out the murder of de la Carta."

"Who?"

"de la Carta, that attorney who was murdered over in Little Havana."

"Murdered?! I thought his cause of death was undetermined."

"Not anymore. He was poisoned with Aconite!"

"With what?"

"Aconite, a deadly poisonous blue flower that was growing just outside the law office."

"A blue flower? Do you have any proof as to who gave this deadly flower to the attorney?"

"Not exactly."

"Not exactly? What does that mean?"

"Just hear me out, Captain. I firmly believe it was de la Carta's gardener who administered the poison since not only would he have knowledge about any of the flowers growing on the property but he'd also have easy access."

"What about the gardener's wife? Isn't she de la Carta's cleaning woman? I suppose you think she is in on it too?"

"Here's what I think happened. Everyone had

already left the office for the evening. De la Carta pours himself a glass of Tequila from his bar and sits down, which explains why he was at his desk but wasn't working. It also explains why he still had his suitcoat on. He then drinks the Tequila that has unknowingly been spiked with this poisonous Aconite."

"Why didn't the blood test show this poison?" The Captain interrupted, sounding a bit annoyed.

"Because you need special equipment to find this particular poison. I'm having the blood analyzed by the DEA as we speak."

"The DEA?! Really, Henderson?" The Captain responded, now sounding more than a bit annoyed.

"Let me finish, Captain. Immediately after drinking the Tequila, de la Carta drops dead at his desk."

"The poison works that fast?" The Captain interrupted again.

"Yes, it is that deadly."

At this point, Detective Henderson noticed the Captain roll his eyes, so he quickly continued.

"The gardener and/or his wife comes in, takes the glass and rinses it out. The poisoned bottle is then replaced with a new, untainted bottle of Tequila. That would clearly explain why there were no fingerprints on the glass or the bottle. It should also be noted that the Tequila glass on the desk was near de la Carta's left hand, yet we know for certain he was right-handed. At some point, the gardener's wife vacuums the carpet as usual, therefore erasing any footprints. Then after vacuuming de la Carta's office and out of sheer habit, she turns the lights off, explaining why he appeared to be sitting at his desk, drinking in the dark. In addition, the air-conditioning was turned off and the alarm was set. Again, part of the cleaning woman's usual routine, which would obviously explain why there was no forced entry or setting off of the alarm."

Detective Henderson finally stopped his monologue and looked at the Captain, waiting for a response.

After what seemed like an eternity, the Captain finally spoke.

"So that's your proof?! A hunch? A wild theory with no evidence to back it up? Not to mention, no motive! And yet, you want authorization to go to Cuba?! To do what?! There is no extradition law there! Are you going to kidnap some random Cuban citizens and bring them here?"

"Of course not."

"Then why the hell should you be given authorization to go there?"

"To try and close this case. I'm sure the gardener and his wife have fled to Cuba since they are from there. Their sons even have a thriving business in Cuba. It would the perfect place to escape to, especially since, as you said, there are no extradition laws there."

"Let's say for the sake of argument, you are correct. Why would we waste resources trying to solve a murder, if it even is a murder, of a drug attorney, possibly killed by two Cubans, who are now back in Cuba and no longer a threat to citizens of this city? If you really believe it was the gardener, his wife or both and you strongly feel that you have enough for an indictment, then get one, issue a warrant and close the file. If they ever try to re-enter the country, they will be picked up and prosecuted."

"And if they live out their lives in Cuba, they will just get away with murder?"

"Guess so."

"And you're okay with that, Captain?"

"Yep."

"Well, I'm not okay with that. I'm not okay with someone getting away with murder. Not on my watch!"

"Henderson, you don't even know if he, she or both, murdered anyone. It seems to me you have nothing except a bunch of unanswered questions and loose ends with not an ounce of proof or even any circumstantial evidence."

In his heart, Detective Henderson knew the Captain was right. He really didn't have enough for an indictment or even enough to take the case to the grand jury for trial and the detective also knew the prosecutor would never sign off on it.

"Let it go, Henderson. This case is just going to have to remain unsolved."

Reluctantly, Detective Henderson left the Captain's office and returned to his desk, looking over the new pile of cases to be solved without much interest.

Several weeks later while sitting at his desk, the phone rang.

"Henderson, here."

"Detective, this is the crime lab. That sample you wanted analyzed of the Aconite finally came back from the DEA lab. You were right, the blood contained poison from the deadly flower."

"Thanks for your trouble but the information arrived just a little too late." Detective Henderson hung up the phone dejectedly, frustrated that this was probably the one case that was going to remain unsolved for the rest of his career.

Chapter Thirty-one

"I want to go home, Federico." Maria said to her husband forlornly.

"We are home."

"No, I mean our real home in Cuba, home with our family, our sons, our friends. I don't want to be here anymore."

"Maria, what's wrong?" Federico rose from his chair and walked over to his wife, who was standing in the doorway of the kitchen. As he tried to put his arms around her, she gently pushed him away.

"I mean it. I've had enough. I want to go back to Cuba where we belong."

"No, Maria, we belong here. There is nothing for us back there. Nothing."

"Nothing! What about our sons? Are they nothing?" Her voice rising with each word.

"I didn't mean that. It's just..."

Maria held her hand up inches from Federico's face, halting any further discussion.

"I've made up my mind, Federico. I'm going home."

"Maria, think about what you are saying. You're actually willing to give up everything we have here in America?"

"What do we have here, Federico? Absolutely nothing, that's what we have and now that Mr. de la Carta is gone, we have less than nothing. So what will happen to us now?"

In Cuba, Federico had owned a popular restaurant serving traditional Cuban cuisine which catered to tourists. He operated the restaurant with Maria and their two sons. Life was good for them and they lived well. At the time, Cuba was considered a tropical island paradise that attracted tourists from all around the globe and its economy was booming. Then suddenly, in December of 1958, Fidel Castro was installed as the new leader of the popular little island. Cuba had prospered under Batista but it didn't take long for this newly installed dictator to bite the hand that fed him. Fidel Castro was a Communist. He quickly aligned himself with the Soviet Union and installed a system of government that would ultimately destroy the beautiful paradise of Cuba. After the installation of Fidel Castro, Cuba became a Communistic country, with Fidel as its dictator. In the beginning, the Cubans loved their new leader as he took control of the wealth of his new kingdom and began to distribute it to the people. Private homes of all foreigners were confiscated and turned over to the people of Cuba, for free. Businesses were taken over by the government and ownership of all businesses by private individuals was prohibited. Sugar plantations and refineries were seized and the non-Cuban owners expelled. They could take nothing with them, leaving behind everything for the new regime. Gorgeous homes, mansions, plantations, were all given, free of charge, to the populace. While families were given the right to occupy these dwellings, the titles to all properties remained with the government. There could be no private ownership under the new rules. Everything would now be owned by the state for the benefit of the people. For the most part, jobs and wages were controlled by the government with everyone receiving the same pay regardless of their occupation. No imports were allowed from the western capitalistic nations and eventually embargoes were put in place, cutting Cuba off from most of the non-communist world, relying exclusively on the Soviet Union for their existence. However, as in anything, there were certain exceptions.

Maria and Federico's restaurant was one of those exceptions. Not only was the restaurant popular with tourists but was a favorite of government officials and high-ranking military. It was liked not only for its menu, but also because it was a perfect spot for government officials to mingle with tourists, enabling them to keep track of tourist visits and on occasion to even making a little extra money by providing services to the visitors. Such services as tour guides, selling highly coveted goods, including cigars that had been pilfered from the factories, arranging car rides in vintage American automobiles or even providing female companionship.

Unfortunately, Federico and his family struggled under the new regime. He had to pay a heavy tax to the government and the officials never paid for their meals or drinks and there was nothing that could be said. As time passed, Federico became more vocal about the conditions in Cuba and he was having a harder time maintaining the quality of food at the restaurant, since many food items were becoming scarce and more expensive.

But the day came when Federico finally had enough. He sat down with his family one night after the restaurant closed and told them of his plan to take them all to the United States to start over in the land of free people. Federico had saved up enough money to pay the passage to the United States. They would leave the next evening from a secluded spot on the shore to be taken by small boat to a larger vessel waiting twelve miles offshore. From there, the couple would leave for Florida where they could seek political asylum. Political asylum was automatically granted to any Cuban who reached the shores of the United States. The family was stunned at hearing Federico's plan. He had purposely kept their escape from Cuba a secret so no one would find out and try to stop them. There wasn't time for any further explanation as his plan was in motion and they needed to prepare to leave immediately. Maria was excited but the boys were not and they had no intention of leaving. They had friends in Cuba, good jobs and besides, they loved their country. They refused to even consider leaving and Maria didn't want to leave without her sons. The family argued throughout the night, with Maria in tears, Federico insisting and the boys adamant. By morning, an understanding had been reached. Since Maria and Federico were nearing retirement and the boys had been running the business pretty much by themselves already, they agreed the boys would remain with the restaurant while Maria and Federico would retire in the United States. The following evening, Maria and Federico boarded the small boat and under the cover of darkness, along with dozens of other refugees, were taken to a waiting fishing vessel to be smuggled to the United States. Maria carried a small suitcase with a few clothing items and a couple of family photos, while the little bit of money that remained after paying for their passages was safely hidden in the lining of Federico's coat. As Maria and Federico climbed aboard the fishing boat, the skipper greeted them.

"Welcome aboard. My name is Captain O'Shaughnessy."

When the refugees safely reached the shores of Florida, the majority of them were greeted by family and friends. There was hugging, tears of joy and more hugging. Watching the refugees happily reunited with family and friends, it suddenly dawned on Federico that he hadn't really thought this all the way through. As he and Maria stood on the shore watching everyone leave, Federico seriously began to doubt his decision to leave Cuba. Maria didn't say a word. She just stood there squeezing her husband's hand with tears rolling down her cheeks. The silence was broken by O'Shaughnessy.

"No place to go?" The captain asked rhetorically.

Before either one of the could answer, Captain O'Shaughnessy offered a suggestion.

"I know someone who might be able to help."

Later that day, Federico and Maria were introduced to Mr. Francisco de la Carta and thus began their new life.

"I don't know what will happen now that Mr. de la Carta is gone, but whatever happens, we'll be better off than returning to Cuba."

"Look at us. We came here to start a new life, a better life and what do we have?" Maria asked tearfully.

"We have our freedom."

"Freedom for what? I'm a cleaning woman, cleaning offices, scrubbing toilets and you are a gardener. When we came to Miami, we had dreams of starting a new restaurant, bringing our sons here..." Her voice trailed off.

Federico knew his wife was right. Their life in Miami certainly hadn't turn out the way he had envisioned. Everything they had in Miami, including their apartment, even their jobs had been provided by Mr. de la Carta and now that he was dead, what was going to happen to them? Mr. Constantine was in charge now and he had not spoken with them about their future with the firm.

How could going back home be any worse than staying in Miami not knowing what their future would be like. Their sons still had the house and restaurant. Maria and Federico could live with their sons and help with the restaurant whenever they needed them. And now that Raul Castro had taken over for Fidel, things in Cuba were getting better. The government allowed family run restaurants, known as paladars, to operate out of people's homes. Even so, many paladars quickly failed, however Federico's sons were astute businessmen and had managed to turn their restaurant into an extremely popular, highly profitable paladar, one that served the city's best food in a bohemian garret atop a magnificent, early 20th century palace, which was once the home of Federico's family. Maria could see Federico was trying to understand her position.

"Federico, remember when you told us we were leaving Cuba, that you had decided that it was the best solution for us? was what was best for us? No arguments, no discussion, you were going with or without us. And because I loved you, I followed you to Miami. Well, now I am telling you that I'm going back home with or without you."

In all the years the two of them had lived in the United States, Maria never stopped calling Cuba home. Federico knew his wife's resolve and realized he wasn't going to be able to stop her. And in that moment, the only decision he had to make was what to pack as he knew he wouldn't stay in Miami without his beloved Maria.

Maria and Federico arrived at the airport two hours early, this time with two large suitcases carrying all their belongings.

As they waited in line to check in for their flight, Federico looked around the concourse nervously wondering if anyone was looking for them. Maria stood as still as a statute, hoping not to draw attention to herself. With thoughts racing through her head about returning to Cuba, reuniting with her sons and friends, Marie started to feel at peace. At long last, they were going home.

Chapter Thirty-two

Maria and Federico were adjusting to life back in Cuba. While Maria was enjoying being with her sons again, visiting with friends and helping at the restaurant, Federico was having a harder time being home. He kept thinking about all that he had given up, all that he went were through to get to the United States, all that he had left behind. Federico had hoped that one day their sons would join them in Miami so they could open a restaurant together and be a complete family again. Yet, deep in his heart he knew Maria was right, it was time for them to leave Miami and return to Cuba. And after all, Cuba was changing. It was the beginning of a new era in Cuban history. A better, stronger Cuba than ever before was emerging. And the more Federico reflected on their lives in Miami, the more he realized returning home may have been a blessing in disguise as well as a new beginning. Federico made a vow to himself to only look forward from that moment on and not dwell on the life they left behind in Miami.

On the other hand, as happy as Maria was to be

back home in Cuba, she couldn't erase the memory of what had happened in Miami. The dark secret she was carrying was eating away at her. She felt overwhelming guilt. Guilt, not so much for what she had done, but for keeping the secret from Federico. She had always been honest and open with her husband, never keeping secrets from him. But this was different. How could she ever tell him what she had done? Federico would never understand. He would never be able to forgive her. Their relationship would never be the same. Federico might even leave her and the mere thought of living the rest of her life without him paralyzed her with fear. Nonetheless, Maria wasn't sure how much longer she could go on living with the heavy burden of such a shameful secret.

As Maria sat in her kitchen, she sorted through how it all began, trying to find a way to explain it all to her beloved Federico so that he would see that she had no choice in the situation, that she had no way out.

It was about two months after they had arrived in Little Havana. Mr. de la Carta was having a late meeting with some clients. Normally, several other staff members would stay in case he needed something but that night he told everyone they could leave, except Maria. He explained he would like her to clean up after the meeting. Shortly after his clients left, Mr. de la Carta called Maria into his office.

"Maria, I would like to speak with you about

something." His tone was softer than usual and he was looking at her differently than ever before.

"I have done a lot for you and Federico, even helping you out when there was no one here for you when you first arrived in Miami. Both of you just standing on the shore with no money, no place to go, no family. Do you remember that Maria?"

"Yes, I remember." Maria answered in a voice barely audible.

"I gave you jobs, paid you more than I needed to and even gave you a place to live."

"Yes." Maria's voice now a soft whisper.

"And I have never asked for anything in return. That is until now."

Suddenly, Maria became frightened by the way Mr. de la Carta was talking.

"As you know, Maria, I am not married and have no steady girlfriend, however there are certain needs men have that only a woman can satisfy."

No, this isn't happening! He couldn't be asking her to do sexual things.

Maria had heard how powerful individuals preyed on refugees, taking advantage of their fears and insecurities, but not Mr. de la Carta. He wasn't like that, at least not until now.

"So, as a small favor, I would like you to occasionally take care of my needs. Not every day, but occasionally."

Maria just stood there frozen in disbelief. Never in her wildest imagination did she think Mr. de la Carta would ask her for sexual favors.

"But Mr. de la Carta, I couldn't, I am married. There are plenty of girls prettier than me, younger than me, who would only be too willing to do those things for you." Her voice pleading.

"Maria, this is just a small favor to show your appreciation for all I have done for you and Federico. Surely, you want to show your appreciation, your gratefulness for all that I have done for you."

"Of course, we are very grateful for all that you have done for us and we will always be indebted to you. But Mr. de la Carta, I couldn't do what you are asking. I just couldn't."

Without warning, the lawyer's voice took a harsher tone.

"I'm not asking you, Maria, I'm telling you. You will do this favor for me."

"Why me?" she pleaded.

"Because I find you extremely attractive and I know I can trust you. And, quite frankly, you're convenient. So do we have an understanding?"

Maria just stood there without responding.

"When I want a favor, I expect you will grant me that favor, without arguing."

Maria felt trapped, yet with her last ounce of

courage, she looked directly into Mr. de la Carta's eyes.

"And if I don't?"

Maria saw a look come over her boss's face that indicated he didn't like her response.

"Let me be perfectly clear, Maria. If you choose not to grant my favors, then I won't need you or your husband around anymore. I will make a phone call to some friends in immigration and immediately have both of you deported."

Maria felt sick. She knew what this powerful lawyer was capable of. There was no doubt in her mind he would do exactly as he was saying.

"And what if we leave Miami before we're deported, go somewhere we can't be found?"

Mr. de la Carta couldn't help but laugh.

"You have no place to go. You have nothing. And if you were to run, what do you think the Cuban government would do to your sons if they were told you were here in the United States giving information to our government about the Cuban government? Maybe you don't care about being deported, however I know Federico would and if you were the one responsible for having him deported, he would never forgive you."

Maria knew he was right and now clearly realized she had no choice, not for only for herself, but for her husband and sons as well. Her thoughts were interrupted by the voice she once trusted.

"So, let's not pretend you won't grant my small favors occasionally. In fact, grant me a favor right now."

Maria just stood there. Everything was blurry, like she was outside her own body. She was numb. Frozen. Trapped.

"Maria, take off your clothes." Mr. de la Carta requested in a soft tone.

She couldn't move.

"Take off your clothes." He repeated in a more demanding voice.

As tears streamed down her cheeks, she began to slowly unbutton her blouse.

The favors continued until Mr. de la Carta's death. Each time, no easier than the time before. Living in constant fear that her husband would discover the true price she was paying for them to stay in this so-called promised land, Maria tried to convince him they should leave and return home, only to hear his constant reply that they were home. She finally quit asking and simply did whatever "favor" Mr. de la Carta forced her to do.

But now safely back in Cuba, the guilt was consuming her. She had to tell her husband, hoping he would understand but fearing he wouldn't. Maria told herself that if he really loved her, he would accept what she had done, what she was forced to do. Nevertheless, whatever the consequences, she was going to tell him, right now, before she changed her mind.

Maria found her husband in the backyard tending to his roses. Ever since they had returned to Cuba, Federico found solace working in the garden. He told Maria that he felt at peace among the flowers. As she stared at him from the doorway, Maria started to change her mind, not wanted to share her horrible secret while he was in his favorite place. However, she quickly reasoned that there was no right time, no right place. This had to be the time. Maria walked across the yard toward the man she loved more than anything, with tears already filling her eyes. When she reached her husband, Federico stood and took off his gardening gloves. Maria threw her arms around his neck and pulled him close. He saw the tears in her eyes and gently held her without speaking.

"Federico, I love you so much." Maria whispered in his ear, her voice breaking.

Federico just kept holding his clearly distraught wife without answering.

"There is something I need to tell you." Maria began.

Breaking their embrace, Federico took a step

back and looked at her. Maria started to continue her confession but Federico reached up and placed two fingers on her lips to stop another word from escaping.

"It's okay. I already know."

And with that said, the couple stood silently in the middle of the rose garden as if they were a statue, holding on to each other tightly while tears of relief flowed down Maria's face.

Chapter Thirty-three

It was barely visible, bobbing in the water just off the bow. The captain slowed the ship as it approached what appeared to be floating debris.

"Why are we slowing down, Captain?" One of the passengers yelled up to the bridge.

The captain didn't answer the young man who had chartered The Poseidon for himself and three of his buddies. It later became known that the four young men were actually members of an immensely popular Hip-Hop band.

Instead, he called down to his first mate, who went by the nickname of Hook.

"What's off the port at about 11 o'clock, Hook?"

"Can't tell for sure yet, Captain, but from here it looks like a piece of wood."

The four young men had now joined the crew at the ship's railing. As The Poseidon drifted closer to the floating debris, they began speculating with excitement as to what the object could be.

"It looks like part of a boat to me."

"Yeah, maybe it's from a sunken ship carrying treasure."

Once The Poseidon was close enough to pull in the debris, there was, in fact, a stern section of a boat, as well as two life preservers, some floatation cushions and a few pieces of splintered wood. Based on the size of the stern section, it appeared to have been a fishing vessel and considering the condition of everything, it didn't appear that the debris had been in the water for very long.

"Do you think there are any bodies out there?" One of the band members asked.

Sensing the imaginations of this young Hip-Hop band were going wild, Hook answered dramatically,

"If there was anyone in that boat, they would have been eaten by the scavengers living below the surface."

"Are you kidding? Why isn't the water red from blood?"

In response to their questions, the first mate suggested checking under the surface for bodies to the wide-eyed group of band members staring into the water.

"Why don't you boys dive in and see if there is anything below the water."

"What??" one responded in disbelief.

"No way!" another one chimed in.

Hook laughed at the terrified expressions on their faces.

"Take some photos of the debris while I call the Coast Guard." The captain yelled down from the bridge.

Even though he was talking to his first mate, the young men took out their phones and began snapping away.

"This is so cool!"

At that point, Hook had heard enough.

"So, you think it's cool someone could have died here and are possibly lying at the bottom of the ocean? Someone whose family is wondering what happened to them. That's "cool" to you?"

"No, of course not. I just meant…." Red-faced, the young man walked away from Hook without finishing his sentence.

As Hook finished taking the photos, he noticed some lettering on the piece of stern.

"Captain, there is some lettering here, maybe IUS. It's hard to tell if it is an I or part of another letter but the other two letters are definitely US."

"What happens now?" One of the band members asked.

"We wait for the Coast Guard to arrive." Hook answered.

"How long do we have to wait?"

The band members enthusiastic interest was now waning.

"As long as it takes." Hook replied.

The young men went back to drinking and started working on what Hook presumed was a new song about the day's unexpected find.

The Coast Guard cutter arrived an hour later.

The cutter pulled up alongside The Poseidon and the Coast Guard officer asked the captain for permission to board the ship.

"Permission granted."

"Are you the one who called this in?"

"Yes sir, Dimitrius, skipper of The Poseidon. Came across some debris about ninety minutes ago. Pulled in a few items."

"Captain Dorsey, US Coast Guard. Mind if I take a closer look around?"

As Captain Dorsey looked around the boat, Dimitrius felt like the captain might be looking for something illegal, especially when he directed the other Coast Guard officer to get the names and contact information of everyone on board. One of the band members took exception and wanted to know why he had to give his information.

"Don't you know who we are? We're the famous band, Rebel Beatz!"

"I don't care who you are. I want your name

and contact information now. You may be a future material witness."

That seemed to appease the young man and he became very co-operative, believing he had a played an important part in discovering the debris.

After getting all the necessary information, the Coast Guard took possession of the salvaged debris and thanked the captain for the call.

"Sorry you had to hang out here until we arrived but we appreciate your cooperation."

"No problem, Captain. Always glad to help out."

"Thanks again. We'll take it from here."

The cutter headed back to the Fort Lauderdale Coast Guard Station. Once back at the station, Captain Dorsey prepared an Incident Report, logged in the items pulled from the area and turned everything over to the Coast Guard Investigative Service. A possible discovery of a boat lost at sea is given priority by the investigative service and the first protocol was to check the list of vessels reported missing in the general area where the debris was found. There is a circulated list of reported missing vessels organized by the name of the boat, the marine region in which the disappearance occurred or the closest country to the area, time of disappearance and last known location.

The investigative team, based on the condition of

the debris and the size of the piece of stern, decided to focus on the last four weeks of missing reports on the list and any reports within a five hundred mile radius in which the debris was found. Unfortunately, everything was just a guess at this point since there really wasn't much to go on other than the few pieces of debris and the letters IUS.

Even armed with detailed information, it would be a daunting task as some ships go missing and simply disappear into the sea without ever being reported or identified. The sea is powerful and no one is its master. The only clue of any help was the lettering on the stern section. It did not appear the US stood for the United States as the fragment of the other letter was too close to the US. It seemed more likely the US was the final two letters of a name. Therefore, on that assumption, one of the investigative agents began looking on the list of missing vessels for names ending in *US*, possibly preceded by another letter with a straight line, such as 'I' or maybe the right side of an h or n.

Although the list had quite a few reports of missing ships within the determined time frame, the investigative agent was able to narrow their search down to just three possibilities. The first name of the three was "The Medius." Pulling up the full report, the agent found "The Medius" had left the island of

St. Thomas three weeks ago and was reported missing by the owner's wife. The couple were in the middle of a messy divorce and one day the husband just sailed off in the boat and never returned. The Medius was quickly ruled out since the size of the boat was much larger than what the team had estimated from the salvaged stern section. Not to mention, there was no mystery as to what really happened to The Medius and its captain.

The second name from the list was "The Genius," reported missing from Cuba about three weeks ago. No additional information was given.

The last possibility was a fishing vessel named "The Aquarius," missing from the Bahamas for two weeks. According to the information in the report, the boat was a charter fishing vessel but had not had any charters in the last six weeks so when the boat wasn't at the docks and the boat's owner, Captain Jack, couldn't be located, a concerned friend called the Coast Guard. Although, there was no response to the Coast Guard's attempts at radio contact, after a brief investigation by the local police, no foul play was uncovered and the case was put on the back burner with the Missing Persons Department. Nonetheless, the Coast Guard investigator felt this was the most promising lead, since the time frame and area fit, plus the size of the missing boat was an exact match for the boat profile determined by the Coast Guard team. Now that they had an exact date of disappearance and origination port, they could develop a possible course the vessel was on before something caused it to come apart.

The investigator checked the logs kept by all Coast Guard cutters regarding any vessels encountered on their shift. He saw there was an encounter at sea on that date but not with The Aquarius.

Even if it was a different boat, maybe the skipper had seen the Aquarius. According to the log, the boat was the O'Sean, owned and operated by a local, Captain O'Shaughnessy.

Chapter Thirty-four

O'Shaughnessy had just finished securing the O'Sean and was heading from the dock to the yacht club bar when he was approached by two men in suits, an unusual sight at a marina.

"Are you Captain O'Shaughnessy?" One of the men asked.

"I am and who might you be?"

"We're here from the Coast Guard Investigative Service. We'd like to ask you a few questions."

"About what?"

"We discovered the remnants of a fishing vessel off the coast and we believe it to be a boat out of the Bahamas named The Aquarius."

"So, what does that have to do with me?"

"We're not sure it does. We're trying to pinpoint how far out The Aquarius traveled before she lost all radio contact and disappeared. Upon checking the Coast Guard logs for any encounters our cutters had with other boats in the area around the time and place we believe The Aquarius disappeared, we saw that the name of your boat was listed."

O'Shaughnessy didn't like where the conversation was heading. He thought about the Cortez incident, as he referred to it, every day and always wondered if it would come back around to him some day. Well, apparently today was the day.

"Our logs state that the O'Sean was in the area and interacted with one of our cutters. Nothing unusual about the encounter, just that you were in the area and we were wondering if you had seen the Aquarius or any other nearby vessels that day."

"What day did you say it was?"

"It was the 14th of last month. You spoke with Captain Dorsey briefly."

"I vaguely remember interacting with the captain but I can't say for sure it was that day, even so, I don't recall seeing The Aquarius. You did say The Aquarius?"

"That's right."

O'Shaughnessy's heart was now beating so hard, he was afraid they could hear it. Stay calm, he told himself, no one knows what happened, at least no one who would say anything.

"What were you doing out there that day?"

O'Shaughnessy couldn't remember what he told the Coast Guard that day or even if they saw anyone else on his boat.

"I possibly had a fishing charter that day."

Why are they asking me what I was doing? What did they think I was doing? What did they see? Did they see the explosion? Or was there another boat out there that saw the whole thing? Unsettling scenarios began to race through his mind and panic started setting in.

"Well, if there is nothing else, I'll be on my way, gentlemen." The captain said as calmly as he could.

"Just one more thing. I ran a check on you, O'Shaughnessy and saw you were once arrested for illegal alien smuggling."

"That was a long time ago and I was acquitted of all charges. Besides, what does that have to do with anything? Why are you bringing that up?"

"Just wondering if you're back to some old habits."

"I told you I was acquitted of all charges. I've never been an alien smuggler and I resent your accusations. If you have any more questions, you can call my attorney."

With that, O'Shaughnessy walked between the two men and headed to the bar, hoping they didn't notice he was trembling.

Chapter Thirty-five

They didn't speak on the ride to Nick's place, both lost in their own thoughts. Nick was trying to figure out exactly how much to tell Rosemarie and she was trying to figure out what he wanted to say to her. She wanted to reassure Nick that no matter what, she would stand beside him, be there for him, always. She didn't know exactly when it was that she had realized she was in love with Nick since it had happened so gradually but she was. Rosemarie never experienced the feelings she has for Nick before. She felt so happy when they were together, felt so safe in his presence. Rosemarie found herself constantly thinking about him when they were apart. And whenever she thought about her future, it always included him. Yes, she was most definitely and completely in love with Nick Constantine and there was nothing he could tell her that would ever change that, absolutely nothing.

Meanwhile, Nick was wondering how Rosemarie was going to react to what he was about to disclose.

He felt sick to his stomach thinking about what a mess he had made of his life. Maybe he shouldn't tell Rosemarie anything but on the other hand, Nick felt if he didn't tell someone, he would explode. The events of that day had started to consume him, constantly playing over and over in his mind. Nick wanted, no, needed someone to tell him it wasn't his fault, to assure him that everything was going to be okay.

"Nick, we're here." Rosemarie's voice breaking the silence.

"Let's go inside." Nick replied, suddenly realizing they had been sitting in the parked car, both lost in thought.

Rosemarie reached over and squeezed his hand.

Once they were inside Nick's place, Rosemarie asked Nick what she should do with the duffel bag the thugs had given them.

"Stick it in the closet for now. Care for a drink?"

"Definitely! If you have it, I'll have an Irish Whiskey."

Nick poured himself a Scotch. When he handed Rosemarie the Irish Whiskey, she noticed his hand was trembling.

Nick took a seat on the sofa and Rosemarie sat next to him, close enough that her leg was touching his. Finishing his drink in one gulp, Nick turned to face Rosemarie.

"Rosemarie, I have something to tell you. Something that I'm not proud of, something so horrible that it may change how you feel about me."

"Nick, there is absolutely nothing you could say that would change how I feel about you."

"I hope that's still true after what I'm about to tell you."

"I promise nothing will change. Please, just tell me what this is all about."

Even with all of Rosemarie's reassurances, Nick was still worried about what Rosemarie would actually think of him once she heard what he had done. Until now, Nick hadn't fully realized how much he cared about Rosemarie and he didn't want to lose her. Nonetheless, he needed to release this heavy burden or go crazy and finally decided to confide in Rosemarie, despite the consequences.

"Do you remember when Frank asked me to oversee something for him and I was gone for a few days?"

Rosemarie felt it was more of a rhetorical question, so she didn't reply but gave Nick an encouraging nod instead.

Nick took a deep breath before continuing.

"Well, he wanted me to help smuggle someone into the country, someone he had to meet with."

"Who was it?"

Nick could hear concern beginning to creep into her voice.

"Javier Cortez."

"The dead guy on our steps?"

"Yes."

And for the next thirty minutes Nick spoke while Rosemarie just listened.

Nick explained in detail the entire plan to bring this wanted criminal into the country. When he reached the part about the fishing boat, he paused for a moment. Should he tell Rosemarie the part about Cortez killing the skipper of the boat and trying to kill O'Shaughnessy? Since he had gone this far, he may as well tell her everything. When he finished, Nick waited for a response from Rosemarie, but there was none. Rosemarie sat frozen, looking at him with a blank stare. No words forthcoming. Just silence.

Nick simply waited, now seriously doubting that he should have told Rosemarie but if not her, who else could he have confided in? She was the only one he trusted. Finally, after what seemed like an eternity, Rosemarie spoke.

"Nick, why? What connection did he have with Frank? Who else knows about this?" The questions kept coming with no pause in-between for answers.

Nick did his best to explain the relationship

between Javier Cortez, the most wanted criminal in the world and their boss

"Are you saying we really worked for Cortez?"

"No, he was just a client. A client who paid the firm a lot of money to be available at a moment's notice for any type of necessary legal work. And now that he is out of the picture, those men that barged into the office, as you heard, want to take over Cortez's spot with our firm."

"Did they kill Cortez?" Rosemarie asked, almost whispering.

"That would be my guess."

"Did they kill Frank?"

Rosemarie was horrified at the very thought. Nick didn't answer.

"So, what are we going to do now?"

Nick was relieved to hear Rosemarie use the word "we" when asking about what was going to happen next.

"There's nothing to do. Those men are now clients whether we like it or not. We're in too deep to do anything but accept it and continue as usual."

"Who else knows about the murder of that poor man on the boat?"

"Just Captain O'Shaughnessy. Everyone else involved is dead. And since I saved the captain's life, I know he won't say anything out of loyalty to me."

"Do we really want to represent these people, Nick?"

"Why wouldn't we? For a million dollars a year and possibly more when we get a case they need our assistance with?"

"But if they killed Frank…"

"There is no indication they killed him. In fact, there is no indication that anyone killed him. The autopsy was inconclusive. For all we know, Frank may have simply died from natural causes."

"I don't think anyone believes that Frank wasn't murdered."

"Well, at this point, no one knows for sure how Frank died."

Nick stood up, went to the liquor cabinet and poured himself another Scotch. He noticed Rosemarie hadn't even touched her drink. After finally bearing his soul regarding this nightmare of horrible events with Rosemarie, Nick thought he would feel relieved but he actually felt worse as he glanced over at Rosemarie, who was still trying to process everything. Nick went and stood in front of Rosemarie.

"After hearing all of this, I would completely understand if you wanted to leave the firm. However, I hope you'll stay."

Rosemarie couldn't believe Nick would think for

even a second that she would leave him or the firm. As she rose slowly from the sofa Nick didn't move and now they were standing just inches apart.

Rosemarie pulled Nick's face towards her and kissed him with the most passionate kiss she had ever delivered. Filled with relief, desire and an overwhelming need for Rosemarie at that very moment, he took her in his arms, and carried her to his bedroom. She wrapped her arms around his neck so tightly, he almost stumbled. Once Nick laid Rosemarie on his bed, they couldn't get each other's clothes off fast enough and hours later, they fell asleep in each other's arms.

The next morning, Nick awoke to the smell of fresh coffee and bacon. He slipped on his robe and went to the kitchen where Rosemarie was cooking breakfast, wearing only a pair of his boxers. Seeing Rosemarie standing in his kitchen happily making breakfast, seem to give Nick the sense of peace he had been seeking. He walked up behind Rosemarie, giving her a hug and kissing her neck.

"Good morning sleepyhead. I thought I would surprise you by making breakfast. I hope you like scrambled eggs and bacon."

"I certainly do. I hope you made enough, I'm starving."

Basking in the glow of their lovemaking, the couple

were all smiles and laughter as they sat down to eat their scrumptious breakfast. Rosemarie and Nick were just finishing their coffee when Nick's phone rang.

His phone rang twice more before Nick decided to answer.

"Slow down, O'Shaughnessy. What are you talking about and how did you get this number?"

Nick motioned to Rosemarie to come sit by him on the couch and he put the call on speaker.

"It doesn't matter how I got this number. You need to do something."

"Something about what? You aren't making any sense."

Captain O'Shaughnessy rambled on about how the Coast Guard came to see him, asking about the missing boat and mentioning in a threatening manner old charges against him.

"Stop and listen to me. Settle down!" Nick interrupted.

"Settle down? Are you kidding me? I tell you, they know something." Captain O'Shaughnessy yelled at Nick.

"Get a grip on yourself, O'Shaughnessy. If the Coast Guard knew anything, you'd be in jail. Besides, there is nothing to know. You did nothing. I did nothing. And no one saw anything because there was nothing to see."

"How did you let this happen, Constantine?"

"I didn't let anything happen. In fact, you may recall, you are still alive by what I DIDN'T let happen."

"What are we going to do? What if someone talks?"

"Who is going to talk? Only four people were there and two of them are dead which leaves just you and me. And we're not talking, so what's the problem?" Seeing the truth in what Nick was saying, Captain O'Shaughnessy began to calm down.

"Just forget the whole incident and go about your life, O'Shaughnessy. If the Coast Guard ever returns, tell them you have nothing to say. Whatever happened that day is over. Understand? It's over!"

"I'll tell you something, Constantine, I'm done with your law firm. I owed Frank but I don't owe you, so lose my number and don't ever call me for any favors."

With that said, the captain hung up.

As Nick stood with the phone in his hand, he thought about Captain O'Shaughnessy's comment that he didn't owe Nick anything. Apparently, the boat captain had forgotten that Nick saved his life that fateful day at sea.

Chapter Thirty-six

After the call from Captain O'Shaughnessy, Nick and Rosemarie discussed what they should do next for the rest of the day. Now realizing that they both felt the same way about each other made it seem that there was nothing they couldn't conquer together. Rosemarie wanted to continue business as usual with Nick as the head of the firm. However, Nick felt that he should confess everything to Detective Henderson and ask for immunity in return for the information. Rosemarie argued that he was being naïve. Nick would never be granted immunity. It was more likely that he would be arrested on the spot and booked on murder charges. Nonetheless, Nick decided to take his chances and go see Detective Henderson the following day.

Rosemarie spent the night and in the morning, Nick told her to wait for him at his place, giving her a passionate kiss goodbye before heading to the precinct. However, just as he was about to walk into the building, Nick suddenly began to have second thoughts about his decision. Maybe Rosemarie was right, maybe he was being naïve. Would they really give him immunity? Deciding he should give his plan more thought and thoroughly look at all his options, Nick turned and headed back to his car.

Rosemarie was beginning to worry. It was after seven pm and Nick still wasn't back. She thought about calling Detective Henderson but if Nick changed his mind and didn't go there, Rosemarie didn't want to explain why she thought Nick might be at the precinct. Rosemarie had called the law office repeatedly during the day but no one had seen him. She thought about going and looking for him but where would she look? As the night dragged on, her imagination began to go wild, creating horrible scenarios as to why Nick wasn't home. By midnight, she was convinced something terrible had happened to him. Rosemarie began calling local hospitals, even the county morgue and was relieved to hear he wasn't lying in a hospital or the morgue. While looking out the window around three am hoping to see something, anything, she saw a vehicle with two people sitting in the front seat. The car was not running. Rosemarie quickly closed the curtains and slumped to the floor to avoid being seen.

Were they waiting for Nick? That must be why he hadn't come home, he couldn't. Nick must have seen them and kept going. Rosemarie felt she had to do something, she couldn't just sit there. Trembling, Rosemarie called 9-1-1 to report 'suspicious activity.' She told the operator she was an attorney and believed it could be a disgruntled client, thus fearing for her safety. Rosemarie described the vehicle along with its location and was told they would send a cruiser by to check it out. Five minutes later, a marked police unit rolled up on the parked car and illuminated the interior with its spotlight. The officer approached the parked vehicle and spoke with the two passengers inside the car. After a brief conversation, the patrol unit drove off. Two minutes later, there was a knock on the door.

"Mr. Constantine, this is Officer Manchu of the Miami Police Department." Rosemarie didn't move.

"Mr. Constantine, are you there?"

Rosemarie opened the door a crack.

"May I see some ID?"

"Of course." Officer Manchu replied, flashing Rosemarie his badge.

"Is Mr. Constantine home?" The officer asked again.

Rosemarie burst into tears.

"Ma'am are you okay? Where is Mr. Constantine?"

Rosemarie quickly regained her composure and not wanting to reveal too much, kept her response brief.

"He left this morning to take care of some business but never came home."

"When was the last time you spoke with Mr. Constantine?"

"This morning."

"And you haven't seen him or spoken with him since?"

"No."

"Did you check with his office?"

"Of course, I did. They haven't heard from him either. By the way, why were you parked outside?"

"Following an anonymous tip he received, Detective Henderson asked us to keep an eye on Mr. Constantine's residence."

"What sort of tip? Did this mysterious caller say where Nick was by any chance?"

"Detective Henderson didn't fill us in on any of the details but don't worry, if Mr. Constantine is indeed missing, we'll find him."

Rosemarie wanted to scream! Of course, Nick is missing or else he would be here at this very moment. Instead, keeping her composure, she politely thanked the officer for his diligence and shut the door.

Rosemarie felt tears welling up once again. Sure, they might find Nick, but would he still be alive?

Chapter Thirty-seven

Detective Henderson hated having unsolved cases on his desk. The detective prided himself on closing his cases, in spite of the fact he was assigned the most difficult ones to solve. Other detectives often turned to Detective Henderson for assistance when they hit dead-ends with their own cases. And the unsolved death of Frank de la Carta stuck in his craw. The fact that the cause of death was undetermined did not sit well with him. If the cause wasn't natural, it was a homicide, plain and simple. He didn't understand how the medical examiner could not determine the cause of death. Something stopped Frank de la Carta's heart.

As a young detective, new to the Homicide Division and on his first homicide case, Detective Henderson asked the medical examiner assigned to the case what the cause of death was.

"His heart stopped. That's the cause of every death, the heart stops. As long as the heart is still beating, there is no death." The Medical Examiner had replied jokingly.

The young detective was not amused. And decades later, Detective Henderson was still not amused by the comment. Something causes the heart to stop and it puzzled him as to why a medical examiner would not be able to determine what caused de la Carta's heart to cease functioning. After all, a medical examiner is a Doctor of Medicine.

Once again, Detective Henderson opened his file on Frank de la Carta. He poured over every page looking for any missed detail, no matter how minor. There had to be some detail, some clue to help solve this case. Something everyone had obviously missed. A minute fact that would solve the issue of what caused Frank's heart to stop. He re-read the medical examiner's report for the umpteenth time. The report indicated there was no illicit drugs, no external injuries, no unusual indications of a heart attack found. No indications of a heart attack? Wouldn't that clearly make this case a homicide?

Detective Henderson turned to the crime scene photos. Maybe he missed something there. Using a magnifying glass to re-examine every inch of every photo, he scrutinized every detail, especially the photo of de la Carta sitting in his chair slumped over his desk with a single glass in front of his right arm. The detective wondered why de la Carta was sitting at his desk. Was he on the phone? Was he meeting with someone? Two desk chairs were pulled up to the desk, yet there was only one glass of Tequila. No legal pad or any other signs of Frank taking notes. Why would de la Carta be sitting there drinking alone? Was he just having a drink before he left work? Detective Henderson poured over the photos for hours. There had to be something he was missing. Still using the magnifying glass, the detective peered at the surface of the credenza to see if he could determine if anything had been removed, leaving a clean space on the surface of the credenza but nothing appeared out of place. Detective Henderson was amazed at how clean the credenza actually was, not even a single speck of dust. If something had been taken, he wouldn't be able to tell. He looked again at the photo of de la Carta's desk and it too was spotless. Perfectly clean. Everything seemingly in its place. There were dozens of photos, as there always were with his crime scenes. Detective Henderson was known by the crime scene investigators to want more photos than any other detective. He often supervised CSI when they were taking photos, insisting on one more from this angle, another from this angle and yet another, until he was satisfied. They never argued with him about the number of photos, they just kept taking them until the detective was satisfied that every possible angle had been photographed.

Detective Henderson knew that the photos were the only thing that preserved a crime scene. Once the CSI team leaves, the body would be removed and the crime scene would be contaminated by everyone coming and going, therefore photos were essential and as far Detective Henderson was concerned, the more, the better.

Detective Henderson learned the value of multiple photos when as a young detective, he was called to a shooting outside an Italian restaurant where CSI was already in the process of taking photos. All the photos taken by CSI were of the body on the street and the surrounding pavement. A few days later, Detective Henderson was notified that the crime scene photos were appearing in a tabloid magazine. He was furious that someone had leaked crime scene photos to the media and went to meet with the editor of the paper, demanding to see all the photos the editor had in his possession regarding the crime scene. Although reluctant to turn them over at first, a threat to arrest the editor for impeding a murder investigation resulted in Detective Henderson obtaining the photos. Looking at the photos, the detective was surprised to see that none of the photos in the possession of the magazine were crime scene photos that the CSI had taken. Detective Henderson eventually learned the photos were shot by a journalist who was on the scene at the same time the CSI team were taking photos. Apparently, the journalist had taken photos of his own and after looking at them closely, Detective Henderson noticed they were shot from a different angle than all the CSI photos and even included vehicles parked at the curb within a one block radius. The detective was able to obtain license plate numbers on a couple of the vehicles and track down the owners, eventually leading to a witness who saw the entire shooting but was reluctant to come forward.

From that point on, Detective Henderson insisted on taking photos at all crime scenes from every angle possible, he was even known to have his CSI photographers lay on the ground and take photos from a prone position.

There had to be something. Somewhere there was a clue! The next photo in the stack was of the temperature control unit showing that the air conditioning was off. Why would it be turned off if Frank hadn't left yet? Maybe he came back to the office after everyone left and never turned the air conditioning back on. The next photo revealed that the light switch was in the 'on' position. Were the lights on when the office manager arrived? Or did she turn them on? Detective Henderson pulled out his initial interview notes to review if the office manager had mentioned anything about the lights. His notes showed she had stated that the lights were off when she arrived and she turned them on. But was she certain? Does it even matter to the case? Maybe, maybe not. The detective, meticulous himself, couldn't help but notice from the photos how clean de la Carta's office was. He closely examined photos of the carpeted floor. No stains, no wear patterns, no footprints in the luxurious pile of the carpet. Detective Henderson placed all the photos of the carpet side by side to get an overall view of the room. Something was wrong. Some photos showed footprints, others did not. How could that be? How did he not notice that before? How did no one notice that there were no footprints in the carpet? Peering even closer at the photos, Detective Henderson also noticed tracks on the carpet made by a vacuum cleaner. Vacuum tracks but no footprints? How was that possible? How did Frank get to his desk without leaving footprints? Detective Henderson went back to the photos of the body. de la Carta was wearing shoes, brown wingtips with hard soles to be exact. There was no way he could have walked across the carpet to his desk without leaving footprints. Henderson looked at more room photos trying to make sense of the carpet photos. There was no other way into the room except through the window, which wasn't really a viable option as de la Carta's office was on the second floor. Whether there was an intruder or just de la Carta in the room, they would have had to walk on the carpet, so why were there no footprints? Is it possible Detective Henderson had found the missing clue he had so doggedly been searching for? Or was it just another dead end?

Six Months Later

Rosemarie was at home when the doorbell rang. She still hadn't figured out what to do with herself since returning to Chicago. Her brothers had been incredibly supportive, even encouraging her to reapply to the City Attorney's Office as a prosecutor. Rosemarie, however, couldn't see herself as a prosecutor after having been on the other side, even with the events that had transpired over the last several years. She couldn't get herself to move forward in any direction and hardly left the house. Rosemarie hadn't heard from Nick in six months and assumed he was dead, dead at the hands of Tito Mendez and his thugs. Even so, she still called Detective Henderson weekly for updates but there was never anything new. Rosemarie began to believe no one was even looking anymore, but she kept checking anyway, refusing to give up hope. At one point, Rosemarie thought about hiring a private investigator to look into Nick's disappearance but her brothers urged her not to as it could bring unwanted attention to their family, thus putting all their lives in danger. When Rosemarie left Miami, she took over two million dollars of retainer money that Tito had given the firm. And for the first two months after arriving in Chicago, Rosemarie was petrified he or one of his thugs would come looking for her and the money. Every time the phone rang or there was a knock on the door, it scared her to death which is why she kept the curtains closed and used headphones to listen to the television, minimizing the noise from her apartment. Gradually, Rosemarie became more comfortable leaving her apartment but there were still moments when she felt she was being followed. Her family was worried about her behavior and didn't understand her crippling fear because what they didn't know is that she had a large amount of a notorious criminal's money. No one knew. As the months went on without incident, Rosemarie began to relax and felt more comfortable being by herself. But the one thing she couldn't get past was Nick. She had fallen deeply in love with him and had pictured herself growing old with him. Rosemarie often had nightmares about what might have happened to Nick, imagining unbearable tortures he must have endured, hoping he died quickly, yet at the same time hoping he was still alive somewhere. However, if he was alive, why didn't he contact her? Was he afraid a call from him would endanger her life? Was he with someone else?

The doorbell rang again. As Rosemarie headed

toward the front door, thoughts began racing through her mind as to who it could be since the only people who came over were family members and they never rang the bell, especially her brothers. They usually pounded loudly on the door, scaring her half to death. Maybe it was Tito or one of his thugs coming to retrieve the money. The thought of someone coming for the money, gave Rosemarie an odd sense of relief. At least it would finally be over. Or perhaps, she could get them to tell her about Nick's disappearance and she could have a little peace of mind knowing what had happened. Even so, with each step her anxiety level soared. It seemed to take forever to navigate the short distance from the living room to the small door that protected her from the outside world. Convincing herself that whatever awaited her on the other side of that door couldn't be worse than the fear she was living with every day, Rosemarie opened the door. It took her a moment to realize that no one was there. Could she have imagined the doorbell ringing? Was paranoia playing tricks on her mind, or even worse, was she losing her mind altogether? As Rosemarie was about to close the door, she caught a glimpse of something laying on the step at the base of the door. It was an 8x10 FedEx envelope. She looked around the front for the delivery truck but saw nothing. As she picked up the envelope, fear began to set in again.

Quickly re-locking the door, Rosemarie brought the mysterious package inside and laid the envelope on the dining room table. Her fear was beginning to give way to curiosity and she started to reach for the envelope but suddenly stopped. Rosemarie's training as a prosecutor told her not to touch the envelope again since there could be valuable information on it such as fingerprints, trace evidence or even DNA.

For the next two hours Rosemarie sat at the table with a glass of wine, staring at the package. Were there pictures of Nick dead or being tortured along with demands for returning the money inside the envelope? Or was it proof Nick was still alive but being held hostage? She contemplated calling Detective Henderson but quickly dismissed the idea. If Nick were alive, Rosemarie would gladly return the money. She didn't want it anyway. She only wanted Nick! However, no matter what she feared, Rosemarie knew she had to open the envelope. Not wanting to destroy any possible evidence on the package, Rosemarie put on a pair of oven mitts from the kitchen drawer. Clumsily and with shaking hands, she pulled the strings to open the flap of the envelope, turned the envelope upside down and dumped the contents on the coffee table. Rosemarie stared at the letter that slid out of the envelope and what looked like a Cuban passport. She looked inside the envelope, there was nothing else. As Rosemarie picked up the letter, she immediately recognized the handwriting as Nick's. Her eyes darted to the end of the letter looking for a signature but there wasn't one. If Nick really did write the letter, why didn't he sign it? With her heart racing, Rosemarie began to read the words on the page:

Rosemarie,

I need you to trust me. I want you to take a flight from Chicago to San Diego as soon as you can. Upon arriving in San Diego, walk across the border into Mexico and take a flight from Tijuana to Mexico City. From there, take a flight to Havana, Cuba. The enclosed passport is valid and the photo is close enough. Beginning tomorrow, I will be at the Havana airport watching all flights arriving from Mexico City, so I can be there the instant you arrive. Once we're back together, I will explain everything. Rosemarie, I love you and am hoping with all my heart that you will come be with me in Cuba. After reading this letter, burn it.

And that was it, nothing more. Rosemarie knew for certain it was Nick's handwriting. Afterall, she had seen his penmanship on numerous legal briefs at the office but was he forced to write this letter? Was this a trap to get her to Mexico? Was Nick really in Cuba? Why didn't he just come home? Why hadn't he contacted her before now? Why a fake passport? Once again, more questions than answers. As Rosemarie re-read the letter, she kept focusing on the words 'trust me.' If she does decide to go, should she tell her family? How would her family of police officers react to her going to Cuba with a fake Cuban passport? Rosemarie realized there was no one to turn to for advice. She was in this alone.

Rosemarie decided she would go to Cuba exactly as instructed in the letter. If it was a trap, she didn't care. She didn't want to keep living in fear and if there was any chance at all that Nick was there...

The next morning Rosemarie wrote a note to her brothers explaining that she was going back to Miami to clear up some things at the old firm and wasn't sure when she would return but would be in touch soon. Rosemarie booked a flight for that afternoon to San Diego, put a few items in a backpack and headed to the airport. On the way, she stopped by her older brother's house and slipped the note into his mailbox. At the airport, she parked her car in the long-term parking lot and headed to the terminal. Rosemarie was amazed at how calm she was, not to mention also very hungry since she had barely eaten in the last twenty-fours and decided to grab a quick bite before her flight. The flight to San Diego was routine and even arrived on time. Upon landing, Rosemarie decided to head straight to Tijuana from the airport rather than spend the night in San Diego. The cab from the airport dropped her off at the Mexican border where she walked across without being stopped. Rosemarie then took a cab to the Tijuana airport, purchasing a ticket to Mexico City on the first flight the next morning since she had just missed the last flight of the day. Deciding not to spend the night at the airport, Rosemarie took a cab to a hotel in downtown Tijuana.

That night she slept fitfully and morning couldn't come soon enough. Rosemarie had put in a wake-up call but didn't really need it as she was up before dawn. After a quick shower, she checked out of the hotel and hailed a cab back to the airport. Suddenly, Rosemarie was no longer feeling very calm. It seemed as if everyone she saw was following her. Was she becoming paranoid or was she actually right? It was with great relief when Rosemarie finally boarded for her flight to Mexico City. After an uneventful flight, Rosemarie approached the ticket counter to purchase a one- way ticket to Havana, showing her fake Cuban passport. The ticket agent took her passport and didn't even seem to notice that Rosemarie didn't look like the typical Cuban. The agent entered the passport into the computer and for the first time Rosemarie began to doubt her decision.

"Senorita."

The ticket agent's voice snapped Rosemarie's mind back to the present.

"Senorita, here is your boarding pass and passport."

"Thank you."

As Rosemarie walked away from the counter, it suddenly struck her as odd the ticket agent spoke to her in English, even though she was in Mexico and was allegedly Cuban. Rosemarie's head was on a swivel. Once again, she felt as if everyone's eyes were on her as she walked through the airport.

Rosemarie arrived at the gate just as they began boarding. She was in the third group to board and the wait was starting to weigh on her. Struggling to remain calm, Rosemarie showed her boarding pass to the flight attendant and found her seat. Moments later, the hatch was closed and Rosemarie was enroute to Havana, Cuba. Not knowing what or even who was waiting for her there, Rosemarie's only prayer was that it was Nick.

Epilogue

It was five years since Detective Henderson retired from the Miami police department. He thought about working with a private security firm or opening his own detective agency but ultimately decided on a life of leisure, hunting, fishing, gardening, all the things he had pictured himself doing once he retired. He relocated to Watauga, Kentucky, a rural community yet not too far from civilization, purchased a home on Lake Cumberland, obtained a dog from the local animal shelter and bought a large screen television to watch every sports game ever played. The detective tried dating a few times but that never seemed to lead anywhere and therefore was resigned to living a quiet, solitary life with his devoted dog named Lady. It would have been the ideal retirement but for one thing. He could not let go of the de la Carta murder in Little Havana. While Detective Henderson had finally figured out for certain *how* de la Carta was murdered, the detective could not prove it and even though he had a strong hunch, he couldn't positively determine who the murderer was. So why couldn't he let it go? After all, it happened almost a decade ago and he was now retired. The detective kept telling himself to let it go but for some reason, he just couldn't. The cold case kept him awake at night due to the very thought that someone had gotten away with murder on his watch. He somehow had to convince himself to move on and enjoy his well-earned retirement. Growing tired of thoughts of the unsolved case flooding his mind during what should be a peaceful time in his life, Detective Henderson finally concluded that karma could work it out, he's going fishing!

Detective Henderson made a trip into Watauga for some new fishing lures. While at the tackle shop, he saw a flyer for a fishing contest in the Caribbean. It was open to anyone for an entry fee of $5,000 and was a three-day event off the coast of Cuba. There were cash prices in four categories, including most fish, largest fish, etc. The contest was sponsored by the newly established Cuban Bureau of Tourism and included dinner with entertainment each evening as well an awards dinner at the conclusion of the tournament.

During his time on the force, Detective Henderson had developed a friendship with a boat captain who had a fishing vessel out of Miami. He wondered if the captain might be interested in putting a crew together to enter the contest if he paid all the entry fees. It sounded a lot more fun than sitting in his living room watching television day after day. After a highly active career, the detective's quiet, sedate life was getting a little boring and going on a three-day fishing trip seemed like the perfect remedy. Detective Henderson called his friend and to his delight, Captain Paparelli was all over the idea. Papi, as all his friends called him, had wanted to enter but didn't have enough money to cover the entry fee.

"I'm in Henderson but on one condition, we split the entrance fee."

Detective Henderson thought Papi might say that and already had a reply prepared.

"Not a chance! I'll pay the fees if you provide the boat, the fuel and a crew. If you don't agree to those terms, it's no deal."

Captain Paparelli could tell by his friend's tone that it was useless to argue.

"You always were a stubborn s.o.b. Henderson but okay, you have a deal. And instead of paying the crew upfront, what do you say we split the prize money four ways?"

Henderson couldn't help but laugh. Papi was already assuming they would win.

"Do you think they would agree to that? What if we don't win?"

"Of course, they will agree to it! Although, if you're going into this contest with the attitude we might not win, you may as well forget the whole thing."

"Alright, let's do it. I'll sign us up and you go round up a crew."

"Will do."

"I'll be down the middle of next week and we can spend a few days together before the fishing begins. See you then."

"Looking forward to it!" As usual, the captain hung up without saying goodbye, believing it to be bad luck to say it at the end of a phone call.

The following week, Detective Henderson arrived in Miami and went directly to the marina to find Captain Paparelli. Walking down the pier, the detective saw the captain on his boat with two younger guys which he assumed were the crew. The captain did not see Detective Henderson approach the boat and was startled when he shouted for permission to come aboard.

"You scared the shit out of me, Henderson! What the hell are you yelling for?"

Both men heartily laughed.

"Good to see you, Papi."

"You, too. Retirement must suit you Henderson, you look well."

"Still adjusting but getting there."

The two young crew members were standing behind the captain, almost at attention and didn't seem to know what to do.

"Henderson, I want you to meet Sandy and Sinker. Two of the best crew members you will ever meet."

Papi gave Henderson a slight wink and a bit of a wry smile.

"Pleased to meet you guys."

Detective Henderson wondered about their names, especially Sinker, but didn't ask. He knew there would be plenty of time to hear their stories later.

"Thought we'd take her out for a test run tomorrow. Help you get your sea legs. Where's your gear?" Papi asked his friend.

"In the car."

"Well, let's put your fishing gear aboard, then we'll go to my place and get you settled."

"There's no need to put me up, Papi. I'll get a motel nearby."

"What the hell are you talking about? Of course, you'll stay with me and that's not up for discussion."

"How's your wife going to feel about you dragging some stranger home?"

"Shit, she left me years ago. Now it's just me and my boat, the only thing I ever wanted or needed." Papi said with a hearty laugh.

The following day Papi took Sandy, Sinker and Detective Henderson out for a test run. They didn't fish but were using the boat's equipment to locate spots with abundant fish so they would know where to head for the contest. Detective Henderson saw several other fishing vessels who were not fishing and surmised they were doing the same thing. Seeing all the boats being helmed by their captains caused the detective to flash back once again to the de la Carta murder and the meeting with O'Shaughnessy, another boat captain. Detective Henderson thought he had put it all behind him yet here he is at sea with his mind flooding with nothing but thoughts of the unsolved murder of de la Carta wondering if he would see O'Shaughnessy out here, wondering what ever happened to that lawyer, Nick Constantine or the cleaning woman from the law firm and her husband, the gardener. He wondered which one of them got away with murder.

"Henderson, are you with us? You look like your mind is somewhere else. Can't have your thoughts wondering off."

Papi's voice jarred the detective back to the present.

"Not to worry, I'm paying attention."

"Good. People get injured by not paying attention."

Friday morning came way too early for the detective as he and Papi were up late, drinking and reminiscing.

"Rise and shine, Henderson."

"It's still dark out. What time is it?"

"0500. We need to get to the boat and be ready to push off at 0700. Don't want to be the last one out."

When they had registered for the contest, in addition to a fishing license, the entire crew received a visa to enter Cuba. Every entrant was also given a list of items they weren't allowed to have on board when they entered Cuba. Among the items prohibited were firearms, apart from one flare gun but with no more than two flares. Detective Henderson always carried his service weapon, even though he was retired. Leaving his gun behind left him feeling extremely vulnerable but Papi made sure the detective wasn't armed when he boarded. Until the day of registration, Detective Henderson hadn't realized they would be entering Cuban waters and at the end of each day would be docking in Havana which is where the catch of each boat would be weighed, photographed and documented before being donated to the locals or he might have given this trip a second thought. The thought of being outside of the United States without his weapon made the detective extremely uneasy. Nonetheless, it was too late to back out now.

By 0700, all twenty-two boats entered were ready for the starting signal, a flare fired over the marina. As the boats were racing to the open waters, Detective Henderson found himself thinking about the de la

Carta murder yet again and suddenly was looking at the name of the other vessels to see if O'Shaughnessy's boat, The O'Sean was among them. Detective Henderson had just a handful of unsolved cases during his career but for some inexplicable reason, this one just wouldn't leave his mind. Will this case haunt me until the day I die?

The day flew by as the fishing was brisk and the crew worked nonstop. Fishing ended precisely at 0400 and any boat caught fishing after 0400 would be disqualified. Even though they hadn't caught any extremely large fish, Detective Henderson felt they had an excellent catch for the first day.

"Pretty meager haul, I must say."

Detective Henderson was surprised by his friend's comment.

"Are you kidding? Look at all the fish."

"That's nothing. The hold should be full and fish overflowing onto the deck. Hopefully, it will be better tomorrow. By the way, how are you feeling Henderson? Think you can get hold up for two more days of this?" Papi asked chuckling.

"Of course! A few drinks tonight, a good night's sleep and I'll be ready to go in the morning."

"Good. We shove off at 0600 A.M."

"Why so late?" Detective Henderson replied with a laugh.

As they pulled into the Havana marina, Papi and his crew were met by Immigration inspectors who asked to see everyone's passports and visas. While one officer was checking documents, two others were checking the vessel. After finding no prohibited items, the two searchers said something to the document inspector in Spanish, presumably giving him the "all clear" since the documents were handed back and with a wave of the inspector's arm, two men showed up pushing a couple of empty carts. With remarkable efficiency, they unloaded the fish and wheeled them over to a scale on the dock. Papi told Sinker to accompany the two men to make sure all the fish made it to the scale and that the weight was recorded correctly.

"You never know who may try to cheat by paying someone to remove a few fish on the way to the weigh station or misrecord the weight." Papi explained to everyone.

Detective Henderson wasn't too surprised his friend believed someone might cheat, it was Cuba, after all.

Sinker returned to the boat with the receipt for the weight and total number of fish. The receipt was in Spanish which fortunately, both Papi and Sinker spoke and the weight was listed in kilograms.

"Just like I thought, pretty meager. We'll do better tomorrow. For now, let's go to the hotel and get a drink."

Papi had reserved two rooms at the five-star Hotel Nacional de Cuba for himself and Detective Henderson. Sinker and Sandy were staying on the boat.

The hotel was extraordinarily beautiful which caught Detective Henderson completely by surprised. Papi chuckled when he saw the surprised expression on his friend's face.

"Everyone has that same surprised expression on their first trip to Cuba. Being in a communist country, tourists expect to see nothing but poverty with a bunch of worn-down buildings everywhere like in the movies. However, in reality, Cuba has quite a lot to offer tourists during their visit, including great old buildings rich with history to tour, delicious food and stunningly beautiful hotels."

Havana certainly wasn't what the detective had expected. His room was well-appointed with a view of the plaza that had rows and rows of 1950's vintage American automobiles that looked brand new. Detective Henderson had read an article about vintage American cars that had found their way to Cuba but he certainly didn't expect to see so many in one place.

"It's so surreal, almost like a time warp. There are signs of modernization everywhere. Beautiful new hotels being built, brand-new city buses traveling down the streets, run-down buildings being renovated. And yet, in the middle of all the new, thousands of vintage American cars fill the plaza." Detective Henderson replied, his mind still trying to absorb what his eyes were showing him.

"The buses you see are all Chinese-made and the renovations are funded by China with all the work being done by Chinese laborers. If you ask me, it won't be long before China owns this country. Anyway, that's enough talk about China, let's check-in and meet back here in an hour for drinks before dinner."

"Sounds good. See you at the bar."

When Detective Henderson arrived at the bar an hour later, Papi was already there sitting at a table, flirting with the server.

"Henderson, I want you to meet my new friend, Cecilia."

"Pleased to meet you. May I get you a drink?" Cecilia uttered in broken English.

"A Hatuey would be fine." Detective Henderson replied with a smile.

"Not a chance. You're in Cuba, you need to try the rum. Cuba has the best rum in the whole world. Trust me." Papi interjected.

"Okay, then rum it is."

"A glass of Havana Club Maestros. Make it a double."

After two more doubles, the guys left the bar and

hailed a cab. A 1958 Oldsmobile convertible pulled up to where the two men were standing.

"Where to amigos?" The driver asked in a thick Cuban accent.

Detective Henderson noticed that there was no meter in the car, no taxi medallion and no rates posted anywhere. He felt a little uncomfortable being at the mercy of the driver.

"Take us to the best paladar in town." Papi instructed the driver.

Seeing that Papi was taking charge of the ride, Detective Henderson's apprehension eased up a bit.

"I know the perfect place." The driver quickly responded.

"How much?"

"For you mi amigos, just five <u>cucs.</u>

Detective Henderson had no idea what a cuc was.

"Sounds fair." Papi replied.

"What the hell is a cuc?" The detective whispered to Papi.

Papi explained to his confused friend that there were two monetary systems in Cuba. One for the Cubans and one for the tourists. The locals use a peso system which is worth almost nothing in American money. The cuc is used for tourists and is the equivalent of approximately one American dollar. Before meeting Detective Henderson at the hotel bar, Papi had exchanged some American money at a nearby bank for cucs since dollars were not legally accepted in most places in Cuba.

During the ride to the paladar, Henderson noticed how smooth the car ran.

"You keep this car running like it was new." Detective Henderson commented to the driver.

"I just put a new Peugeot engine in."

"A Peugeot engine?"

"Si, amigo. They fit perfectly."

The driver explained that there were no parts available from the United States for American cars, but they could get plenty of car parts and engines from France for the Peugeot. And any car parts that they couldn't get imported from Europe, they simply made them. The cab ride took about six minutes to get to the restaurant. When the driver announced they had arrived, Detective Henderson looked around but didn't see a restaurant, only multi-family homes.

"Here you are, amigos, the best paladar in all of Cuba."

Detective Henderson gave Papi a quizzical look as they got out of the car.

Papi thanked the driver and handed him five cucs.

"Will you need a ride back, mi amigos? I can come back in one hour."

"Make that an hour and a half and you have a deal."

"You got a deal, amigo. Gracias."

Papi laughed at the concerned look on his friend's face.

"Relax, detective. Follow me."

Detective Henderson followed Papi but not without a great amount of skepticism.

"This is the latest thing in Cuban dining. A paladar is a privately owned restaurant operating out of the owner's home. The Cuban government supports this new way of dining, especially since all profits are split between the owner and the government but it is also the hope that word will spread that Cuba can offer more revolutionary foods than just the traditionally known rice and beans thus increasing the tourist trade." Papi explained as they entered the paladar.

"A table for two, gentlemen?" The American hostess asked.

Immediately, the hair on Detective Henderson's arms and neck stood up. His stomach instantly churned. He knew that voice. And sure enough, standing directly in front of him was none other than Rosemarie Callahan.

Rosemarie froze. This can't be happening, not after all this time. She wanted to run, warn the others but she couldn't move. She told herself there was nothing to worry about. They were in Cuba. There was nothing this man could do to her. They had many friends in Cuba, including important people within the government who ate at their restaurant. People who would protect them. After what seemed like an eternity, Rosemarie finally gathered the courage to speak.

"Detective Henderson, it's been a while. What brings you to Cuba?" she asked, trying to stay calm.

"Rosemarie, right?"

"You two know each other?" Papi asked in disbelief.

"In another life." Rosemarie responded.

Detective Henderson noticed her nervousness.

"To answer your question Rosemarie, I am here on a fishing trip."

"Aren't you going to introduce us Henderson?" Papi asked.

"This is Rosemarie Callahan. Rosemarie this is an old friend of mine, Captain Paparelli."

"Pleased to meet you, ma'am. Any friend of Henderson's is a friend of mine."

Neither Detective Henderson nor Rosemarie bothered to correct Papi's mistaken belief that the two of them were friends. After the introductions were made, the three of them awkwardly stood there without speaking.

Rosemarie finally broke the long moment of silence.

"Would you like a table?"

"We would love one." Papi replied with a smile.

He couldn't wait to hear how his friend knew this lady since there was an undeniable tension between the two. Rosemarie seated the gentlemen at a table by the window and handed them each a menu.

"May I get you a drink?"

"Two glasses of your best rum. Actually, make it two doubles." Papi said, ordering for himself and Detective Henderson.

After Rosemarie left the table, Papi turned to his old friend with a grin.

"Okay, now tell me, what's the deal with you two?"

Rosemarie was visibly shaking by the time she reached the bar.

"Nick, you are not going to believe this!!"

"Believe what?" Nick asked.

"Guess who I just seated?"

"Castro?" Nick answered laughingly.

"Detective Henderson!"

"From Miami?"

"Yes, from Miami."

"Did he recognize you?"

"Of course."

"What does he want?"

"He and his friend just ordered drinks and then they are going to have dinner. What should we do?"

"Serve them. We have nothing to worry about. I'll take the drinks over and say hello."

"Nick, are you sure?"

"Positive."

While in the middle of telling Papi the story of the murder of de la Carta, the murder he never solved and still haunts him to this day, he received another shock.

"Hello, Detective."

"Well, I'll be damned. You are still alive."

Now Papi was really intrigued. Who was this guy? Is he involved in the murder Henderson was just talking about?

"So, Nick, I see you and your law partner have relocated to Cuba."

"My wife."

"Well, congratulations to you both. But why Cuba?" Detective Henderson asked.

"Are you asking out of curiosity or for some official reason, Detective?"

"I'm retired now and just down here fishing."

"And you just happened to run into us? That's a little hard to believe."

"It's true. I had no idea you guys were here."

"I can vouch for my friend." Papi interrupted.

"I understand he is a Captain. Is he retired also?" Nick inquired of the detective.

"Relax, Nick. He is a boat captain."

"What made you choose this place to eat?"

"The cabbie picked the place."

Nick felt a bit relieved as he left the two gentlemen at their table and returned to the bar.

For the next hour, the two men ate and drank as Detective Henderson told his friend the complicated, unsolved murder of Mr. Francisco de la Carta. After dinner, they ordered more drinks and dessert. The men had so completely lost track of time that they hadn't even noticed they were the last ones left in the restaurant. Nor did they realized that the cab driver had arrived as promised and was still waiting outside.

"Will there be anything else, gentlemen?" Rosemarie asked as she placed the check on the table.

Detective Henderson, now feeling the effects of all the rum, looked up at Rosemarie.

"Rosemarie, I need to know what happened. This case haunts me every second of every day. I can't seem to let it go."

The detective's words were slurred and pleading.

Rosemarie walked away without responding.

A few moments later, Nick appeared, pulled up a chair, looked at Detective Henderson and asked,

"You want the whole story?"

"From beginning to end. And don't leave out a single detail!" The detective said emphatically.

Papi suddenly remembered that the cab driver had probably returned to pick them hours ago and may still be waiting for them.

"Wait, before you say another word, let me check on the cabbie." Papi said as he headed to the door.

Seeing that the cab driver was indeed outside waiting for them, Papi paid him ten cucs to continue to wait for them and went back inside to hear what Nick was about to reveal. Rosemarie locked the door behind Papi as he sat back down at the table. And for the next two hours, the four of them sat at the table as Nick told Detective Henderson and Papi everything, all about the smuggling venture, the murder of de la Carta, the million-dollar retainers, how he fled to Mexico to escape Tito Mendez and everything in between. He even explained how de la Carta had forced Maria, the office cleaning woman, to perform sexual flavors in order to stay in the United States. Detective Henderson had already figured out that the pretty but extremely poisonous blue flowers were the cause of death but couldn't ever figure out how the poison had been administered. And why? However, thanks to Nick, he now knew the how and the reason why. The only detail Nick didn't divulge was the actual murderer. Was it the office cleaning woman, the gardener, or someone else? Although, for some reason it didn't seem to matter anymore. He had all the other answers. It was time for him to let this case go, once and for all. As Detective Henderson stood up from the table, he shook Nick's hand and thanked him profusely. Rosemarie unlocked the door for the two friends and as they left, Detective Henderson turned to Rosemarie.

"Congratulations again on your marriage."

"Thank you."

As they were entering the cab, Detective Henderson looked back at the Constantine paladar and from the upstairs window he saw two people looking down. He couldn't be sure but they looked exactly like a cleaning woman and a gardener he had once met, a whole other lifetime ago.

CPSIA information can be obtained
at www.ICGtesting.com
Printed in the USA
BVHW030257080922
646534BV00007B/79